THEY HAD COME IN SEARCH OF GOLD—

but what they had found fossilized within its asteroid tomb was something more ancient than they could comprehend. Erin was reluctant to try to explain to Dent why she was suddenly positive that it was absolutely vital to put the fossil skeleton aboard the *Mother Lode*. She couldn't have told him why, she just knew that it had to be done.

She used the laser carefully, hoping to detach the humanoid skeleton from the bones of whatever life-form was lying under it. But the protrusions from the humanoid's shoulder blades were fossil bone that formed a ball and socket joint much like the hip joint, and from that joint the long, delicate bones swept outward in a graceful ellipse.

"Dent," she whispered.

He heard, for he had been standing directly behind her, watching as she cut away the matrix to expose two features of the humanoid skeleton that were definitely nonhuman.

"Wings," Erin whispered. . . .

ZACH HUGHES
MOTHER LODE

DAW BOOKS, INC.
DONALD A. WOLLHEIM, FOUNDER
375 Hudson Street, New York, NY 10014

ELIZABETH R. WOLLHEIM
SHEILA E. GILBERT
PUBLISHERS

First Printing, December 1991

1 2 3 4 5 6 7 8 9

DAW TRADEMARK REGISTERED
U.S. PAT OFF. AND FOREIGN COUNTRIES
—MARCA REGISTRADA.
HECHO EN U.S.A.

PRINTED IN THE U.S.A.

CHAPTER ONE

The X&A ship U.P.S. *Rimfire* blinked into normal space a quarter of an astronomical unit from the bustling spaceports of the administrative planet Xanthos. The officer on the navigation bridge, Lieutenant Erin Kenner, studied the scanners carefully and waited for clearance from Xanthos Central before giving engineering the order to make the last of an epic series of blinks. *Rimfire* disappeared instantaneously to reappear at a two-hour, sublight distance from her assigned orbit. Erin buzzed the captain's quarters.

"We'll be ready to go to debarkation stations in two hours, Captain," Erin said, as she punched orders into the board to start the ship moving. After over five years in space every man and woman on board was more than ready to feel a planetary mass underfoot. An almost tangible current of excitement was running through the ship.

Captain Julie Roberts, dark haired, almost spare in her service blues, looked as if she'd spent the last two hours in front of a mirror instead of having a quick nap in her cabin. When she came onto the bridge, she checked the scanners and frowned. "Heavy traffic?" she asked.

Erin had never seen so many ships congregated in one area of space, but she made no comment. Julie Roberts punched the communicator. "Xanthos Central, *Rimfire*."

"*Rimfire*, Xanthos Central, go ahead, please."

"Xanthos Central, *Rimfire*. Concerning your assignment of position. The designated area looks a bit crowded to me."

"*Rimfire*, Xanthos Central. Hold one."

There was a pause. The communicator speakers hissed the subliminal, forlorn audio signature of limitless space.

"Look, Captain," Erin Kenner said.

The congregation of ships, large and small, was sorting itself out into two long files curving off into the distance on either side of *Rimfire*'s assigned orbit. The communicator came to life.

"Rimfire, Xanthos Central. Captain Roberts, you will bring your ship to the assigned position to enter orbit and to receive a salute from units of the fleet."

"Damn," Julie Roberts said. She looked at Erin Kenner and shook her head. "Well, Lieutenant, there goes our plan to have dinner planetside."

Erin used power to augment the gravitation of the planet, let *Rimfire* fall slowly. In the engineering spaces the largest blink generator ever constructed was doing its eerie thing, drawing a combination of radiative, electromagnetic, and gravitational forces from the nearest star. Under Erin's skillful control the ship rotated neatly around a ninety degree turn, adjusted speed, cut back power.

"Nicely done, Erin," Julie Roberts said. "I'm going to be sorry to lose you."

"I'll miss this part of it," Erin said. "I'll never be able to play with so big and expensive a toy again."

Ahead and to the sides the evenly positioned ships of the X&A fleet glowed like giant fireflies as all external lights were turned on at the same instant. For hundreds of miles in front of *Rimfire* space flares filled the empty blackness with pyrotechnic display.

"All hands, all hands," Julie Roberts said, after turning on the in-ship communicators, "check your nearest viewer. I do believe that we're being welcomed home."

Rimfire's swim through space seemed to those in the ships who were greeting her to be slow, although the velocity of the entire armada was high enough to balance the planet's gravitational pull against the effect of the first law of motion. Signal lights blinked out the ancient visual code of welcome. Fleet Admiral Flying Bird, a Healer from Old Earth and commander of the space arm of the Department of Exploration and Alien Search, spoke briefly to the officers and crew of *Rimfire*. His voice echoed throughout the giant ship. Men and women who wanted nothing more at the moment than to get off the ship winked at each other as if to shrug off the admiral's sincere praise.

"Ah, shucks, Admiral," Erin Kenner said, "t'weren't nothin'."

All *Rimfire* had done was to circumnavigate the galaxy.

Just under six years ago she'd blinked away from Xanthos toward the periphery, leaving behind the last, scattered stars and entering the black void of intergalactic space. As she did the exploration crawl, traveling only instrument-scan distances in any one jump of her powerful generator, she left behind her a string of blink beacons that would allow others to do in weeks what had taken her years to accomplish, to circle the Milky Way Galaxy around the rim of the disc's horizontal plane. She had been built to do the job, and she had done it well. In one expedition she had accelerated galactic exploration enormously, for now a ship could follow her beacons to a position opposite any given point in the galactic disk and begin exploratory penetration at a point which would have taken years to reach if it had been necessary to pick a laborious path between the stars.

Rimfire's long and lonely voyage was important because of the nature of the blink drive. Even in the crowded heart of the galaxy, distances were measured in light-years and parsecs. There was, of course, more space than matter, but a blinking ship had to avoid all material objects during its period of semi-nonexistence while blinking. In the two known instances where a blinking ship had made contact with another object while in a state of transition a process of molecular breakdown had welded the two objects into one solidity. Therefore, when traveling in unexplored space, a ship was limited to blinks only as great as the distance that could be surveyed by her instruments and predetermined to be free of stars, planets, asteroids, or particularly dense clouds of space dust.

After *Rimfire*'s voyage, a ship could travel outside the galactic plane and reach a point on the other side of the galaxy faster than she could travel in a more or less straight line between the stars. The distances were greater via the out-galaxy routes, but a blinking ship covered a jump of a thousand parsecs as quickly as one measuring half an astronomical unit.

Captain Julie Roberts was right in guessing that the ceremonies would be time consuming. By the time *Rimfire* had been saluted, orated to, honored, and boarded by an assortment of brass including the elected president of the United Planets, Erin Kenner had been off watch, had eaten, slept, showered, watched a few hours of programming from Xanthos to catch up on what had been going on in the inhabited areas of the galaxy, and was pulling another watch on the navigation bridge.

The ship was at orbital secure, her drive systems down, the big blink generator humming quietly at a power setting sufficient to keep the flux drive active and to provide electrical power and three-quarters New Earth Standard Gravity. The brass had departed. The ship's shuttles were dropping away and flashing down planetside, each of them packed to the maximum with the lucky ones who had drawn first liberty.

Erin leaned back in the command chair, her long legs propped up. Maintenance hadn't touched up the paint on the console in recent months. Two worn spots in the U.P. issue gray showed that Erin wasn't the only one who assumed a casual posture while on post. She was dressed in X&A shipboard duty wear which consisted of neatly cut blue shorts, comfortable white overshirt, and flesh-tone hose. On her ash-blonde hair perched the little go-to-hell spacer's cap. Her badges of rank and station were embossed on the cap and on the shoulders of her shirt, Navigator First Class, Lieutenant of the X&A Space Arm. Over her right breast was her blue and gold nameplate. Over the left the logo of *Rimfire*. She was a small woman, five-feet-four-inches in height, one-hundred-and-twenty pounds. She was just over thirty years old. She'd spent the last twelve years of her life in the service, four of them at the Space Academy on Xanthos, the last six standing watches on the navigation bridge of the *Rimfire*. She had developed the faraway gaze of the deep spacer, but the tiny squint lines at the corners of her large, almond-shaped, sea-green eyes were becoming. Other than that her skin was flawless. Her nose, she felt, was just a little too cute to be dignified. Her lips were wide and full.

She looked up as a tall, mature man came through the security door onto the bridge. Her feet dropped to the floor.

"As you were," the newcomer said. "How's it going, Erin?"

"Slow," she said.

"That eager to leave us?"

She shrugged. "Yes and no," she said truthfully. "I haven't seen my father in six years."

"As I remember it you're from Terra II."

"New Earth," she corrected automatically, for Earthers felt that the formal name of their planet was a bit stilted.

Lieutenant Commander Jack Burnish knew very well that Erin was a New Earth girl. He knew quite a lot about her, for until she had learned quite by accident that he had a wife and family on Delos III, she had held nothing back from him.

"Commander?" she asked formally, breaking the silence. "Is there something I can do for you?"

"Erin—" He moved closer. There was a pained look in his eyes. For a moment she remembered, and felt that soft, sliding, melting feeling in the pit of her stomach. She shook her head, tossing her short, ashen hair.

"Erin, I—"

"If you have no business here, Commander, I *am* on watch, you know." Her voice was cold, service standard.

"I loved you," Burnish said.

She looked at him evenly for long moments, her face set in serious lines, before she smiled and said softly, "Bullshit."

"I hope you find what you're looking for back on Terra II," he said.

She opened her mouth to correct him, but remained silent. For two years she had thought that she'd found the universe in Jack Burnish's arms. She'd always been a sucker for older men, although she would have fought any head-shrinker who tried to hang a father complex on her. She was by no means a promiscuous girl. There'd been a boy at the Academy, and then Jack, and after she'd found the holo-tape from Jack's wife and children there'd been two others, quite discreetly, aboard *Rimfire*. The ship had been a long, long way from home, with years stretching ahead before she made the last left turn and headed back into the starred regions of the Milky Way Galaxy and that little grouping of suns and worlds that made up the U.P. Sector. Jack's deception had left her empty and very, very lonely. With the others she was simply trying, unsuccessfully, to fill the void inside her with shared passion.

For the last three years of *Rimfire*'s voyage she had kept to her own bed. She had learned that without love the act of coupling was almost comically sweaty, strenuous, undignified, quickly finished, and in the aftermath somewhat damaging to one's self esteem.

At the end of her last watch aboard *Rimfire* she put on a full dress uniform, tucked the last few items of her personal gear into her bag, and went to knock on Julie Roberts' door.

The captain was in gown and slippers.

"I'll be leaving on the next shuttle, ma'am," Erin said.

Julie rose, gave Erin a solemn salute, then came to put her arms around the younger woman. She squeezed, stepped back. "You are a good officer," she said. "If you change your mind, your rank and position will be reserved for you for a period of six months."

"I know. Thank you."

The captain smiled. "Thanks, but no thanks?"

"I'm afraid so."

"We're getting a unit citation. Leave your home address with personnel and I'll have yours sent along to you."

"I will, thank you.' "

"Have a good life."

"And you," Erin said.

The shuttle dropped away from the big ship. Looking back, Erin saw the harsh outlines, the dingy, service gray paint, and felt a moment of sadness. In a way it was like leaving the womb, for the ship had been her home, her haven in a completely hostile environment. The crew had been her family while ship and complement were at awesome distances from the nearest outpost of human exploration. *Rimfire* looked worn and old and tired and that was odd, for there was nothing in space to erode her original sheen, to dull her paint.

Thirty minutes later Erin was on the ground. She had fourteen hours to wait before catching her flight to New Earth, so she was in no hurry to exit the shuttle. She waited for the more eager crew members from *Rimfire* to get on with their planetside liberty before leaving her seat. A few of them called out one final good-bye.

She was the last one off the shuttle. She stepped out of the hatch and had to reach for the railing of the boarding ramp as dizziness swept over her.

''You'll be fine in a minute,'' said one of the shuttle's crew from behind her. ''Ain't it a bitch? You breathe recycled air for long enough and the real thing hits you like a good belt of booze.''

She breathed deeply, tried to define the smell of the air. The answer was that there was no smell. No scents, no flavorings, only an exhilarating keenness and a feeling of clean purity. For years she'd lived with the subliminal odors that accumulate when a closed ship recycles air and organic wastes. On Xanthos, where industry was prohibited, there was a purity to the air that really did seem to intoxicate her.

The planet was one huge city. From Xanthos the lines of command and administration extended over parsecs of space to the various U.P. planets and beyond into the areas of exploration, to dim and distant planets not well suited for human habitation, to Old Earth, the planet from which space-going man had emerged thousands of years in the past, to her home, New Earth, where the space travelers had struggled against long odds to overcome the loss of all technology and their own history to blast their way back into space on the ravaged resources of a planet.

After checking into an X&A B.O.Q., she placed a blink call to New Earth to tell her father that she would soon be on her way home. She was told that there'd be a two-hour delay. She went out onto the streets and walked. Civilization buzzed, hummed, honked, whistled, roared, whispered, sang about her. Humanity swarmed, making her feel just a bit ill at ease. She envied the Old Earth Power Givers, females who could soar above the crowded street, their tiny, jeweled scales reflecting the lights. Now and then she saw a Healer, one of the males who was so highly valued in X&A because of his ability to explore places that were deadly to the Old Ones, meaning ordinary men like those who had left the home planet before the Destruction. Once and only once did she see a third form of the race that had mutated on Old Earth after the Destruction, a Far Seer, his bald, pointed head gleaming, his eyeless face moving from side to side as he made his way unhesitatingly among the throngs. One never saw the fourth Old Earth mutant, the idiot savant Keeper, in public.

She took a moving sidewalk to a shopping complex and marveled at the richness of goods on display. After buying a few luxuries for herself and gifts for her father, she ate alone in a beautifully decorated little restaurant that specialized in the cuisine of the Tigian planets, drank two glasses of a beautifully dry Tigian wine.

The communications blink routes to New Earth were still jammed. She had a lovely night's sleep in her room on the B.O.Q. with the windows open. She had to bundle up under heavy covers, but the unladen sweetness of the air made it worth it. She had a leisurely breakfast next morning, tried to call New Earth again without success, left the B.O.Q., grabbed a taxi, and was soon aboard a passenger liner enroute to Tigian I, II, and III; Trojan V; Delos; and New Earth. The bed in her stateroom was prepared. She stripped to her singlet, punched a Do-Not-Disturb message into her communicator, and slept.

Her stateroom was, when compared to her quarters aboard *Rimfire,* luxurious. There was no limit to the amount of water she could use, so she filled the bathtub until she could slide down and soak with only her face showing. She lolled in the bath for an hour and emerged feeling wrinkled but good. The food in the ship's dining room was excellent. Her fellow passengers seemed to be a cross section of United Planets society, although most of them were considerably older than she. She was polite enough, but made it clear that she was not interested in socializing. When the ship cleared the three Tigian planets and settled in for the extended trip to Trojan, the captain invited her to the bridge. He was a distinguished man with gray hair and grayer eyes, a veteran of the Service. He asked questions about the circumnavigation.

"Incredibly dull," she said, "after the first few thousand parsecs."

They indulged in did-you-know exchanges. Both of them had known Dean Richards, first captain of the *Rimfire*. Neither of them had ever met Pete and Jan Jaynes, who had earned a huge bonus by bringing *Rimfire* back from entrapment in dimensionless space during the big ship's maiden voyage when her blink generator malfunctioned.

The conversation was pleasant, but it caused her to wonder if she'd made the proper decision in leaving the Service. She knew and understood people like the polite, sophisticated man who captained the luxury liner. The civilians who laughed, clinked glasses, dropped flatware, talked at the top of their voices in the dining room seemed to be a separate species.

But, she told herself, it would be different when she was back among her own kind on her home planet with her father. That thought sustained her as she rested in her stateroom, hydrated her skin in the bath, ate more than she should have eaten in the dining room, explored the spacetown around Trojan V's port. And then she was looking down on home. Terra II. New Earth. No uncomfortable space-suited transfers to shuttles for passenger liner customers. Liners dropped through planetside clouds and weather, generators roaring on flux, using the occasional guidance jet, to land featherlike on hardpads set among manicured lawns and exotic plantings.

She had not been able, as yet, to notify her father of her coming. She had decided, when one last attempt to call had been frustrated on Delos, to surprise him. She gathered her bags, hailed a taxi, and gave the driver an address a full thirty miles away, on the outskirts of Old Port.

"Sure you can afford this, Lieutenant?" the driver asked.

"Has there been inflation in the past six years?"

"Does a bear defecate in the woods?"

"If it's that bad, maybe you'd better give me an estimate," Erin said.

The driver let his eyes drift up and down her well-shaped body. His gaze lingered on the ship's patch over her left breast. "Say, you're from the *Rimfire?*"

"Yes."

"You with her all the way around?"

He had a tattoo on his forearm that told Erin he was a veteran of X&A Service. She talked Service talk to him. "Does a bear shit in the woods?" she asked.

The driver laughed heartily. "As it happens, I live in Old Port and I was just thinking about heading home when you got aboard. "Tell you what, Lieutenant, this one's on me."

She tossed her bags to the floorboard and took a seat. The hydrocar leaped forward. "I was in the Service a few years back," the driver said.

"Yep," Erin said. "I noticed."

"Battle cruiser. Went out with the peace force that occupied Taratwo. That was before your time."

"I'm afraid so," Erin said.

The driver was looking into the rearview mirror. He had read her name tag, but it hadn't registered until he spelled it out backward from the mirror. He said, "Kenner. Kenner. Say, you wouldn't be John Kenner's girl?"

"I am," she said, smiling. "Do you know my father?"

An odd look took possession of the driver's face. The hydrocar slowed, stopped. He turned to stare at her, his mouth dropping. "You don't know, honey?"

Her heart thudded. "Know what?"

"Well, damn," he said.

"Please, what is it?" she asked.

"Honey, I hate to be the one to have to tell you, damned if I don't."

"Something has happened to my father?"

"He died just last week," the driver said.

CHAPTER TWO

John Kenner had built his retirement home on high ground overlooking a peripatetic river which, like many natural features on Terra II, had an Old Earth name of lost meaning. The Canadian wound its way among wooded, rolling hills past the line of rocky bluffs from which the Kenner house overlooked the river and, on the far side, the ancient scars of deep mining that had devastated the area in the Age of Exploitation. The centuries had healed the wounds to the planet's crust, but there were people alive who still remembered when the Canadian ran red and oily as buried petroleum and mineral wastes were weathered to the surface. Man, in his frantic rush to get back into space, had once again raped a planet, although he had not, as in the case of the home planet, poisoned it fatally with the by-products of nuclear, chemical, and biological war.

A concerted drive to return New Earth to her original beauty had been initiated two hundred years before Erin Kenner was born to a retired fleet marine sergeant major who had married in middle age.

The air was sweet in the midlands of the western continent where John Kenner had built his stone, glass, and polished wood retreat. As a part of the rehabilitation of Terra II, billions of trees had been planted. Tough, hardy grasses had been imported—after careful study—from distant planets to take root in the scorched slag heaps and the scars of the deep surface mines. A climate change that had threatened to give New Earth a permanent overcoat of ice had been reversed.

The planet wasn't a garden spot like Delos III, but it

offered privacy and a pace of life that was less hectic than that on Xanthos or the bustling Tigian planets. A man of modest means could own, as John Kenner did, a tract of land stretching half a mile in three directions from the house on the sandstone bluff overlooking the river.

"You'll always have a place to come back to, Erin," her father had told her when she went away to the Academy at eighteen. "It's yours." He winked. "I hope you don't mind if I enjoy it until you're ready to take over."

Erin could just barely remember her mother as a pretty, gentle woman who told her young daughter stories of her life on a pleasant agricultural world lying in-galaxy from the main body of U.P.

Erin was named for her mother, who had died when her daughter was seven, leaving Erin to form the closest of bondings with her father.

For six years she had looked forward to coming home, and now that she was here John Kenner had been dead five days. As she entered the house in which she had grown up, she had a feeling that her father would emerge from his office or from the kitchen where he had loved cooking dishes from recipes he'd collected on a score of planets. That, of course, did not happen. She was very much alone.

Winter had come to the mid-continent. The outside temperature was just above freezing, but it was warm in the house because the climate control unit had been left on. John Kenner had liked the house to be warm. With a smile of fond memory Erin went to the control unit and lowered the temperature four degrees.

As usual, the house was immaculately neat. The bed was made up in her father's room, where he had died in his sleep. Perishable foods had been removed from the kitchen storage units, although the pantry was stocked with staples and canned goods. In her father's office—he preferred that to calling it his den, saying, "I'm not, after all, some kind of animal,"—she found the same perfect order. She sat in his chair and stared at the holo-stills on his desk. The images were familiar. There was her mother, big Erin, with baby Erin in her arms. Erin at six, in miniature, looking as if she were alive, with a puppy in her arms and with her front teeth missing. Erin as a teenager in her first formal gown.

Tears clouded her vision. She had not yet wept. She let it come in a flood of stomach wrenching sobs, for there was no one in the house to hear and she was more alone than she'd ever been.

She put her head down on her father's desk as the sobs lessened and there began in her mind that age-old game of *if only*. *If only* Rimfire had finished her job a couple of weeks early. *If only* she had never left home. *If only*. . . . But *Rimfire* had not finished earlier; and she *had* left home, encouraged by her father to make a life of her own.

But *if only* she had been able to see him just once more. *If only* she'd been at home to comfort him in his last moments.

"When we face the death of someone dear to us, honey," John Kenner had said beside the grave of Erin's mother, "we weep for ourselves. We may think we're weeping for the dead. We're not, but that's all right. We're weeping for ourselves, and that's permissible because it hurts so damned badly. God knows how badly it hurts, so he gives us tears to wash away the pain that makes us think that it might be best to just give up and join *her*. The tears help us get through it and go on doing what we have to do."

Remembering, Erin wept harder. She was so lost in her misery, weeping, as her father had said, for herself, that she didn't at first notice a small sound at her feet. It was only when she felt a light touch on her knee that she lifted her head quickly to look into a pair of steady, large, chocolate brown eyes peering up at her from a bedraggled mop of blond-brown canine hair. In his last letter to her via blink beacon, her father had told her about his new companion.

"Well, hi," she said, snuffling mucus, reaching for a tissue. "Hi, there."

The dog was standing on his hind legs, forepaws on her knee, his liquid, warm eyes seeming to express concern. He was quite small, weighting only seven pounds.

"I know you," she said.

He made a little sound.

She reached down to pick him up. He leapt away, stood looking at her with his unwavering eyes.

"You're Mop," she said. "Dad named you that because he said when you lie down you look like an old-fashioned rag mop."

At the sound of his name one of the dog's floppy ears stood up.

"I'll bet you've been lonely," she said. "Come here."

Mop was doubtful. He crept closer. Erin didn't move. He put his paws on her knee, lowered his head so that his chin rested between his paws, and looked up at her.

"Oh," she said. This time he allowed her to pick him up. "Poor little fellow," she crooned. "Who's been looking after you?" Mop licked her hand politely, just once.

There was space on New Earth to allow old-fashioned burial of the dead. The Kenner family plot was situated two hundred yards from the house in an area of knee-high grass dotted with purple and yellow wildflowers. The dirt on John Kenner's grave was still fresh. Mop the dog, who had guided her down a pathway familiar to Erin because it led to her mother's grave, sat down and looked solemnly at the mound. The headstone had been in place since the death of John Kenner's wife. On her father's slab only the date of death had been left blank. She made a mental note to find out who could carve the letters and numerals into the stone.

A cold wind crept up the skirt of her dress uniform. As if reminded of his loss by the moaning of the wind through the trees that outlined the burial plot, the little dog lifted his head and howled.

"I know how you feel," Erin said, her throat tight, her eyes stinging.

Mop howled again and her own grief burst out of her again in harsh sobs. The dog stopped howling, came to look up at her with concern. She knelt next to him and said, "It's all right to howl. It hurts. If howling makes it feel better, howl your head off." She threw back her head, looked up at a leaden, winter sky that promised snow, and turned her sobbing into an imitation of the dog's cry of loneliness. After one questioning tilt of his head, Mop joined her and the joint howls of anguish soared upward, out, and away to be absorbed in the dull, chill air.

Night. She went from room to room turning on all of

the lights, Mop following her every step. She discovered his water and food dishes in the kitchen, saw that both basins were stocked. Someone had been looking after him. He followed her to the main room of the house where a front wall of glass gave a view of the Canadian. The river was up from heavy rains in the hills to the west. Muddy water filled the wide channel from bank to bank. In the summertime, she knew, there would be only a four or five foot wide trickle of clear water making a runnel down the center of the half-mile wide, sandy riverbed. In the glow of the lights on the patio, big feathery snowflakes began to fall and, although it was warm and comfortable in the house, she shivered.

She tried the holo, flipped through the available channels, turned the power off. The image of a newsman in business dress faded quickly from the viewing square. Mop was sitting in front of her, his long hair hanging to the deep pile of the carpet.

"So what do you think?" she asked.

He barked twice, with some urgency.

"You *are* kidding me," she said. "You really don't want me to let you out."

The dog barked excitedly.

"Out?"

More excited barking, a run toward the glass wall. She opened a door. The dog dashed out. Snowflakes and a cold wind hit him in the face. He ran back in faster than he had run out.

"So?" she asked.

He lay down and assumed his mop pose, head between his legs.

"Well, if you can hold it, all right," she said. "However, I am not accustomed to cleaning up after some hairy little bugger like you."

It was too early to go to bed. She had talked with no one other than the taxi driver who had known her father. She was sure that John Kenner had had his affairs in order, but she imagined that there'd be some matters that would require her attention. At that moment her plans didn't go past calling her father's bank and, if he'd had one, his attorney. She went into the office and opened the middle drawer where her father had kept his bank book. The bank balance was small, under two hundred standard credits. The current power bill, unpaid, was stuck in the checkbook.

She began to explore other drawers in the desk. John Kenner had prided himself on having a clear title to the house and three hundred acres of reforested hills and rolling meadowlands. With New Earth becoming more and more popular as a quiet haven, such retreats were accruing in value. The Kenner place, should she decide to sell it, would bring a good price.

There was a chrome steel strongbox in the bottom drawer. She punched in her mother's birth date as the combination and the box opened. The first piece of legal paper she opened was a copy of her father's will. No surprises there. Everything had been left to Erin Elizabeth Kenner. But under the will was a blue-wrapped mortgage on the house and land. Less than a year ago John Kenner had borrowed to within a few thousand credits of the value of his property. Instead of leaving his daughter a valuable piece of real estate free and clear, John Kenner had left her a sizable debt.

"So, Mr. Mop," she said to the dog, who had climbed to her lap and then to the desk to lie there watching her as she riffled through the drawers, "what is this?"

The doorbell rang. The dog leapt to the floor, barking.

"I hear, I hear," Erin said. She detoured past her bedroom, got her regulation X&A hand weapon from her bag, held it behind her as she walked to the side door which was the house's front door, facing west. It was strictly illegal for her to have a Service issue hand weapon, but if every retired X&A officer who had managed to hang onto a saffer were arrested, the Service would have to work overtime to discover another planet to be used as a prison for them. Bearing arms was still looked upon as one of the personal freedoms, and saffers were, after all, inexpensive. X&A didn't make too much effort to prevent the taking of one deadly souvenir by a departing officer.

Erin looked through the viewer and saw a tall man, young of face. His unruly brown hair was sprinkled with snowflakes. Mop was still barking frantically, but in a different tone, as if he were thoroughly excited.

"All right," she said. "That's enough." The dog paid no attention. In fact, the pitch of his bark rose.

"Who?" she asked, after pressing the button that activated the talk-through.

"Miss Kenner?"

"Yes, who are you?"

"I'm Denton Gale. I'm a friend of your father's."

She opened the door, letting the X&A saffer hang down by her side in plain view. Mop rushed toward the visitor, yapping happily.

"Hey, Moppy," Gale said, bending to rub the dog's head. Mop's stubby tail was doing overtime in circles. The young man picked him up and rubbed him, then looked at Erin. His eyes widened when he saw the weapon.

"You won't need *that,*" he said.

"I hope not," she said.

"Look, if you'd feel more comfortable if I come back during the day—"

On the hardpad she saw an aircar, sleek, silver. "I apologize for my caution," she said. "I suppose if my little buddy there knows you—"

"I work at the port," Gale said. "I rebuilt the computer on the *Mother Lode* for your dad."

"Run that by again?" she said.

"Look." When he smiled he looked very young. "You're letting all the warm air out and, quite frankly, I'm freezing."

"Come in."

"I heard that you had come home," he said, as she closed the door. "I would have been here in daylight, but I had an emergency call."

She stood in the center of the room, the saffer held behind her. "Gale?"

"Denton Gale."

"And you work on computers?"

"Yes."

"And you did some work for my father?"

"On the *Mother Lode,*" he said. "You won't saff me if I sit down?"

She laughed. "Sit. I've been gone for six years. The last letter I had from my father was almost a year ago. What is a Mother Lode?"

"A Mule Class space-going tug."

"Good God," she said, sitting down weakly.

"You didn't know?" Gale asked. He had deep, dark brown eyes, a regular, pleasant face, a mouth that smiled easily and attractively.

"I've had a lot of surprises lately."

"He bought it just under a year ago. She's in good shape. Really. She was on service with the Trans-Zede Corporation. She was one of the last Mules to be built, as a matter of fact."

"What in hell did my father want with a Mule?" she asked.

Gale shrugged. "I didn't ask."

"What does an antiquated space-going tug cost?"

He named a figure that was within a few thousand credits of the face value of the mortgage she'd found in her father's desk.

"The reason I came over tonight," Denton said, "is because the pad rent is due on the *Lode*. The port's government operated, you know—"

"No, I didn't."

"Well, it is. And they get pretty damned sticky if the pad rent is late."

"How much?"

"A hundred and fifty credits for the month."

"Fine." That, along with the current power bill, would clean out her father's checkbook.

"If you like, I can take the check with me," Gale said.

"I'd appreciate that." She went into the office, wrote the amount. "How do I make it out?" she called.

"Canadian County Spaceport Authority," he answered.

"You're sure that's not you?" she asked, coming out of the office waving the check.

He laughed. "Nope. I'm 'The Computerman, the Century Series a Speciality.' "

"Antiques," she said. The Century Series of computers was two generations older than the Unicloud computers on *Rimfire* and all current X&A ships.

"But solid," he said. "Look, my office is at the end of the main administration building. I'll be glad to show the *Lode* to you any time."

"Can you help me sell her?"

"I guess so," he said.

"If the weather isn't too bad, I'll come over tomorrow."

"Fine."

"Give you a cup of coffee before you go?" She didn't know him, but he had a nice smile and the house seemed so empty with only the little dog for company.

"I really do need to run. I've got a rush job on a freighter that's scheduled to lift for the Tigian planets tomorrow."

"Thank you for coming by."

He smiled, and for the first time his eyes showed that he had noticed that she was a girl. "My pleasure."

She watched his aircar lift off and zoom up and away. The snow was heavier. The ground was turning white. Mop had followed them out. He lifted one leg and left a liquid message on a bush and then ran to wait for her at the door. She went to the library and pulled down a reference book.

Mule Class tugs had been in deep space for almost fifty years. Thousands of them had been built on Trojan during the last half-century. A Mule was a stocky looking brute, knobby and squarish. She was overpowered, built with a blink generator that could take her on half a dozen jumps without recharging, hefty enough to enclose the largest ship within her fields and jump with her in an electronic embrace. Spaceships, after all, were just electronics and mechanics. Electronic things and mechanical things had not changed since some Old One on Old Earth invented the wheel. Machines broke down. Electronic circuits failed. And if enough of them broke down or failed at the same time, a ship carrying a crew and a valuable cargo or a ship with a load of passengers was stranded in space. That's where the Mules came in. Some space tugs were government owned. Most, however, were free enterprise. At specified sites on every blink route space tugs were stationed. There was fierce bidding for the more traveled

routes, for the salvage money that came to a space tug and
its owners when a big ship had to be piggybacked to a
repair yard by a squat, dwarfed Mule made fortunes.

Although the Mule was hailed all over the civilized galaxy as the most dependable ship ever put into space, she
had been replaced over the past ten years by the newer,
larger, more comfortable Fleet Class tug, built by the same
Trojan shipyards that had produced the Mules.

Erin first saw her Mule on a day when snowdrifts were
piling up against the side of the port buildings. She had
drifted over in her father's aircar, Mop sitting beside her,
tongue lolling in excitement at being able to *go*. She was
given a landing spot at least two hundred yards from the
administration building. After a few doubtful steps in the
snow, Mop decided that it was frisky time. He dashed
back and forth, made mock attacks on her legs, bit at the
falling flakes.

Sure enough there was a sign over a door that said THE
COMPUTERMAN, The Century Series a Speciality. She
entered without knocking. Denton Gale sat with his feet
up on his desk. He dropped his boots to the floor and
stood, smiling. Mop jumped into his chair and demanded
attention. Denton rubbed the dog's head as he said, "I
didn't think you'd come today."

"Well, I couldn't wait to see my inheritance," she said
with a wry smile.

"Let me get my coat."

The *Mother Lode* sat squatly on a pad another two hundred yards away through snow and icy wind. Denton
punched a code into the airlock.

"Mother's birthday," Erin said.

"This is a pretty secure port," Denton said. "Even if
someone figured out the code you wouldn't have to
worry."

Ship's smell. A hint of silicon lubes, that almost intan-
gible scent produced by banks of electronics at work, the
odd tang to the recycled air that meant a Blink generator
was in operation. The *Mother Lode* was on standby. Her
automatic monitoring systems purred and hummed. The
control bridge had been freshly painted. The command
chair was newly upholstered in synthetic leather.

"He had her completely overhauled," Denton said. "She's ready. You could take her anywhere."

"I've just been there," Erin said, for the hatch had closed behind him and she was closed in, encapsulated once more in metal, and although it was the cold, winter air of New Earth outside instead of the harsh vacuum of space, she suddenly felt lonely.

"Still want to sell her, huh?"

"Yes."

"I just wish I had the money to buy her," he said.

"I wish you did, too."

"I haven't had a chance to ask around. If you want me to, I will."

"Please do."

He touched buttons on the console. An electronic hiss accompanied the brightening of the computer screen. "Know anything about the Century?"

"We had one at the Academy in my first year, then it was replaced with a first generation Unicloud."

"The Century will do everything a Unicloud will do."

"But slower," she said.

"True. But how vital are a few nanoseconds?"

"Most of the time, not vital," she said.

"There was some senility in the cloud chambers when I first began work on her," Denton said. "Nothing serious. Required recharging the Verbolt fields. Reloading. You'll find that she's as crisp as new."

"I don't really anticipate—"

A beeper at Gale's waist buzzed. He put the instrument to his lips, identified himself. Erin, examining the controls of the Mule, didn't hear the communication.

"I have to run over to the office," he said. "Someone wants to give me some money and I find that to be one of the more rewarding aspects of having my own business. If you'll wait here, I'll be back in a few minutes and I'll show you the rest of the layout."

Erin nodded. In a careful search of the house she had turned up nothing to indicate why a retired spaceman— who had said repeatedly that if he never had to breath recycled air again he would be happy—would put his entire assets into a spaceship. She went into the Mule's living quarters. Crews of two had spent long months in the large and luxurious private cabins aboard the *Lode* when she was on space duty. On the *Mother Lode* one cabin had been converted into a control room for mining equipment attached to the ship's squarish hull. The remaining cabin was equipped with a terminal to give access to the ship's library.

She returned to the bridge, turned on the computer terminal, punched information up idly, saw that the *Lode* was stocked with a rather magnificent library of books and visuals.

"My boy," she told Mop, who had jumped up onto the bed, "I think Mr. John was planning to be in space for a long time. Now the question is, why?"

Mop cocked his head as if to echo her question.

"Why would he name the ship the *Mother Lode?* That's a mining term. My father? Going mining?" She shook her head, turned off the terminal, continued her search. In the engine room the huge blink generator was a solid bulk. Even in repose it emanated a force that lifted the short hairs on her neck. The gym contained the usual exercise equipment. The galley was stocked with enough concentrates to feed a dozen men for a year. She went back to the control bridge and reactivated the computer. She was checking files when Denton Gale returned.

"Ah, so you decided to get acquainted, after all," he said.

She shrugged. "Denton, why did my dad buy this ship?"

"He didn't say and I didn't ask."

"Come on. You worked with him. He must have given you some hint."

"Only her name."

She nodded. "That has occurred to me, but I can't really see John Kenner going off into deep space to prospect for gold."

He laughed. "He was a nice fellow."

"Yep," she said, and suddenly she missed him like crazy. She turned back to the computer. "Not many files."

"Nope. The star charts and navigation tables are in the

root directory. Internal operations and monitors, ditto. Library is in a separate sub-file.''

"I saw that. There's nothing personal listed in the directories. Nothing that my dad put in himself.''

"No.''

"You've looked?''

He grinned. She was not unaware that Denton Gale was a well-constructed, smooth-muscled young man of considerable masculine appeal. He had sun-smiles at the corners of his eyes to match her space squint lines. The way he looked at her told her that he was not unimpressed by an ash blonde woman in spacer's blue.

"Damn,'' she said.

"What?''

She shook her head. She'd been joining Denton in the mating dance of the juveniles, and she wasn't in the mood for games of that sort. "I've forgotten how to check hidden files on a Century,'' she said.

"Unless you have the entry code there's no way to do it short of cooking the X&A black box.'' The black box, required equipment on any space-going computer, held everything that went into the Century whether from the ship's automatic recordings of position and direction or by manual feed from an operator, kept it secure from meddling, under seal, available for official examination should it ever become necessary. Accidents in space were rare, but when the inevitable happened the black box, destructible only by atomics or by being tossed into a sun, gave the reasons. The black box was sacred. To tamper with it was a felony serious enough to lose a man his license *and* his liberty. X&A was jealous of its police powers in space.

"Did you try Mother's birth date?''

He smiled and nodded. "And your dad's birth date and his Service serial number.''

"If you have something to do, Dent, I think I'll stay here and tinker with this old crock for a while.''

"There is some paperwork. I'll be in the office.''

"Thanks for what you've done.''

"No problem,'' he said.

She punched in an order for coffee. It was a thick, heady brew, her father's favorite, made from Delos beans and rich, synthetic cream. Mop indicated that he'd been on board the ship before by going to a service area that had obviously been installed for a person of just his height to paw a little red button that delivered a Mop-sized milk bone.

"Well, aren't you the spoiled one," she teased, as he crawled under the command chair and began to consume the tidbit with unhurried satisfaction.

She began to punch codes into the computer. Her own birthday. The day of her mother's death. The date of her graduation. The date of her father's retirement. When she ran out of numbers, she began on names. Erin. Elizabeth. John. Kenner. Mop. Nire, which was Erin backward. Htebazile, hers and her mother's middle name spelled backward. The computer clicked and hummed, hissed in electronic satisfaction, displayed a typed letter.

The letter began, "Dear Erin."

"Oh, Moppy," she moaned, as she read. "He went senile."

It was a long letter. It told of a visit from an old shipmate who had come to New Earth specifically to see John Kenner. And then she knew why her father had mortgaged his retirement retreat to put everything he had and could raise into an antiquated space tug. The old shipmate had been a member of a prospecting party that stumbled onto a belt of space debris orbiting around a dim and distant sun, debris so rich in heavy metals, including gold and the platinum family, metals so vital to the new age of exploration that one trip to the belt would make a man rich.

"Oh, Dad," she whispered.

The old shipmate had died, leaving the space coordinates that would lead his friend, John Kenner, to the rich belt of ores. There it was, a star chart. She had to check references to orient the relatively small area shown on the chart with the United Planets zone. The distances involved could best be measured in thousands of parsecs. If, indeed, John Kenner's old shipmate had gone there, deep, deep into the hazardous, star-crowded heart of the galaxy past the mysterious Dead Worlds, he had traveled far. Past the Dead Worlds the blink routes extended only a few light-years.

"Mop, he was going to go off the established routes," she said. "What do you think of that?"

Mop thought it was time for a little loving. He licked his chops, leapt into her lap, and threw himself onto his back so that she could rub his chest.

"What are we going to do?" she asked. "What do you think?"

"Wurf," Mop said contentedly.

"You're a helluva lot of help," she said. "Here we are, owners of a Mule equipped for deep space mining, in possession of a treasure map and enough food to last us for three or four years and that's it, buddy. The old home place is mortgaged to the hilt. If we could sell this *mother*—" She was using that element of the tug's name in another context, and that set the ship's personality in her mind. "—for enough to pay off the mortgage, we'd be damned lucky."

She had saved most of her salary during the years of deep space probing aboard *Rimfire*, but a fleet lieutenant didn't earn enough, even in six years, to become rich. She might be able to unload the *Mother*, redeem the old homestead, and squeak by for a few years on what she had saved.

"The question is, Mr. Mop, do I want to? What about you? Would you rather stay at home or go—" One ear came to attention, for "go" was one of his favorite words. "—Blinking and creaking off into the unknown?"

"Wurf," Mop said, waiting for her to say "go" again.

Two days later Denton Gale came to the house with an offer on the *Mother*. "I hate to tell you how much they said they'd pay," he said.

"In that case I don't want to hear," she said.

"It's less than your dad put into her."

"Mother jumping—" She caught herself. "How much less?"

He named a figure thousands of credits below the amount owed on the mortgage.

"Tell them eff them and the horse they rode in on," she said.

Inheritance laws were simple on New Earth. Racial guilt for the spoliation of the planet settled by the only people to escape the Destruction sent U.P. money in great sums to the government. Tax loads were light on New Earth's citizens. There was no governmental bite into John Kenner's estate. The *Mother Lode* and the mortgage encumbered family home were transferred to Erin's name without undue red tape and an offer to buy came not for the Mule but for the Kenner house and lands.

The snow had melted quickly, leaving the clay-rich earth puddled and muddy. Until she'd had to visit her father's attorney's office, Erin had not been out of the house since the first day she'd gone aboard what she was coming to think of as that *Mother,* John Kenner's Folly.

"So you see, Miss Kenner," the attorney who had settled her father's estate said smoothly, "it is quite a generous offer. You would realize some five thousand credits over and above the payoff of the mortgage and legal fees."

"Legal fees, if any, will be paid by the buyer, if any," Erin said in a steely tone, her sea green eyes squinting.

"Perhaps that *could* be arranged," the attorney said doubtfully. "I must tell you, however, that my client is quite eager to settle on New Earth and is examining other properties."

"Bless his little heart," Erin said.

The lawyer raised his eyebrows.

"Don't try to con me, my friend. I've been screwed by experts." She rose to leave his office. "You may tell your client that I am considering his offer, but that I would consider it more strongly if he added five thousand credits to the price."

"I'm afraid that's out of the question."

"Tough titty, then," Erin said. She didn't ordinarily use spacer vulgarities, but there were times when she found a bit of shock to be useful, or, at worst, satisfying. "He's the one who seems to be eager."

She found herself on the approach to the aircar pads of the port, cleared herself for landing, said to the Mop dog, "Now why the hell are we here, partner?"

Mop didn't say. He ran ahead of her to greet Denton Gale at the door to Gale's office. Dent had seen John Kenner's old aircar come in and was waiting. He opened the door, lifted Mop, rubbed his chest, winked at Erin. "The weather is a bit nicer than it was when you were here before."

She pushed past him into the office. He put Mop on his desk where the little dog curled himself into a ball and took a little practice nap.

"Dent, did you talk with that old shipmate of my father's who came to him with this tale about a gold mine?"

"Once or twice. He came by here with John a couple of times when they were shopping for the *Lode,* asking me about computers and electronics. He was an older fellow. At the time I thought he was a bit fragile to be planning to go back into space."

"Obviously you were right," she said.

He sat on the edge of the desk, motioned her to take his chair. She sat, crossed her legs. She'd dug into a trunk at the house to find cold weather slacks and had been quite pleased to find that other than a bit of rather becoming tightness in the seat, she fit well into clothing she had not worn since she was eighteen.

"Any particular reason why you ask?"

"Ummm," she said.

His face was haloed by backlighting from the windows. He was smiling. He was one handsome son-of-a-bitch. She felt that sliding, melting feeling and answered his smile.

"Not thinking of going out there to take a look, are you?" He looked upward, making the standard physical reference to space.

"What do you think?"

That often used phrase caused Mop to lift his good ear.

"I think, Erin, that you are the most beautiful girl I've ever seen."

"Now where did that come from?" she asked disgustedly.

"Here," he said, touching his chest.

Her reaction was out of proportion to his infraction. She used a couple of choice spacer expressions on the way out of the office and was in the aircar jerking it aloft and toward the house before she realized why she was so angry.

It had not been Dent's compliment that had sent her flee-
ing from his office but her reaction to it. Once before when
she'd been lonely she'd turned to casual male arms for
comfort and she had never forgotten the stomach-sinking
feeling of self-loathing when the brief spasms without love
were over. Now she was lonely again, and she'd seriously
entertained the idea, at least for a moment, of seeking
solace in Denton Gale's arms.

Her decision was made by the time she found the attorney's com-number. A secretary answered. "Yes, Miss
Kenner. As a matter of fact, Mr. Atherton has been trying
to reach you."

"Glad you called, Erin," the lawyer said. "I relayed
your message to my client and I was rather surprised to
find that he is willing to go an extra five thousand for
occupancy within thirty days."

"So? I should have asked for ten, huh?"

Atherton cleared his throat. "He is quite eager to take
occupancy."

"Throw in another five for the furnishings and a used
aircar and he can have it right now."

"I'll get back to you within the hour," Atherton said.

The sale was closed before the end of business next day.
She left the only home she remembered, taking with her
nothing more than books, pictures, holo-tapes, a few music capsules that brought back youthful memories, and the
Mop's bed. Her savings and the equity from the property
had been converted into universal credits to be drawn on
at any bank in the U.P.

She spent a day checking and double-checking *Mother*'s
store of goodies. Her father had stocked the ship well. Her
only purchase was several cases of Tigian wine and a few
cases of liver flavored nibbles for the Mop. Once she saw
Denton Gale come out of his office and look over toward
the *Mother*, but he did not put in an appearance. She lifted
ship without saying good-bye to the only person on New
Earth other than a lawyer whom she knew by name.

Once out of the planet's gravity well she set multiple
blinks into the Mule's big and powerful generator and
within a half hour *Mother* had traversed the most traveled
routes within U.P. territory, putting parsecs behind her.

Each time the ship blinked, making for that funny little feeling in the stomach, Mop looked up, lifted one ear, and yawned. During recharging, when there was nothing to do but wait while old Mr. Blink's miracle accumulated energy from the stars, she slept, read, sampled the holo-pictures, and wondered if, after all, her mother had had any children that lived.

"You," she said accusingly to the Mop dog. "It's all your fault. You're always so damned eager to *go.*"

Mop's good ear lifted. His tongue came out and he panted excitedly as if to say, "Where, where, go where?"

CHAPTER THREE

Dressed in athletic shorts and shirt, breasts bound to prevent soreness from bouncing, Erin ran down a New Earth country lane between rows of flowering trees. The sun was warm on her back. The sky overhead was pellucid blue. She'd done half a mile, had a mile and a half to go.

Beside the moving track a long-haired little dog sat watching with puzzled interest. He rose, yawned, and stretched, went to lift one leg against a roadside tree.

"No, no," Erin said.

The dog was confused. The holo images looked real, but when he tried to go into the woods to find bigger and better trees to irrigate, he bumped into the wall. He came back to cock his head and look up at Erin as she ran lightly on the moving belt. He apparently decided that it looked like fun and jumped onto the belt, lost his footing, and went rolling back past Erin's feet.

"You just have to get the hang of it," Erin said. She slowed the belt, picked Mop up, put him directly in front of her. The belt carried him backward, but he began running, fell back between Erin's legs and almost tripped her. He finally got the hang of it and, as she increased the speed of the exercise track, ran ahead of her, looking back over his shoulder once with his tongue lolling out.

After a few more humiliations such as running into the far wall of the gym when he decided to dash ahead, and being tossed tail over head off the moving belt, he got the swing of it. Within a week he was leaping on and off the belt as he saw fit, could pace himself to the speed of it, and, looking quite proud, Erin thought, could even double back, running with the belt, to make a mock attack on her pumping legs.

"This is one thing I hate, hate, hate about space," she told Mop, as she toweled off after a shower. "Exercise for the sake of exercise is—" She paused. "Your young ears should not hear what I was thinking."

She let the shower stall finish drying her with a gentle zephyr of soft, desert air.

"And so," she said, "here I am, halfway to hell-and-gone, half bonkers, talking to a hairy little pooch."

Mop cocked his head charmingly and said, "Wurf."

"And now, sir, it is inspection time. Shall we go?"

The magic word. Mop leapt up, did a horizontal 360, a complete turn in the air, and scampered toward the door.

The human body's bio-clock adjusted itself to the axial rotation of two planets so much alike that their days differed by mere seconds. On board the *Mother Lode* ship's clocks measured New Earth hours. Each day at a specific hour Erin made a complete round of *Mother*, checking all systems and all structural features. *Mother* was a sound ship, but, space being the most unforgiving environment faced by man, one could not be too careful. In the big empty a particularly swift and unpleasant death lay just beyond a few inches of hull. A pinpoint penetration of that hull by some speeding particle of debris, if not repaired immediately, could bleed the air away. Not even the technology aboard the most advanced of ships, such as *Rimfire*, could create oxygen out of nothing. *Mother* had only the air she'd carried with her from New Earth. So once every twenty-four hours the ship's captain and first mate, Erin and Moppy the Dog, strolled the corridors, poked heads into cargo and engineering spaces, scanned the sealed food and water storage chambers, gazed meaningfully at the bolt heads that held the multilayered hull together, pored over the autologs that recorded the ever-mysterious workings of the generator, punched test buttons on various electronic circuits, and in general went over the *Mother* from her square stern to her square bow.

The inspections were made during the periods when *Mother* floated motionless in the blackness, less than a mote among the ever more dense fields of stars. After a charge things were a bit more interesting as Erin programmed blinks into the computer and punched them in one by one until the huge generator's charge was depleted. The little ship hurled itself down the star lanes toward the fiery heart of the galaxy.

There came a time when the blinks were shorter, when the course became a zigzag made necessary by the density of the stellar population. Actual travel was instantaneous, but preparation for that travel began to take more and more time so that weeks became months.

She had leisure during the charging periods for exploring the contents of the library, and for getting to know her companion. "You are, sir," she said, as Moppy offered his right paw for shaking, "a rather remarkable fellow. You don't snore. You don't take up much of the bed. You know that your duty is to keep my feet warm at night and that all you're expected to do during the day is guard against boogers and to get a smile on your face and keep your big mouth shut. Men could learn a lot from you."

Moppy rolled over and said, "Uhhhhh," which was his way of saying, "That's nice, Erin. Rub my stomach."

She was quite rapidly running out of charts. Winds of radiation swept past *Mother* as she floated in the hard, hard light of the crowded star fields. After each jump she was reminded of the difference between the Century Series of computers and the state-of-the art Unicloud aboard *Rimfire*. With millions of points of reference the old Century chuckled to itself for minutes before confirming position. There were times when Erin was tempted to cut the process short. She was, after all, still on established blink routes. However, from her first year at the Academy she had been taught to check and double-check. There was only one recorded case of it happening, but if some natural force, say the gravitational pull of an errant comet, had moved a blink beacon a substantial distance from its surveyed location, a ship using the coordinates of the beacon on which to base a blink might end up inside the atomic furnace of a star or become blended atom to atom with some small, dark body.

As she moved ever deeper toward the star-packed core she began to develop a claustrophobic feeling of being hemmed in by stars: orange stars, red stars, blue-white stars; M stars and K stars; visual binaries and eclipsing binaries; variable stars—Cepheids and RR Lyrae stars, SS Cygni stars and R Corona Borealis stars; large stars and medium stars and blue giants and old, tired, dark, shrunken stars dead by nova in a time so remote that it was meaningless to a mere woman of New Earth who had the life expectancy promised to the men of Old Earth in the one surviving piece of Old Earth literature, the Bible. "The life span of man shall be a hundred and twenty years." *Genesis 6:3.*

She was just over one-quarter through her allotted time, if, indeed, she proved to be average; but as she jumped *Mother* carefully toward a dense cluster of New York type stars it seemed that time had slowed, that she would use up too much of her ration of years before *Mother* reached her destination.

The New York cluster blocked a straight-line blink route into an area of space, less crowded among the harshness. The blink routes took her around the cluster and, the generator depleted, *Mother* was motionless in space within optic range of a small grouping of stars that were huddled together as if for company in a sort of cul-de-sac in space surrounded by glittering oceans of old, huge, central core monsters.

The sac stars had families. One member of the planetary grouping of the star nearest her came onto her view screen when she punched orders into the computer. The world was one of several that had given mankind the shivers for centuries.

Planets were not common enough to be ignored. Planets among the dense star fields near the core, some 10,000 light-years from the U.P. sector, were even more rare. Any ship coming into the sac would take a close look at the world known as D.W. One, and would see one principal reason why man had constructed huge fleets of ships and had armed them with the most deadly weapons that technology could supply.

D.W. One, the first of the Dead Worlds to be encountered by a ship coming in from the periphery, had been killed with a totality that belied the difficulty of the feat.

Man could denude a planet of forests, eliminate thousands
of animal species, poison the atmosphere and the oceans
with his wastes, but it was pretty damned difficult to kill
a planet and leave it intact. A planet buster could fragment
a world and leave nothing more than a belt of asteroids,
but what had been done to the Dead Worlds was even more
impressive, for D.W. One and several of her sister planets
in the sac were dead from the inside out. Although she
was old, she should have had a molten core. That she did
not was one of the mysteries that had kept astrophysicists
guessing and caused all U.P. exploration ships to go
armed. If the planet killers ever came sweeping in from
the vastness of space, man, so fragile in his frame of
bones, tendons, cartilage, and flesh, would need protection. Thus, on *Rimfire* and on all other major ships of the
X&A fleet there were weapons that *could* fragment a world
if necessary.

Once the planets in the sac had lived. Although there
were no clues to the identity of the race or races that had
peopled the Dead Worlds, unidentifiable rubble on the ravaged surface of D.W. One proved that there had been a
technological civilization there. Now even the top soil was
gone. The ground up nonbiodegradable debris of a technological civilization was scattered over a surface that was
nothing more than inert rock. And into a flat, continent-
sized area of the rock the killers, the race that had destroyed twenty living planets, had carved a warning. The
message was not in words, but in symbols. An eye. A
world, a stylized building and other, more obscure images.

There was disagreement as to the exact words intended,
but all of the experts agreed that the message carved into
the bones of a continent was a warning: "Look at this
world and tremble. Build not, for we will return."

Erin turned off the optics, shivered. Then, perversely,
as if to prove to the vast emptiness around her that she
wasn't *really* spooked by the mystery of twenty dead
worlds, she checked the library index and watched a docu-
history that told of the initial discovery of the worlds in
the sac, and ended with the account of the last licensed
scientific expedition to the sac by six graduate students

aboard the *Paulus*, under Laconius of Tigian. The *Paulus* had disappeared, had vanished as completely as the race that had lived on the Dead Worlds. Every holo-drama fan could name the six students who had disappeared with Paulus.

Of course, ships did evaporate into the nothingness of space from time to time, but the fact that the *Paulus* had disappeared while on a trip to the Dead Worlds had inspired writers, good and bad, to go into spasms of speculative creativity.

Aside from the Dead Worlds docu-history, the *Mother*'s library contained no less than three holo-dramas based on the loss of the *Paulus*. Erin watched two of them while waiting for the generator to charge and then, before the big power source was fully ready, she blinked onward and past the sac into the star fields and to the end of the line, as far as established blink beacons were concerned. From there on she had only the star chart in *Mother*'s computer, a chart compiled by her father's old shipmate who, she felt, may or may not have known a black hole from his own dusky posterior orifice.

She wanted a fully charged generator. She watched the third holo-drama about the Dead Worlds in which a rather sick minded writer presented the theory that giant lava beetles had hatched deep down in the fiery magma of the interior of the planets and had eaten the life from within before, in desperate hunger, they had emerged to crumble into tiny, unidentifiable bits everything they didn't eat.

To get the taste of that one out of her mind, she selected the documentary version of the X&A expedition to the colliding galaxies in Cygnus and the finding of the Miaree manuscripts written in the language of the second alien race, the Artonuee, of which U.P. explorers had found evidence.

She told herself that she'd had enough thinking about aliens, about planet killers and the Cygnus races who joined each other in death. She had spent her time of awe and wonder as an undergraduate, speculating with others on the nature of the female ruled Artonuee and the very masculine Delanians, and about the nature and the source of power for those who had devastated the Dead Worlds.

But back in college on New Earth she'd been a long way from either the colliding galaxies in Cygnus or from the twenty worlds in the sac. Out here, alone except for a polite, gentle little dog, surrounded by the eternal glow of the core worlds, the possibility of coming face to face with the planet killers was a bit more real.

Look on this world and tremble. Build not, for we shall return.

With a fully charged generator she double-checked the visuals, ran a deep-search with all available ship's instruments, and, holding her breath, took the first blink from coordinates on the star chart drawn by her father's old shipmate. She and the ship arrived. As she prepared for the next jump, Mop came to her and politely asked to be held. She took him into her lap.

"You're nervous, too?" she asked.

He licked her thumb. Just once.

"Don't blame you, little buddy," she said. "But hang in there, huh?" She poised her finger over the button. "Heeeeeere we go."

After the little wrench to the system that is standard with a blink, she looked at the viewers. Still lots of stars. Still closer to the core. And it took still longer for the computer to chuckle its way to a conclusion about location, for the stars around them were not included on the ship's charts and the computer had to backcheck behind them until it found a familiar correlation.

Once again, and again, and a long wait for charging with a storm of solar winds eddying and seething around the ship, straining the capacity of the radiation shields built between the hulls.

"One more time," she told Mop. She pushed the button. *Mother* leapt. Mop sat down, his long hair hiding his rear legs, lifted his sharp little muzzle toward what the ship's gravity told him was the ceiling, and howled.

Erin jumped, startled. "Don't *do* that," she said.

Mop lifted his nose and howled once more, then lay down with his nose between his front legs.

Erin felt little sheets of shivers running up and down her spine. She punched in an all-direction scan, watched the screens closely. Stars and more stars. Then, toward

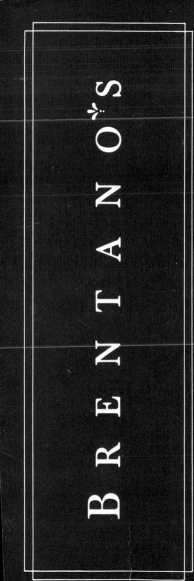

the core, oddly enough, a big blackness. She punched in magnification, her heart pounding. She hadn't really expected to find an isolated binary so near the galaxy's heart. But there they were, two stars of equal brightness. She punched in orders. Optics whirred into position. The twin stars were separated by 9.5 astronomical units, had an orbital period of 44.5 years. The mass of the nearer sun was .96 of the sun of New Earth, the star by which man measured all others. The farther star was slightly larger in mass than the New Sun, which accounted for the fact that, even though it was more distant, it had the same apparent brightness as the nearer star. The nearer star was sterile, alone in its assigned volume of space. The other had whelped.

She had to make a short Blink to get near enough for the ship's instruments to pick up the family of planets circling the more distant, larger star.

So far everything on the chart was checking out. She put the *Mother Lode* on flux and, while she gathered data and recharged the generator, had a bath, gave Moppy one—much to his disgust—dried her hair and his with a blower, and then held Moppy up to the viewer to show him the sights. The ship flew past two uninhabitable planets, one a frozen ball of ice, the other a gas giant.

"Well, my boy," she told Mop, "it's just the way Dad's old buddy said it was."

She felt herself becoming just a bit excited as *Mother* neared her destination. She was quite close, astronomically speaking, before *Mother*'s sensors could pick up the belt of asteroids located roughly in what would have been the star's life zone. Beyond the asteroid belt were two small bodies, one not much larger than a respectable moon, orbiting so close to the sun that they were nothing more than scorched rock.

Not all life zone planets were number three planets, but most were. Once, apparently, this sun had had a third planet, a world positioned in that relatively narrow, highly critical area just close enough to a sun to condense water, not close enough for the water to boil away, and not far enough away for the water to freeze permanently.

Now, in the orbit of the third planet, the ship's instru-

ments picked up a band of rubble. The jum
extended far and away, curving in both direc
a ring of space rubbish all around the sun. Sh
fall closer, whistled when the optics showe
really crowded in there, that the chunks of ro
large and small, were so close together that
among them was going to be, at best, thrill
the ship directions. Gyros whined. The ship t
taking up an orbit parallel to and at a safe
the asteroid belt.

She jumped when *Mother*'s detectors ping
but before she could act a chunk of rock t
interplanetary freighter rolled past not ove
away. The tumbling asteroid didn't make a r
as debris sometimes did in the more amateu
eras, but even without sound it was menaci
send Erin scampering to the controls to put
between her and the belt.

She had a good sleep before approaching
again. Then, heart pounding, she turned the
tors to maximum power and upped *Mother*"
She zapped in close to the belt, holding
matched velocity with the nearest large ro
was tumbling slowly. It had ragged, sharp ed
no friction, no nothing in space to weather
big on one relatively flat surface as a city bl
on the other three sides. She edged the ship
on the detectors. Not much happened.

She moved on to make another nerve-rack
to a slowly tumbling rock mountain and used
again. Nothing. It was four hours and several
later that she pulled up alongside a smaller
and turned on the detectors to hear them si
of heavy metals. She did some fine turning

"Well, Mr. Mop," she said, "There's gol
hills, after all."

It was challenging as hell to bring the sh
closer to the slowly tumbling chunk of mas
One little misjudgment and it was one hell
home. She edged up to a flat surface, tease

the core, oddly enough, a big blackness. She punched in magnification, her heart pounding. She hadn't really expected to find an isolated binary so near the galaxy's heart. But there they were, two stars of equal brightness. She punched in orders. Optics whirred into position. The twin stars were separated by 9.5 astronomical units, had an orbital period of 44.5 years. The mass of the nearer sun was .96 of the sun of New Earth, the star by which man measured all others. The farther star was slightly larger in mass than the New Sun, which accounted for the fact that, even though it was more distant, it had the same apparent brightness as the nearer star. The nearer star was sterile, alone in its assigned volume of space. The other had whelped.

She had to make a short Blink to get near enough for the ship's instruments to pick up the family of planets circling the more distant, larger star.

So far everything on the chart was checking out. She put the *Mother Lode* on flux and, while she gathered data and recharged the generator, had a bath, gave Moppy one—much to his disgust—dried her hair and his with a blower, and then held Moppy up to the viewer to show him the sights. The ship flew past two uninhabitable planets, one a frozen ball of ice, the other a gas giant.

"Well, my boy," she told Mop, "it's just the way Dad's old buddy said it was."

She felt herself becoming just a bit excited as *Mother* neared her destination. She was quite close, astronomically speaking, before *Mother*'s sensors could pick up the belt of asteroids located roughly in what would have been the star's life zone. Beyond the asteroid belt were two small bodies, one not much larger than a respectable moon, orbiting so close to the sun that they were nothing more than scorched rock.

Not all life zone planets were number three planets, but most were. Once, apparently, this sun had had a third planet, a world positioned in that relatively narrow, highly critical area just close enough to a sun to condense water, not close enough for the water to boil away, and not far enough away for the water to freeze permanently.

Now, in the orbit of the third planet, the ship's instruments picked up a band of rubble. The jumble of rocks extended far and away, curving in both directions, making a ring of space rubbish all around the sun. She let the ship fall closer, whistled when the optics showed that it was really crowded in there, that the chunks of rock, asteroids large and small, were so close together that maneuvering among them was going to be, at best, thrilling. She gave the ship directions. Gyros whined. The ship turned slowly, taking up an orbit parallel to and at a safe distance from the asteroid belt.

She jumped when *Mother*'s detectors pinged a warning, but before she could act a chunk of rock the size of an interplanetary freighter rolled past not over a half mile away. The tumbling asteroid didn't make a roar of threat, as debris sometimes did in the more amateurish space operas, but even without sound it was menacing enough to send Erin scampering to the controls to put more distance between her and the belt.

She had a good sleep before approaching the asteroids again. Then, heart pounding, she turned the ship's detectors to maximum power and upped *Mother*'s speed a bit. She zapped in close to the belt, holding her breath, matched velocity with the nearest large rock. The rock was tumbling slowly. It had ragged, sharp edges. No rain, no friction, no nothing in space to weather it. It was as big on one relatively flat surface as a city block, rounded on the other three sides. She edged the ship closer, turned on the detectors. Not much happened.

She moved on to make another nerve-racking approach to a slowly tumbling rock mountain and used the detectors again. Nothing. It was four hours and several fruitless tries later that she pulled up alongside a smaller chunk of rock and turned on the detectors to hear them sing out loudly of heavy metals. She did some fine turning and nodded.

"Well, Mr. Mop," she said, "There's gold in them thar hills, after all."

It was challenging as hell to bring the ship closer and closer to the slowly tumbling chunk of mass and inertia. One little misjudgment and it was one helluva long walk home. She edged up to a flat surface, teased *Mother* into

followed the tumbling motion, hit the guidance jets, yelped
as the landing gear contacted the rock.

Mop said, "Yipe."

"*Now* you're worried?" she asked, as she adjusted the
field to include the big rock and to effectively attach it to
the ship. She let the computer measure the roll and tumble
and fed impulses into the flux drive and guidance jets until
the disturbing motions were stilled and the ship and rock,
held together by the power of *Mother*'s giant generator,
sailed serenely along without so much as a wobble.

"My boy," she said, "things are looking up."

There was a huge vein of gold directly under the ship.
She took up station in the second crew's cabin, which her
father had turned into a control room for the mining equipment. Soon an extractor arm was using a laser to boil rock
away from the vein of gold and, before the end of her first
work day, she had not just *some* gold, but pounds of gold
aboard ship. Gold so pure that it seemed to glow.

When the vein of almost pure gold ran out she moved
ship, using the extractor arm to pull *Mother* to a new position. There was gold, but it wasn't nearly as pure as the
first vein. She lifted ship and spent several days trying to
find another source as rich as that of the first day. After a
week of it, she came to the conclusion that she was not
going to get rich in a matter of days, that the first vein had
been a fluke. Not that there weren't fortunes contained in
the asteroid belt. There was enough gold and platinum
metals and silver to make her one of the richest people in
the U.P., but it wasn't going to be all that easy. The *Mother
Lode* wasn't going to go home laden with nuggets of pure
gold, but she would go back with very, very rich ore filling
all available cargo spaces. Heck, it might even take two
or three trips out there to make her as rich as she decided
she wanted to be.

She started loading gold-rich ore. It was picky work.
First the areas containing gold had to be searched out by
instrument, then *Mother* had to be positioned. The ship
couldn't sit on a needle point of rock, so some very rich
sounding areas had to be bypassed in order to find a fairly
flat landing place. Moving in and out of the tumbling,
crowded asteroid belt ceased to be so thrilling she could

hardly stand it and came to be just spine-tinglingly terrifying.

She'd been working for just under a month when she decided to scout around a bit before attaching the ship to another asteroid. She circled the sun in an orbit outside the belt. The density of the belt was about equal all the way around. She saw chunks that were large enough to make fairly respectable moons for a small planet. She had forgotten her loneliness. She had her work. She had very good company. Mop was not demanding. He fed and watered himself by pushing on his Mop buttons at his station. He had been trained to use an ingenious little pad in the exercise room that broke his body wastes down into recyclable liquids immediately and pulled the smells in behind them. He didn't talk a lot. In fact, except for that meaningful grunt which said, "Please, Erin, rub my belly," he'd been silent since his disturbed howling had chilled Erin.

On the opposite side of the orbital ring of debris she jockeyed *Mother* down onto a flat surface, stabilized the tumble, put out the extractor arm, and began to load ore that was the richest she'd seen since the first day. The detectors were humming merrily about gold and she was humming a little song that had been rewritten with some rather ribald lyrics by the junior officers aboard *Rimfire*. She was just about ready to knock off for the day when there was a clear tone, a vibrant, piercing tone that jerked her to attention. She stopped the movement of the arm and focused a viewer on the biter at the end. The vibrant, piercing tone of alert continued to sing in her ears. She saw something a bit lighter in color than the gold bearing rock, reached back to kill the foreign object alert, turned on a powerful light, lowered the viewer until its nozzle almost touched the biter at the end of the extractor arm.

"Woah," she whispered.

All around her was the vacuum of space, the coldness and emptiness, the uncaring, glaring stars. The nearest planet, a bit larger than New Earth, was a chemical swamp with surface temperatures hot enough to ignite paper, if there'd been any oxygen in the poisonous atmosphere. Nearer the sun were the two cinder planets, lifeless rock baked by the solar storms. Far away, out past the chemical swamp planet, was a frozen, airless ball of ice. And at the tip of the excavator arm, still half encased in the matrix rock, was a fossilized skull, a skull that looked up at her with dark, eyeless sockets, a skull that had to be incredibly ancient, and was very damned definitely humanoid.

Man had been twice in space. A very few had soared upward from Old Earth on the fire of primitive chemical rockets. Centuries later man had broken the bounds of planetary gravity once more, this time with the help of old Billy Bob Blink's invention that made star travel less dangerous and much less time-consuming. Man had been in space for the second time for thousands of years and in all that time he had encountered intelligence only in the mutated forms of life that had survived the Destruction of Old Earth. He had found evidence of alien intelligence, but the aliens were all dead—the residents of the Dead Worlds and the two races who clung together in a clasp of death as galaxies collided in Cygnus.

The decades of work on Old Earth since the reunion had taught man much about himself. From her classes at the Academy Erin knew that life on Old Earth had begun millions of years in the past, but that man, himself, was a relative newcomer. The humanoid skull staring up at her with its blank, dark eyes was as old or older than the anthropoid remains that had been discovered in fossil form on Old Earth since the reunion. Here, then, was evidence of another manlike race. Whether or not the skull represented intelligence she could not guess, but she knew that X&A scientists would consider it to be of more importance than the gold and gold ore she had stowed in *Mother*'s bins.

She moved the extractor arm slightly. The skull was still attached to the matrix rock. "Well, damn," she said.

Mop looked up questioningly.

"I can't believe I'm going to do this," she said.

Mop followed her to the air lock and watched anxiously as she worked her way into a suit.

"Sorry, fella, this trip isn't for you," she said.

She took the dog to the control room, closed the door behind her, felt panic for one moment not because she was *scared,* but because if anything happened to her *out there,* Mop would be left all alone to punch out his food and water until it was all gone and then—

"Oh, damn," she moaned, as she closed the helmet and sucked air.

"Oh, shit," she said, as the inner hatch closed and a pump whined as it evacuated air from the lock.

"Balls," she whispered, as the outer hatch opened and she stared out into the big empty.

CHAPTER FOUR

She felt stiff and heavy as she stepped out of the hatch onto the ship's ladder. She could never get enough oxygen into her lungs while she was imprisoned inside a flexsuit. The feeling of being slowly suffocated was psychological, for the air mixture in the suit was richer than that aboard ship. She halted for a moment before turning around to adjust the tool kit strapped to her back. The hatch started to close behind her. She did not hear it, of course, but she felt the slight vibration of its movement coming up through her boots. She turned and was mesmerized as the opening narrowed. When the crack closed and the hatch snugged itself into its seal, she felt panic.

What if?

What if the hatch lock didn't respond to her instructions when she was ready to go back into the ship? She had only a few hours of air. With the oxygen gone, she would never decay. She would be held on the surface of the asteroid by the field of the ship's generator until, perhaps years from now, the generator used up its full charge and cooled. Would she then drift away from the rock to tumble free in her own eternal orbit around an alien sun?

She had performed extravehicular work before, but never alone. There had been times when teams of crewmen in suits had swarmed over the outside hide of *Rimfire* to check her condition, but each man had been teamed with another. Every spacer who had faced the void knew the devastating effect of looking at the big empty through an impossibly frail faceplate from the doubtful security of a

flexsuit. It was S.O.P. to never, never, send a man outside
the ship without a buddy.

There near the core, with legions, hoards, multitudes of
brilliant stars surrounding her, she felt more isolated than
she had felt while space walking in the nothingness outside
the galaxy when she had to look in one direction to see
the misty mass of the Milky Way, when there was nothing
but blankness on three sides.

She was dwarfed. She felt as if she were being infinitely
diminished. She turned and with a shaking hand punched
the entry combination into the lock. The hatch began to
open. She took a deep breath and let it out, canceled the
open order, turned her face up toward the viewport in the
control room. She saw the shaggy face of Mop. His sharp
nose and alert eyes followed her movement as she climbed
down the ladder. She waved and said, "Hold the fort,
buddy. I'll be back before you know it."

The *Mother Lode* was in harsh sunlight. The surface of
the asteroid was not level so that the ship seemed to be
tilted. From the inside the lopsided stance had not mat-
tered, since the reference for the senses was the ship's own
gravity which made her deck down regardless of her position. Standing outside, the breath of the nuclear furnace
that was the nearest star raising the temperature on the
surface of her suit, Erin felt momentary dizziness as she
looked up at *Mother*. She took a deep breath. The hiss of
air was loud inside her helmet. On all sides around her the
shattered remnants of a world kept pace, most of them
tumbling slowly. She was in the middle of an eerie sea of
motion made up of the glaring, brutal, unfiltered sunlight
reflecting off sunward planes and angles and the absolute
blackness of space that was echoed on the dark sides of
the asteroids. And over and under and to all sides were
the cold, many-faceted faces of the core star fields.

In the shadow of the ship the suit's coolers changed tone
as their function was reversed to heating. The light attached to her helmet came on automatically. She pointed
it by moving her head, approached the extraction arm,
stepped down into the trench. It was pleasing to her to see
the light bouncing off flecks of pure gold, but that pleasure

passed when she focused her attention on the thing that was partially exposed near the biting end of the arm.

She placed the work kit on the barren stone, removed a hand-held, laser powered cutter, a tool developed especially for mining. A sensor guided her to a setting that would not harm the fossil bone. She applied the laser to the matrix rock around the skull experimentally, saw that the setting was perfect. The enclosing rock melted away.

For a few minutes she forgot her appalling isolation, did not lift her eyes to see the harsh sunlight or the crowded stars, concentrated on the job at hand until she could lift the skull free. She placed it on the rock at the side of the trench and cleaned it with the laser beam.

She had not been wildly interested in the subject matter covered in the one course in paleontology that had been required at the Academy. Following the fossil record of the evolution of the Tigian tiger was, at best, dull. Only a few days had been allocated to the discussion of the work being done by technicians in anti-radiation gear on Old Earth, where the hardened remains of the Old Ones, man himself, were being unearthed. Before going extravehicular, she had punched in orders for the scant material on the development of man. The skulls of the Old Ones, Earthmen, were identical to those of modern man. This had inspired various interpretations. One cynical school of thought had it that God had given up on man, that after the Destruction He had determined that man was His greatest failure and had abandoned any further development. Others, more upbeat, believed that, as the Bible said, man had been created in God's image, and was thus perfect, needing no evolution from the form that had been developed prior to the Destruction.

The mutation of the Old Ones into Healers, Power Givers, Far Seers, and Keepers after the Destruction was, depending on one's viewpoint: 1. The power of God exemplified, since divine miracles were required to preserve life on earth. 2. The work of the evil one, perverting the perfection of God's finest creation into ugly and malignant forms.

Fortunately, the first view, or more moderate adaptations of it, prevailed in U.P. society, allowing the mutants from Old Earth to be valued and welcome members of the race.

But the fossil skull that grinned at her, all teeth intact, eye sockets black and empty, was not that of some mutated form or of some alien. Her knowledge was limited. She was not an expert in the field, but she'd looked at pictures just minutes before exiting the ship and the images were fresh in her mind. This fellow had been the guy next door. He was man. Modern man. And that was very damned interesting since, if she remembered correctly, it took a few million years to turn living bone into stone.

She used the mining laser to check the area where the skull had spent an eon in sleep. She melted out a lightning bolt of pure gold and held it in her hand, but there was no sign of other fossilized bones. *Mother* spoke to her. The husky voice of the computer said, "You have been extra-vehicular for one hour and twenty-eight minutes."

No problem. She had four hours worth of air and a ten minute reserve. She melted out another small vein of gold, put it into her specimen pouch, examined the rock near the trench, said, "Well, to hell with it."

The suit's coolers sizzled into action as she stepped back into the light. She looked up and around. The skull in the pouch on the outside of the flexsuit pressed against her thigh as if reminding her that once it had housed the soft, mysterious things that made up an intelligent brain. The stars pushed down, dazzling her eyes. The tumbling rocks of the asteroid belt seemed to be moving toward her. She ran in pure panic, clambered up the steps, mispunched the combination to the lock, screamed out good, solid, spacer profanity that had originated in the less desirable areas of a score of planets. Her frantic eyes looked up, saw Mop sitting on the little ledge of the control room viewport, his mouth open, his tongue hanging out.

"Hi," she said, calming enough to punch the right combination into the lock.

The outer hatch closed with an unheard but felt clang. Air hissed into the lock. The inner door opened and she peeled out of the suit, first removing the two samples of gold and the skull from the outside pouches.

"Well, my friend," she said, holding the skull in both

hands, for it was, after all, heavy stone. "I can't say I care too much for the garden spot where you decided to spend eternity."

She was just a little bit ashamed of herself. Mop greeted her as if she'd been gone for ages, leaping, making mock attacks, hoisting his rear and lowering his head between his front paws in his "look-at-me-I'm-charming" pose. She ruffled his soft hair, picked him up. He threw himself over onto his back in the crook of her arm with a gusty sigh and allowed her to rub his chest and belly. When he had had enough he began to wiggle. She put him down, punched up a very stiff drink, sat in the control chair. Mop took his place on the console and lay down, his head held up alertly, ready for conversation.

"Mr. Mop," she said, "looks to me as if this belt of rock was once a planet of considerable size."

Mop said, "Wurf."

"Which makes you think, doesn't it?" She took a long sip of her drink. "The U.P.'s planet buster could have done this to a planet. Did, as a matter of fact, to a few Zede worlds during the Zede War, but that was just a thousand years ago, and our friend, there—" she shifted her eyes to the skull—" is very damned definitely more than a thousand years old."

Mop lifted his right paw, asking for a handshake. She complied, held the paw. "What we should do, I guess, is send a blinkstat back to X&A right now."

Mop cocked his head.

"Yeah, you're right," she said. "We've got everything we own tied up in this expedition. Dad's money, too. Everything wrapped up in this *Mother*. I don't know how much gold we've got aboard, but I do know this. We report our friend, here, to X&A and this whole belt will be off bounds until it's searched for other fossils. That means that you and I wouldn't live long enough to get back to digging gold."

She had released Mop's paw. He scratched her hand gently, demanding her touch. She held his paw again.

"What I think is this," she said. "I think we will wait to mine this particular rock. What I mean, sir, is this."

Mop cocked his head. "We haven't even seen this rock, have we?"

Mop didn't say anything.

"If you ever want me to take you *go*—" His right ear shot up. "—you'd better agree with me."

"Wurf," he said.

"Good," she said, nodding. "And we won't see it until we're good and damned ready to see it, will we? If you *ever* want to *go?*"

"Wurf," Mop said.

"Because our friend there has waited an eon or two already. I think he can wait until a nice, deserving young girl and a rather splendid pooch are so rich that the U.P. tax men can't take it all away from us." She picked Mop up and ruffled the blond hair on his head. "So rich that waiters will bow and shop women will give us shit-eating grins. So rich that we'll buy you a diamond-studded collar. Would you like that?"

"Ummmmm," Mop said, meaning, "rub my belly, Erin."

She had to go back out again to place a coded beeper in the trench before she covered it over with debris. She did it quickly, without looking up and around at the silent, watchful stars or the slowly tumbling remnants of a world. When she was aboard once more she moved ship, found a nice pocket of gold, and went to work. Three weeks later the cargo space of the *Mother Lode* was heavy with ore. The generator was fully charged. *Mother* went flashing back down the blink routes toward civilization.

The latest edition of the United Planets' Directory told her that the best place to sell her gold was a mining world on the coreward frontier of the U.P. sector. She punched a query into the computer and the old Century hummed and chuckled and came up with routes to the fourth planet of a class G sun a few thousand light-years away.

She had let her hair grow during the months in space. She felt that she was a bit old, at thirty, to wear her ash blonde tresses shoulder length, but there didn't happen to be a hair care center nearby, so she blinked into communicator range of a rather cold looking planet called Aspiration and got landing instructions for the port in the principal city, Wiggston. She was told to stay aboard until customs checked the ship. Mop, able to see paved pads, snow, a few scraggly trees, buildings, and other items that might need irrigating, was going bananas, leaping and whining to go out. Erin tried to reason with him in vain. She called Wiggston Control.

"Look, fellas," she said, in her sexiest voice, "I've got a little dog over here who is about to burst something internally because he wants to go outside so badly. We've been in space for a few months. May I have permission to walk around outside on the pad?"

"Let me speak to your captain," the controller said.

"You're speaking to the captain."

Silence.

"Wiggston Control, this is the *Mother Lode,*" she said in irritation. "Permission to walk my dog, if you please."

"Your animal must go into quarantine," the controller said.

"The hell you say."

The controller's voice was harsh. "Do not open your hatch, *Mother Lode.* Do not allow your animal to exit the ship under any circumstances until our animal importation people are at your ship with a sealed transporter to take your animal to quarantine."

Silence on Erin's part. Then, "How long is your quarantine period?"

"Six months."

"Permission to lift ship," Erin said.

Silence.

"Wiggston Control, *Mother Lode.* I request immediate permission to lift ship."

"Permission refused," the controller said. "You have broken the laws of Aspiration. Your animal must be put into quarantine."

"You and the horse you rode in on," Erin said, as she pushed instructions into the computer. *Mother* quivered and lifted. An angry voice was on the communicator. Erin turned it off and juiced the flux drive. Mop whined as the g forces pushed him down onto the console forcefully.

Just in case the good people of Aspiration were *really* assholes, Erin turned on the detectors. If anything looking

like an armed ship came toward her she was ready to blink
to hell out of there, although blinking while in a planet's
gravitational well was against the rules. However, no ships
appeared. She kept *Mother*'s flux drive pumping full power
until she was well clear and then punched in a blink.

"What do you think?" she asked the Mop.

Mop, freed of the g forces of the quick getaway, lifted
his head and looked pitiful.

"Sorry about that," she said, "but I don't think you'd
have liked an Aspiration prison for pooches."

The U.P. Director said that there were refineries on
Haven, a planet just a few blinks down the routes. This
time she was more careful, checking on Haven's attitude
toward small dogs before going down.

"Tell your captain," the controller at Havenport said,
"that your ship and crew *and* the little dog are welcome
in our city."

"You're speaking to the captain," Erin said.

Silence.

"Ah, good, *Mother Lode*, you have clearance to land
on pad A-10. Make your approach vertical from 90 angles.
What service do you require for your ship?"

"Nothing more than offloading," Erin said.

Hardpad A-10 was near the eastern edge of Havenport,
and it was lined with green lawns, shrubbery, and *trees*.
Erin cracked the hatch as soon as *Mother* had settled, put
a harness and leash on Mop just to be sure his enthusiasm
could be controlled, and went out into air that smelled of
the refineries smoking up the skies around the city. Mop
was whining in his excitement. After a few satisfying, leg-
lifting efforts, he looked up at her as if to say, "Why are
you doing this to me when there are *trees* just over there?"

"All right, buster," she said, taking off his leash. "But
you stay close."

Mop tore around in circles. He'd learned to run quite
well on the moving belt in the exercise room, but there
was no substitute for grass, open spaces, the occasional
planting that needed hiked-leg attention, and *trees*.

After a quarter hour of watching a busy little dog checking each object that rose above the level of the lawns for
messages left by fellow canines and leaving volumes of

meaning himself, she clapped her hands to bring Mop running and took him back aboard ship.

There were two messages on her communicator, both from refinery representatives. She returned the calls. Yes, good yielding gold ore was very welcome on Haven. The price, U.P. standard, thirty-two credits per troy ounce of refined gold less ten percent for the cost of refining. Both reps offered the same price. She called one other refinery, pretended to be a reporter for a Xanthos-based holo-magazine, and was told that the going price for gold was thirty-two credits per troy ounce less ten percent for refining. She rewarded the first man who had called her by selling him her cargo.

She supervised the offloading. Mop, on a leash, cringed at the noise. A cleaning crew went to work in the cargo hold as soon as the ore was offloaded. She and Mop followed the ore carriers to the refinery and visited the office.

The man who had originally contacted her was six-four, weighed in at a solid-muscled two-hundred-ten, had a go-to-hell cowlick in his sandy hair and a lopsided grin that, he felt, was irresistible to all persons of the female persuasion. "What's a sweet little thing like you doing coming into Haven all alone with a cargo of gold ore worth a few hundred thousand credits?" he asked.

"I'm not alone," she said, rubbing Mop's blond head. "And I had hoped a million or so credits, not just a few hundred thousand."

His name was Murdoch Plough. He grinned. "Well, we'll see." He reached out. "Cute little feller, ain't he?"

Mop growled deep in his chest.

"No, Mop, you can't eat the nice man," Erin said.

"Real killer, is he?"

"His father was a Tigian weretiger," she said.

He laughed deep in his chest. "Well, we'll know in a few hours, little lady. I hope it is a million, but I sure can't figure out why a sweet little thing like you wants to go traipsing around out there in the big dark all by her sweet little self."

She stood up. "Oh, I find it rather restful," she said. "You can call me aboard *Mother Lode* when you've completed the refining."

"Now you don't want to go running off," he said, coming around his desk quickly to take her arm.

Mop growled.

"Easy, killer," Murdoch said. To Erin he said, "Look, you've been in space a long time. It would be my pleasure to buy you a real steak and to show you the sights of Havenport."

"Thank you," she said. "I have some housekeeping to do aboard ship, and I want to restock some food items."

"I can handle that for you," Murdoch said, letting his hand travel up her arm.

"I can handle it myself," she said. "And I'd appreciate it if you'd quit handling my arm."

He laughed. "Now, little lady—"

Mop lunged from his position in Erin's right hand and sank his sharp little teeth into Murdoch's index finger. Murduch yelped and leaped back.

"Isn't it odd, Mr. Plough, that nobody will listen when I tell them what a mean little son-of-a-bitch my dog is?"

Mop growled deep in his chest.

"I'll be waiting for your call, Mr. Plough," Erin said.

Murdoch Plough called late the next day. He did not use her name. "We have your check ready for you, Captain," he said.

"Good," Erin said. "How much?"

"Well, I have some bad news for you," he said. "When we put the ore through the refining process, we discovered that most of the gold content was of very low purity. Lots of contaminants, you know. It lowered the yield and increased refining costs. If you'll check your contract, you'll see that the standard ten percent charge is increased to twenty percent if there are certain impurities. However, the good news is that you have just over four-hundred-thousand credits worth, even if it wasn't pure stuff."

"Bullshit," Erin said. She switched off.

She dressed to go out. Mop was dancing, thinking that he was going to get to *go*. When she told him that he had to stay and guard the ship, he went into Erin's cabin and sulked, refusing to come out to say good-bye. She checked a town directory, hailed an aircab, gave the driver an address.

It took a half hour for the assay office, licensed by the Haven government and the United Planets Department of Mining and Heavy Metals, to tell her that her gold samples were of very high purity, just a few points less than refinery pure. She had saved back the pretty little lightning bolt in gold that she had removed from its matrix rock and one nugget that she had selected at random. She went next to the Haven office of X&A and, after showing her discharge card, was immediately escorted into the office of an overweight X&A planetside commando wearing the leaves of a colonel.

"Ah, Lieutenant Kenner," he said, offering his hand, "you're a bit late, but I think we can waive the six month limit on separation from the service and get you your old rank and position back within one year."

"Thanks," Erin said. "That's not why I'm here."

The colonel's face fell. "Well, have a seat," he said. "What *can* I do for you?"

"Colonel," she said, "for years, ever since I entered the Academy, I've been told that the Service always looks after its own."

"That is very true," he said.

"I'm not sure, but I think I'm getting a royal screwing here on this wonderful little planet."

He raised his eyebrows, but not because of her language. Spacers were, he knew, an elitist bunch and they liked to show their toughness with shock talk.

She told the colonel about her gold ore, showed him the assay figures from the government approved testing facility. He nodded and reached for a communicator. He winked at her and said, "Lieutenant, if you won't consider this a sexist suggestion, there's a pot of fresh coffee just outside the door. I'd love to have a cup, and you're more than welcome to join me. White and sweet for me, if you please."

She went out of the office and poured. She heard him ask for the Planetary Attorney General's office. She was back in the room, putting his coffee in front of him when he said, "Sam, how the hell are you?"

It was good coffee and it was good talk she heard. He was only a groundbound colonel, but he was X&A, the voice of the most powerful agency in the civilized galaxy. He had the attention of Sam, the Attorney General. He grinned at Erin, winked as he listened. When he switched off he was still grinning.

"Lieutenant," he said, "I think that if you'll visit Mr. Murdoch Plough again in about two hours you might find that he has refigured the worth of your ore."

Erin rose, kissed the colonel on his cheek. He had the grace to blush. He laughed. "If you didn't leave any lipstick on my cheek, do it again. It's about time I made my wife a *little* jealous."

"It's true," she said.

"Yep," he said, nodding. "We do take care of our own."

Murdoch Plough did not rise from his desk when she entered his office after being announced by his secretary. He looked up sullenly, stared at her for a long time before he spoke.

"It seems, Lieutenant Kenner, that there was, ah, a bit of a mix-up in the assay of your ore."

The fact that he called her lieutenant told her that he had received some sort of a communication from on high. She nodded.

He threw a gold-tone check across the desk toward her. She picked it up and read the figures—1,000,456.54 C. Over one million credits. On a certified check.

"Thank you. I do appreciate the fast work."

Plough had evidently thought about the situation. "Will you be selling again, Lieutenant?"

"There is that possibility," she admitted.

"We here at Plough are always interested in doing business," he said.

"I'll remember that," she said, "while also recalling that you did your best to *give* me the business."

She turned and was gone before he could reply. An hour later, having survived a wild greeting from a lonely little dog, she was lifting the *Mother* for space. Two blinks away from Haven the routes crossed. A right turn took her back toward the galactic core and the mining belt. A left turn and she was on the way to X&A Central and a serious conference with the Service scientists. It was decision time. The generator didn't need charging, but she put it on refill mode to buy time to think, went into the exercise room, stripped to her briefs and walked as she thought. If she went to X&A on Xanthos and showed them Old Smiley, the friendly fossil skull, the rocks would be fenced off by an X&A electronic cordon and there'd be no more gold for Erin Kenner. She had a million credits. With a million credits she could find a quiet little backwater on a frontier planet and live comfortably ever after. On Xanthos, however, where the bright lights were, a nice apartment would cost five thousand credits a month, sixty thousand a year. A sporty aircar went for over a hundred thousand. A million wouldn't last her a lifetime on Xanthos, or on any other metro planet.

It was a tough decision. She was, after all, a loyal citizen of the U.P. She'd just been shown, on Haven, that the Service took care of its own. X&A had paid for her education and had given her the training that had enabled her to navigate to the gold belt and back in safety. Being ex-X&A, she had her share of the induced xenophobia that haunted a race face-to-face in three dimensions with the big, unexplored dark. She shared the knowledge that entire civilizations, multi-planet cultures, had passed into oblivion before man fought his way into space for the second time. She knew why the United Planets maintained a huge, heavily armed fleet of ships in service and in mothballs. Although the power that had devastated the Dead Worlds was unknown and, therefore, doubly awesome, mankind *hoped* that his weapons would be adequate to face an emergence from deep space of *things* like those beings who could kill a world from the inside out.

It was her duty to report her findings, of course. Perhaps study of the fossil remains in the belt would give man more information on what had happened to at least three advanced races who were no more.

Ah, but there was another possibility. The skull she'd found could have been seeded onto the planet which had been shattered into asteroids. Old Smiley might be the only humanoid fossil in the whole belt.

"Mr. Mop," she said, shaking hands at Mop's request,

"Wouldn't it seem to you that our friend can wait a few months longer for his moment in the limelight?"

Mop sighed.

"After all, he's been in cold storage in the middle of a rock for maybe a million years."

Mop cocked his head.

"It would be nice, though, if you and I had some help out there, wouldn't it? With a couple of men to help us we could do two or three more loads in short order."

"Wurf," Mop said.

She thought about it. She considered going back to Haven and asking the X&A colonel to recommend a couple of good men, good workers. She quickly decided against that. One cabin on *Mother* had been converted into the mining control room. There was one bunk bed, high on the wall, in the mining room. Not enough space for two hired hands. And *Mother* was a small ship. To share a ship as small as a Mule two people had to be very good friends. Trouble was, all of her friends were still in Service.

Except.

"Hummm," she said.

"Uhhhh," Mop said, looking for a belly rub as he rolled over.

"You sort of liked Denton Gale, didn't you, Mr. Mop?"

Mop grinned as she rubbed his chest and belly.

"He acted civilized," she said.

Mop said nothing.

"True, he was my father's friend, not mine."

"Uhhhh," Mop moaned.

"We could share the exercise room and the library with no problem, and he could sleep in the mining control room. What do you think?"

Mop, having had enough rubbing, wiggled to be put down. She put him on the deck and he went to paw a chew bone from his personal dispenser.

"You're a helluva lot of help," she said. "Comes time for a heavy decision and you clam up."

Mop crawled under the control chair to eat his tidbit. She turned left, but not to go to Xanthos. Soon she was blinking rapidly down established routes. At beacons she encountered other ships lying on charge. *Mother*'s sensors warned her of the presence of vessels in her blink line, but the Mule was not equipped with the highly advanced detection gear that had become standard issue for X&A ships after Pete Jaynes rediscovered how to tune a blink generator to frequencies other than standard. Such equipment would have told her as soon as she left Haven that she was being followed one blink behind by a sleek deep space miner equipped with a Unicloud computer and the latest detection equipment. The deep space miner was still with her ninety days later when she blinked past the administration planet and toward New Earth.

CHAPTER FIVE

Perhaps it was her proximity to civilization that brought out a feeling of guilt as Erin blinked the *Mother Lode* into orbit around New Earth. Before asking for landing instructions she sent a blink to X&A Central on Xanthos inquiring about the whereabouts of the *Rimfire*. Her intention was, at that moment, to settle for what she had, to go to her former commanding officer, Julie Roberts, and put Old Smiley into the captain's capable hands. However, *Rimfire* was on the opposite side of the galaxy, preparing to penetrate inward toward unknown areas. Going to X&A Central to turn over her discovery to strangers had little appeal and left room for cupidity to reassert itself.

Mother settled gently onto her gear at the same hardpad assigned to her when John Kenner first brought her to Old Port. She told Control no, she did not want to renew the monthly lease on the hardpad, that she would be only a temporary visitor.

Mop was in familiar territory. He scampered around the hardpad and greeted beloved bushes with a gaily hoisted leg before leading the way at a frantic run toward Denton Gale's workshop. He arrived at the door ahead of Erin, announced his presence with frantic barking, and leaped into Denton's arms, wiggling, whining, licking Denton's hands and face in delight when the door was opened. Mop was still demanding attention when Erin reached the office.

"Hi," she said.

"Now if you were as glad to see me as this little rascal—" Denton said, grinning.

"Well, I can't wriggle my rear as fast as he does," she said, moving her hips.

"Fine fellow that you are, Moppy," Denton said, "on her it looks better." He ruffled the dog's hair, pulled on his scrubby tail, put him down on the floor, said to Erin, "Come on in."

It was early autumn on New Earth. Erin, Mop, and the *Mother Lode* had been gone almost a year. She had scanned the areas surrounding the port on the way down, had seen little change except that the new owner of the Kenner home had built white fences around the entire property.

Denton Gale had not changed. He still looked exuberantly youthful. The sun lines at the corner of his eyes gave them a permanent smile. His shop and office were as cluttered as ever.

"You left in a hurry," he said, as he walked to a table to pour coffee for two.

"Yes," she said.

He handed her a steaming mug. Mop had jumped from a chair to the top of the service counter that separated the workshop from the office area. Erin sat down. Denton leaned against the counter, a tall man, his brown hair slightly mussed. "I hope that your trip was successful."

She nodded. "Dent, what are your plans for the future? What do you hope to accomplish in life?"

He grinned. "You come back here to talk to me about my innermost dreams?"

"Yes," she said, "if you want to put it that way."

He looked at her intently, realizing that she was serious.

"Would making inordinately large amounts of money interest you?"

His grin broadened. She wondered if his genes were that good or if he'd spent a lot of time in a dentist's chair.

"How large?" he asked.

"Obscenely so."

"I'm told that the U.P. Penal Service is quite humane," he said, "but I have no desire to spend any portion of my life in a work camp on some frontier planet."

"That's me," she said, "the master criminal." She stood up. Mop's right ear came to attention and he bailed out from the top of the counter to land with a thump at Erin's feet, ready to *go*. "Bring your coffee," she said.

"Yes, ma'am," he said with mock humbleness.

In the control room on the *Mother Lode* she handed him her bankbook. He looked at her inquiringly, eyebrows raised, opened it. At the bottom of the page was a figure of a few thousand credits. "Well, you had this much when you left here, didn't you?"

"Turn the page," she said.

He turned the page, did a classic double take, brought the little book closer to his face, whistled. His eyes showed his interest when he looked up.

"By being more selective in gathering ores we can gross more than that on the next load," she said.

"We?" He handed her the bankbook, sat down in the captain's chair. "You have my attention."

She darkened the room, punched instructions into the computer. On the main viewer the harsh light of the asteroid belt made Denton blink. *Mother* sat alone in solitude. She had taken the holos on her last extravehicular excursion from a distance of about a hundred yards. Large and small chunks of space debris were visible, patches of glaring light and inky blackness. The scene changed, shot from a holo on the extraction arm. In artificial light the yellow gleam of gold made streaks on the rock sides of an excavated trench. Close up shots showed the dramatic lightning bolt of pure gold that Erin had extracted from the matrix rock, a pile of pure nuggets next to it.

"So it was mining that your dad had in mind," Denton said.

"It took me four months to fill *Mother*'s cargo space."

"Sounds simple. Why do you need me?" He laughed. "Or is it that you're overwhelmed by my masculine charm?"

She said stiffly, "I'm offering a straight business deal. One third of the gross. Working partners. Twenty-four hour operations. You work, I sleep. I work, you sleep. And that's it, period."

"What's the rush?" He pushed buttons, returned the holo to its beginning, watched the tumble of the asteroids again.

"Are you interested?" she asked.

"I have a few things to clear up here."

"Time is important," she said. "How important are those things when compared to one third of three payloads bringing in more than one million credits each?"

"Not very, come to think of it," he said. "A million for me, huh? But why just three trips?"

"I'll tell you if you decide to come with me."

"Okay, but I want half. You've made a million. Three more trips at, say, a total of four or five million and you won't be hurting."

"A third or nothing."

"Okay." He stood up. Mop made his begging sound, wanting to be noticed. Denton patted his head. "Too bad, Moppy, I thought maybe we'd be shipmates."

He was halfway out the open hatch before Erin said, "All right, damn it. Half."

He turned. "It's not that I'm greedy. It's just that I hate working twelve-on and twelve-off."

"Sure."

"How soon do you want to leave?"

"Now."

"A couple of weeks. That's the best I can do."

"Two days, three at the most."

"I'll do my best, but even with the prospect of being quite rich I'm not going to just close down a business I've busted my—back to build."

"I won't be unreasonable, but I won't wait weeks."

"You were going to tell me why the rush."

"Sit," she said, punching in the holo-tape that showed the first view of Old Smiley.

The import of what he was seeing hit him with the holos of her cleaning the skull. He waited until a close-up filled the viewing area. "Old?"

"I'm no expert. A million years, maybe."

"And you haven't reported it."

She shook her head.

"So that's the rush."

"I figured another few months, a year, wouldn't matter. It isn't as if Smiley is a threat to the security of mankind."

"Ummm."

"My dad sunk everything he had into this mother of a ship. I had visions of coming home, caring for him in his declining years, living in genteel poverty on the old home place. I came home to find him dead and the house and lands mortgaged up to the hilt. I think I owe it to his memory not to throw away the opportunity he wanted for himself."

"With what you have already, you could buy a place like the Kenner house."

"Yes, I could."

"But you want more?"

"Don't you?"

There was a long silence. "Yes, I do." He turned off the holo, brought up the lights. His eyes squinted. "What would X&A do if they found out you've delayed reporting an important find?"

"The laws are very strict. Ten to fifteen years in a penal colony."

"What if you—we—simply do away with it? The skull."

"No. I couldn't do that."

"No, I guess not." He sighed. "Well, then."

"We go to the belt. We work our asses off. We haul at least three, maybe four loads of the finest ore we can dig to Haven. We keep our eyes open for more fossilized bones. And then we call in X&A and show them where we found the objects—*on our last trip to the belt.*"

Denton winked, picked up the dog, who grunted and threw himself onto his back in the crook of Denton's arm, indicating that he wanted his belly rubbed. "What about this hairy little scoundrel? Can we trust him to keep his mouth shut?"

"Uhhhhh," Mop groaned in pleasure.

Erin found herself smiling. Dent was so good with the dog. Any man who liked dogs couldn't be all bad.

She shook her head. "Nothing personal, Dent, but I want to reemphasize that this is strictly a working arrangement."

"I get the message. One question. Do we hot bed it, since the other cabin has been converted to mining control?"

She smiled coldly, led him by the arm to the door of

the mining cabin, pointed to the folded bunk bed on the bulkhead. He shrugged. "That makes it seventy-five twenty-five, my way."

"You and the horse you rode in on," she said.

"All right, Captain," he said, his voice heavy with sarcasm. "Although it will be a terrible struggle for me to resist your charms, I will control my animalistic impulses. I will sleep like a bat, hanging to the bulkhead. I will work twelve-on and twelve-off. Any other orders, ma'am?"

Her face had gone stiff. "If that's your attitude, there's no need beginning it," she said.

He held up one hand, shook his head. "No, it's all right. I promise I'll be a good boy."

She clapped her palm to her forehead, looked up, rolled her eyes. "I shouldn't do this," she said. "I know I shouldn't do this."

Mop came to put his forepaws up on Denton's leg, asking to be picked up. "You're outvoted, lady," he said. "The hairy member of the crew likes me."

Denton sold his business to a large corporation that had been gobbling up small operations all over New Earth. His sporty aircar went into storage, along with a few personal items from his rented apartment. Erin, impatient to be off and away, told him that he'd have the money to buy a new and far more luxurious aircar, that it was silly to store things like music reproduction equipment.

"Want me to throw away my baby pictures and stamp collection, too?" he asked.

Actually, he was not quite ready to leave his entire life behind, and, in spite of her eagerness to be underway, Erin understood. He needed to know that he would have something to come back to. She had felt the same kind of wrench while gathering the personal things she had brought aboard *Mother* from her home.

It took three days. *Mother* lifted off the hardpad into the nightside, orbited briefly as Erin punched in multiple blinks. By the time the generator was drained and ready for recharging, they were light-years from New Earth. During the charge period they settled into a routine that would become familiar. Twelve hours on duty, twelve off.

Only one of them at a time in the small exercise gym. No meals taken together.

With a fully charged generator *Mother* blinked again, and again, and just behind her, one blink back, the sleek, armed, deep space miner followed.

CHAPTER SIX

Dent watched nervously as Erin maneuvered *Mother* into the stream of asteroids, working her way toward the center where she had found the fragments containing the richest ore on her previous trip. The detectors spotted a promising site. Mop said "yipe" when the ship settled against the tumbling chunk of rock. Dent loosed a long sigh. Erin pretended total nonchalance, although each time she attached *Mother* to an asteroid it was pucker time. She balanced out forces with the flux drive and with steering jets until ship and rock flowed through space without tumbling. There were less than six hours left of her shift and Denton had been awake for eighteen hours.

"You're going to need some sleep," she said.

"Now that the excitement's over?"

"What excitement?"

He laughed. "I'm familiar in theory with the extraction equipment, but it might be a good idea to have you go through the procedures with me."

She was thinking that at the end of his next twelve he would have gone thirty-six hours without sleep. A tired man was a careless man. X & A axiom. She, herself, would use the rest of her watch making minute measurements to be sure that their neighbors in the crowded asteroid belt were not being pushy and moving in on *Mother* as she sat on her rocky perch.

"All right," she said. She led the way into the mining control room. He had moved a locker from the gym to store his clothing and personal possessions. The bed was neatly made, although the movable partition that separated it from the rest of the room was pushed back. At least, she thought, he wasn't a slob. She ran him through the checklists, operating procedures, and buttonology for the biter and extractor. Within an hour he was handling the equipment well. It was a rich deposit and the weight of ore built quickly in *Mother*'s hold.

"Won't take long at this rate," he said.

"All the deposits are not this rich," she said.

She glanced at the clock and saw that they were two hours into Dent's watch. The tension of taking the ship into the belt, the stimulation of finding a good ore field, all drained away, leaving her exhausted. "I'm declaring a holiday," she said.

"In honor of what?"

"You name it," she said, rising, stretching. "In observation of the day they lopped off Mop's tail."

"A truly significant day."

"You've been up over twenty-four hours. I'm beat, too. I think we both need a good eight or ten hours' sleep, and then we can settle down to serious work."

"You talked me into it, Cap'n."

She was asleep moments after she pulled the light coverlet over her. At some time during the "night" she heard or felt the vibrations caused by the mining machines, thought about getting up to see why Dent had gone back to work, turned over and was fast asleep again.

When she woke again, she'd been asleep for over nine hours. She had a solid breakfast before going to the cabin that was a combination of Dent's quarters and the mining control room. Mop greeted her at the door, leaping up joyfully, acting as if it had been months since he'd last seen her. Denton was seated in the control chair. The weight gauge showed that he'd loaded several tons of ore.

"Looks as though this vein is about to play out," he said.

"Couldn't sleep?" she asked.

"Slept for a couple of hours. I'll have twelve hours to catch up now."

"I'll take it, then."

"I think if we moved ship about a hundred feet toward that sharp extension—"

"Readings are good in that direction?"

"Yep."

"Well, if you've pretty well exhausted the vein—"

"You're going to trust me with moving her?"

"You'll have to do it sooner or later," she said.

"Okay. Just check behind me before I do anything," he said.

She watched closely. He used the remote control panel in the mining room to lift *Mother* with her flux drive and lower her without so much as a jar to a spot just over a hundred feet away.

"Well done," she said.

He nodded, positioned the biter, and sampled the rock. A gleam of gold appeared in the viewer. Gold and something else. "Damn," Erin said.

"What? What?" he asked, startled by the tone of her voice.

"On the surface," she said, "just to the right of the trench."

It took him a while to see it. The telltale was a difference in texture more than shape. She pointed it out to him on the viewer. "Two separate pieces," she said. "That jagged end there—"

"Ah, yes," he said.

Mop protested loudly when both of them left him alone and disappeared into the air lock. Once again Erin had that feeling of disorientation as she stepped out of the lock onto the asteroid, but since Dent was directly behind her she did not have the sense of almost panicky loneliness that she'd experienced while going extravehicular on her first trip to the belt. She demonstrated the use of the laser cutter to Dent, adjusting it to flow away rock and leave the fossilized bones intact.

One bone had a large knob extending just above the surface. As the matrix stone melted away it was apparent that the knob was part of a knee joint. The small bones of the feet of the two partial legs were scattered, but seemed to be complete.

"When the crust of the planet was shattered," Erin said, as Dent put the specimens into separate bags, "the break occurred just here." Her voice was made slightly metallic by the radio. She indicated the jagged end of one leg bone.

"The rest of him might be in one of the other asteroids," Dent said.

"I'm no expert," she said, "but they look humanoid to me."

"Yep," he said.

"We'll have to watch very carefully."

"We could mark this one and move on."

"No. This is a rich ore field. Let's work it."

Once they were back inside the ship she had to insist that Dent go to bed. He took one last look at the fossils, grumbled a bit, went into the bath and stayed half an hour before closing off the partition around his bunk area.

Mop leapt into Erin's lap and climbed up onto the console to take his place beside the main viewer. Erin scratched him behind the ears and whispered, "We have to keep quiet, Mr. Mop." Mop curled up and closed his eyes. Erin began to hum softly. The hours passed. The weight of ore grew in *Mother*'s storage areas. Denton emerged, pulling down his jumper, after only six hours.

"Can't sleep?" she asked.

"You're going to have to learn another tune."

"Oh?" She made a face.

"If you're going to hum throughout your watch, you're going to have to learn a few more songs."

"Oh, hell," she said. "I'm sorry. I didn't realize that I was doing it. It's habit, I guess."

"Not that I don't like music—"

"All *right*," she said. "You've made your point."

"Maybe I can insulate the partition."

"No, I'll be quiet."

"Maybe I could sleep in the other cabin."

"No," she said quickly. Then, "Look, I'm sorry, Dent, but I have a thing about that. I think a bed is just about as personal as underwear."

"Your skivvies wouldn't fit me," he said. "Much too small."

In the next week, *Mother* mined surface ore fields on three different asteroids. No more fossils were found. The relationship between Erin and Dent was unchanged. He had apparently adjusted to sleeping behind his partition while she was at work, and she remembered, most of the time, not to hum as she manipulated the biter and the extractor. It was Mop who brought about a change in the routine.

The little dog's stub of a tail was the barometer of his feelings. Usually it was perky, a cocky little spike pointing stiffly upward and slightly forward. It was a sturdy stump of a tail, and it was lowered only when Mop was asleep. When he started carrying it tucked under, Erin was concerned.

"Come to think of it, I haven't seen him punch out a nibble for himself lately," Dent said.

Erin pushed the button and offered Mop a tasty little artificial bone. He sniffed at it, lowered his head, lay down with his muzzle between his paws. "What's the matter, partner?" Erin asked, picking him up. He rolled onto his back in the crook of her arm, closed his eyes, sighed.

Erin ran the tip of her finger over his nose. It was dry, sandpapery. "He's sick," Erin said, looking at Dent with her eyes wide and full of concern.

It took them a couple of days to figure out why the dog was under the weather. The first clue was that when Erin went to bed Mop was not content to lie down and keep her feet warm. Instead, he barked to be let out of the cabin.

"Dr. Gale has the answer," Denton announced one "morning" when Erin entered the mining room. "The problem is that Mr. Mop has no one to relieve him."

Erin was still feeling a bit sluggish from sleep.

"Huh?"

"You work twelve hours and rest twelve hours," he said. "Ditto for me. Our little buddy here has to keep you company while you're on watch and then he goes to work immediately to keep me company." He spread his hands. "Not even a superior pooch like Mr. Mop can be on duty twenty-four hours a day forever."

"Oh, pooh," she said.

"Now you think about it."

She thought. When she was alone on the ship, Mop had slept at her feet for the eight hours or more she was in bed. "I'll be damned," she said. "Well, I'll just force him to stay in the cabin with me during your watch."

But Mop fretted, paced, leapt on and off the bed, begged politely to be let out the door.

"He's a very conscientious canine," Denton said. "You're keeping him from what he sees as his duty."

"One more night like last night," Erin said, "and I'm going to pull his hairy ears off."

"The only solution," Denton said, "is to work a normal day."

Actually, Erin had been thinking the same thing. Most of the time the work of extracting ore from the rock would go faster with two people at the controls in the mining room, one operating the biter and the laser, the other working with the extractor.

"I'm thinking of myself, too," Dent said. "I'll sleep a lot better with some peace and quiet."

Mop had a few fitful naps during the first watch under the new arrangement. With two people working, the ore poured into *Mother*'s storage with pleasing swiftness. At the end of the watch Erin took Mop to bed with her. He showed the same pattern of behavior as he had exhibited previously, so she opened the door to her cabin and left him free to roam the ship, checking out the mining room and Denton's bed when he cared to do so. When he saw that the lights were off and that Dent was asleep, he returned to Erin's cabin, jumped up on the bed, rolled onto his back with his legs in the air and slept for ten hours without so much as moving. The stub of a tail was a flag of cheerfulness when he joined Erin and Dent for breakfast.

Extracting ore was a repetitive job that had become a matter of routine. As they worked they made comments about the density and color of the rock, speculated on the method of destruction of the planet that had once followed the orbit that was now a huge ring of debris. Since Erin felt guilty for not reporting Old Smiley and The Legs to X&A, she never mentioned the fossils. Dent asked questions about her time in Service and she recounted the routine of life aboard the *Rimfire*.

Like Erin, Denton had been born on New Earth. Unlike

her, he was not widely traveled. Before shipping with her on the *Mother Lode*, he told her, he'd made one trip to Delos to take a course on how to recharge the Verbolt cloud chambers that were at the heart of most computers. His childhood had been a happy one, as had hers. His parents had died within the same year when he was twenty years old. He had never owned a dog.

"My dad always used to give me dolls when I was a little girl," she told him. "What I wanted was a bicycle, or a pellet gun. One Christmas he gave me a beautiful baby carriage lined in white silk. Charlie Frink and I were playing road construction and I filled it up with dirt, pretending it was an earth mover. It was very, very black dirt."

It was a comfortable, easy relationship. There were no demands made from either side. When the working watch ended, Erin went to her cabin or to the gym. Now and then they had a meal together or watched a holo-drama sitting in the comfortable control chairs on the bridge. Mop was more than happy with the new system. Once or twice a night he'd leave Erin's bed to check on Dent. The doors to both cabins were left open so that the dog could perform his duty of looking after both of them.

It *seemed* logical, since production had actually increased, to continue the system of working together. It *seemed* safe. After all, during her first trip to the asteroid belt, she had been alone and had left *Mother* to look after herself during her sleep hours. Each "night" before retiring one of them would check the ship's detection system and set the audible alarms. While they slept, *Mother*'s little electronic gadgets sent out beams to confirm that the neighboring asteroids were keeping their distance, chuckled their way through internal checks of the recycling plants, measured the sleeping power in the blink generator, probed the temperature in the food bins, and performed dozens of other tests, checks, and analyses.

But the *Mother Lode* was not equipped with the latest detection gear which would have enabled her to warn Erin and Denton that stealthy search beams were playing on and through her metal hide, beams that told the man who operated the originating instruments that the routine had changed aboard the Mule, that now the Alpha patterns of the two-man crew showed that both slept at the same time. Nor could *Mother* see through the considerable mass of the asteroid on which she was currently perched. So it was that the sleek, fast, well equipped mining ship that had followed the *Lode* from the day that Erin first left Haven was able to wend her way through the belt and give an almost casual shove to a tumbling, roughly rectangular slab of stone that measured a hundred yards on its long axis. For a period of several hours the tombstone-shaped asteroid closed on *Mother*'s blind side.

When contact came, a small protrusion on the tumbling slab brushed across a distended node of stone on the asteroid contained in *Mother*'s field. The two masses were traveling at the same speed in their orbital path around the sun. The differential in inertia was represented mainly by the slab's tumbling motion. As the slab came near, it was affected by the field being put out by *Mother*'s generator. The brushing contact altered the vector of the large asteroid only slightly, and slowed the tumbling motion of the slab minutely. Now the slab was being drawn toward *Mother*'s asteroid by the ship's field, and being impelled by its own motion. As it tumbled, it would have been apparent to an observer, had there been one, that the most massive end of the slab would impact solidly within a matter of minutes.

Aboard *Mother* the first brushing contact sent a faint tremor through the ship. Sensors trembled, searched, sent signals to the computer. A quick search of near space showed the ship's systems nothing that was a cause for alarm. "Underneath" the ship the sensors found solid matter. All was well.

But there happened to be a rather efficient biological sensor at work aboard the *Mother Lode*. Mop the dog had experienced every motion that was possible aboard a ship of *Mother*'s size. When the very slight tremor of contact vibrated upward through the legs of Erin's bed, he rolled onto his feet and put all of his senses to work. When he was agitated, or doubtful about something, his neck seemed to get longer as he held his head high, perked up one ear.

"Wurf," he said softly.

"Ummmf," Erin said in her sleep.

The hair on Mop's back rippled. He felt a difference in the ship's field, for it had strengthened itself to account for the additional bulk of the tumbling slab that was swinging slowly, so slowly, to smash its heaviest end directly into *Mother*'s asteroid.

Erin was galvanized into frenzied motion as Mop sounded off, "Yap-yap-yap-yap," in a near-hysterical, high-pitched bark that brought her to her feet, standing up in bed, yelling, "What? What? What?"

"What's going on?" Denton yelled, his voice carrying across the control bridge through Erin's open door.

Erin leapt to the floor and dashed for the bridge. Since she'd been leaving her door open, she'd taken to sleeping in shortie gowns. The one she wore that night was blue and set off her ash blonde hair well. Lights came on automatically as she ran onto the bridge. She punched up the computer. There was something vaguely wrong. Mop was still yapping. Her hair seemed to want to stand on end.

"The field," Denton said, as he ran out of his cabin pulling on a pair of jeans. She noticed, although it didn't register at the moment, that he had a nice chest and that his arms were strong. He noticed, and it *did* register, that it was evident through the thin material of the gown that she was a natural ash blonde, and that her waist was even smaller than he'd thought.

She punched instructions. The field was showing almost double the mass of the asteroid that they were mining. Mop was yapping warning. She had a feeling that the next few seconds were critical, but a quick search of near space showed no danger. She punched in an order and saw that the sensors had recorded a small tremor only four minutes ago. With a sudden chill running up her back she searched near space again, selected a vector, killed the ship's field and gave power to the flux drive. *Mother* jerked away from her rocky perch with a suddenness that sent Mop to his belly on the deck and caused both Dent and Erin to reach for support before the ship's gravity adjusted.

Behind them, the tumbling slab smashed with all of the inertial mass of millions of tons into the asteroid just va-

cated by *Mother*. Rock shattered soundlessly in the vacuum of space. Erin found an opening in the belt and sent
Mother soaring outward, racing away from chunks of rock
that seemed to be pursuing her.

At a safe distance, Erin stabilized the ship. "Keep an
eye open," she said, "in case some of the mothers come
after us." She motioned with one hand to indicate that she
was talking about the shattered particles of the asteroids.

"You wanta tell me what the hell happened?" Dent
asked.

"In a minute."

"What are you doing?" he asked.

She was at the food dispensers. "I'm going to give Mr.
Mop a full two ounces of our best and most tender steak."

Mop had a sensitive digestive system. He was, after all,
a small dog. Giving him two ounces of steak was the
equivalent of a man of Dent's size eating four pounds.
Both Erin and Dent knew from experience that people
food, as much as Mop loved it, upset his tummy, which
cause him to have diarrhea, which tended to make him
very messy and very smelly at the rear.

"Two ounces?" Dent asked.

"Yes."

"Well, he's your little dog."

"Yes, and if it upsets him I'll wash his rear end," Erin
said. "Because if it weren't for him, we'd be dead."

Denton adjusted a viewer, saw a growing cloud of rock
particles behind him. "Think he'd want three ounces?"
he asked.

Erin bent over to give Mop his treat, felt a draft, realized that she was dressed only in her shortie gown, stood
up quickly, saw Denton looking at her with a musing smile
on his face.

"Nice," he said.

"Son-of-a-bitch," she said.

"Give the dog his treat," he said, as Mop danced
around on his rear legs.

Erin knelt and began feeding the dog the bits of savory
meat. Denton's eyes on her seemed to generate warmth
deep inside of her.

CHAPTER SEVEN

With her superior detection equipment the *Murdoch Miner* could keep track of the *Mother Lode* either from a distance or at close range if the *Miner* was hidden from *Mother*'s sensors by intervening rock. For some time those aboard the rakishly designed ship were content to observe the actions of the converted Mule as she went about her work, although personal relations aboard the *Murdoch Miner* were not as congenial as aboard the Mule.

Ordinarily the *Miner* operated with a four-man crew consisting of two married couples who got along very well together because the women were sisters who had an impartial regard for the cousins they had married. Over a period of several years the four had discovered that a certain amount of change and variety enlivened the dull routines of space mining. Into the smoothly working and cozy arrangement the boss, Murdoch Plough, had tossed a disruption that muddled things up as severely as if someone had dropped a piece of durasteel into the gears of a complicated machine.

The disruption was named Gordon Plough, and since he was the little brother of the boss, thus making it necessary to put up a good front, the sisters had to keep to their own respective beds, wear more clothing than usual, and be careful of what they said.

The situation was a pain in the hootchie, and it threatened to get worse before it got better, because little brother couldn't make up his mind what to do about the Mule that was keeping the *Murdoch Miner* from the richest gold deposits anyone aboard her had ever seen.

In fairness to Gordon Plough it had never been simple being the younger brother to a self-made man. It hadn't even been easy when they were boys because Murdoch had always been big for his age and had taken great pleasure in making life as painful as possible for Gordon.

Now that they were both men, Gordon thought that his older brother liked him well enough, but still looked upon him as a kid. He wasn't. He was twenty-nine years old and he'd always felt that if Murdoch would ever give him a real chance he could prove that he could do more for the Haven Refining Company and the mining interests than be some kind of errand boy.

Gordon's chance had come when his brother put him in charge of following the *Mother Lode* to, it was clearly understood, if not stated openly, discover and take possession of one of the richest gold sources in the galaxy. Just how Gordon was to accomplish the job had been left up to him. In spite of the fact that the *Miner* had been functioning well under her captain of some five years, one of the male cousins, Gordon was now captain of the ship and, since it was his first real command, he was determined to make the most of it.

The *Miner* had been in space for months. The cousins, Sam and Kim Maleska, were getting more and more fed up with Gordon Plough's constant orders and his indecision. Not the least of their frustrations was the fact that their customary shipboard social life had been put on hold by having a representative of the company aboard. It wasn't that Murdoch Plough was a prude, it was just that the cousins feared management might think that a crew that was having fun wouldn't get the work done. They hadn't been able to play musical beds since leaving Haven and they were discovering that you never miss a good thing until you have it within your reach but can't grab it for some reason or another.

"Gordon," said Sam Maleska one morning after weeks of sneaking around the belt spying on the *Mother Lode*, "I sure would like to get cracking on a few of them gold bearing rocks."

"Patience," Gordon Plough said. "Why should we do the work when we can let them do it for us?"

It took Sam a while to figure that one out. He told Kim and the sisters, "I *think* he's planning to let the *Mother Lode* fill her holds and then hijack her."

"Hell," Kim said, "we could work twice as fast as they can. This ship was built for mining."

"I think he's scared," said Caryl. On this trip Caryl was the blonde. It was sister Cherry's turn to be the brunette.

"I think he's a pussy," Cherry said. She tugged uncomfortably at her tunic. She was accustomed to wearing nothing more than a loose, transparent, hip length tee and briefs while aboard ship. "Why don't one us just let our finger slip and blast hell out of that Mule?"

"Get it over with," Caryl agreed.

"Blasting her would leave teeny little scraps floating around," Sam said. "The scraps might be found—" He lifted his eyebrows and spread his arms to indicate the vastness of space and the impossibility of the captain's fears. "Our captain doesn't want to risk having a piece of the *Mother Lode* identified at some—"

At that moment Gordon Plough came into the lounge.

"And here he is now," Kim Maleska said.

"I know that you've been wondering why we have delayed the completion of our mission," Gordon said pompously. "I think you will be pleased to know that we are going to take action."

"When?" Caryl asked, with a flip of her blonde hair.

"Soon," Gordon said. "First we have to find some way to catch both of them out of the ship."

"Why?" Sam asked. "Let's just hole her with a laser and then toss her into the sun."

"There's always the chance that she might get off a distress signal if we do that," Gordon said. "No. She's got to go into the sun on her own power and without any possibility of a message being sent."

"Can't see how some sombitch can send a stat while his lungs are blowing up in decompression," Kim grumbled.

"That's why my brother put me in charge of this operation," Gordon said. "He wants things done *right*."

"If you don't want to put a hole in her with a laser,"

Sam said, "how about if she gets busted open by accident?"

Gordon made a face. He had to admit that an accident would be almost as good as what he had in mind. "An accident would be neat," he said. "But it would have to be catastrophic and instantaneous."

It was Cherry who arranged the "accident" that would have smashed the *Mother Lode* in the collision of two asteroids.

"You see," Gordon said, his voice rising in anger, "I told you so. I said, 'Look, men, let's not be hasty.' "

"You hear him say that?" Sam asked Kim.

"I didn't. You hear him say that, Cherry?"

"I didn't," she said. "You hear him say that, Caryl?"

"Well, maybe I didn't say it in words," Gordon said, "but you know what I was thinking."

"Oh," Kim said. "Well, sure." He looked at Sam with his eyebrows raised. "We always know what you're *thinking*, Cap'n."

"Now what if she sent off a stat?" Gordon asked.

"She was too busy saving her ass to think about sending off a stat," Kim said. "What would she send? Help, help, a big rock tried to smush me?"

Sam Maleska came to his feet. He was a big man, well over six feet, and he affected a huge, bushy, black beard that made him look quite uncivilized. "Cap'n," he said, "with all respect, if you don't come to a decision pretty quick I'm gonna forget that you're the brother of the boss and take it on myself to kick a little ass."

"Are you threatening me?" Gordon blustered.

"You hear me threaten the cap'n?" Sam asked, arms spread.

"I didn't hear him threaten the cap'n," Cherry said. "Did y'awl?"

"Not me," Kim said.

"Me neither," Caryl said, tossing her blonde locks.

As it happened Caryl was on watch when the air lock of the *Mother Lode* opened and two flexsuited figures descended to the surface of the asteroid. She lost no time in waking the others. The captain assessed the situation and came up with a plan. It wasn't a good plan. Sam said to

Kim, "This sucks." But it was a plan. At last they were going to do *something*. Since there were five of them and only two members of the crew of the *Mother Lode*, it didn't really matter if the captain had come up with what was, really, a lousy plan. Five of them would handle two quickly and easily.

"Listen and listen good," Gordon said.

Sam and Kim looked at each other and rolled their eyes.

"We'll take them by surprise," Gordon said. "Use a narrow beam on the saffers. We don't want to leave pieces of them scattered around. Just hole the suits and then we'll put them on board their ship and set the ship's generator to blink her into the sun. Everyone got that?"

As it turned out it wasn't a bad plan after all, it was just that it didn't work for Gordon Plough and the crew of the *Murdoch Miner*.

CHAPTER EIGHT

There was nothing wrong with the *Mother Lode*'s warning systems. For two days Erin and Dent checked and rechecked, working the old Century Series computer hard. When Erin was satisfied that Murphy's Law had been at work, that the tumbling slab of debris had, quite naturally, taken the very worst approach so that the bulk of the asteroid on which the ship sat blocked detection, she sighed, said, "Well, that's it," and was ready to go back to work. But it seemed that the incident with the straying asteroid had changed their luck.

Time and time again Erin eased the ship close to a grim, barren, spinning mountain of rock only to find that there were no heavy metals or if there were they were buried deeply. *Mother* was equipped only for shallow, surface mining. She didn't have the tools to drill a thousand feet into stone to test the source of some very strong readings on the detectors.

When, at last, the instruments buzzed happily, having located gold deposits near the exterior of an asteroid with convenient level areas, she attached *Mother* to the rock with the strength of her field and was pleased when rich flakes and nuggets were extracted immediately. Soon the comfortable work routine had been reestablished. She had forgotten that Dent had well developed arms and a muscular chest with just enough hair to make him look masculine.

The sensors on the digging arm sounded the presence of fossilized bone late in a watch. "Oh, damn," Erin said, stopping the biter from deepening a trench.

"There," Denton said, pointing to the viewer screen.

The bones were lighter in color than the matrix rock. Three arching bands were visible. "Nothin' to it but to do it," Dent said. Erin followed him to the air lock, suited up. Mop was voicing his protest.

"Guard the ship," Dent told him.

"Hush," Erin said, as the dog continued barking.

Mop did not hush. He barked energetically long after the inner hatch closed.

"You'd think," Erin said, as she stepped down onto the bare surface "that you'd get used to this after a few times."

Denton lifted his helmeted head, turned a full circle. Near them, sunward sides reflecting dazzling light, were a few asteroids. Over them, under them, and to all sides there was the harsh glare of the core stars.

"I won't miss this part of it when it's over," Dent said. He was carrying the laser cutter. He positioned himself over the curving bones and began to melt away the matrix. Slowly a rib cage emerged.

"Small," Erin said.

" 'Bout like a six-year-old child," Dent agreed.

"There haven't been any fossils where the gold is in veins," she said. "Only in this softer rock."

"This type of formation must have been near the surface of the planet's crust," he said. "Notice how it's layered, as if it were formed by sedimentary action. And I'd guess that the gold is a placer deposit, washed down from some mother lode."

The fossilized skeleton was disjointed, but below the rib cage lay a large pelvic bone and long thighbones. Arms, neck, and skull were not to be found. It took over an hour to free the bones and bag them. Erin headed back toward the air lock, Dent directly behind her. She reached out her hand to punch the entry code into the lock, but her finger did not make contact. She felt a sudden sense of disorientation. With nightmare slowness the *Mother Lode* lifted and drifted away from her outstretched hand.

"Hey," she cried out.

Dent jetted away from the surface of the asteroid as *Mother* accelerated, moving toward the black emptiness of space. For a few moments it seemed that he would catch the ship, but she was moving too fast for the jets of the suit. He and the ship became glowing little stars almost lost among the vastness.

Erin watched in shocked silence. The small brightness that was Denton Gale grew until she could make out his suited arms and legs. And then he was landing beside her.

"Erin? Hey?" His voice was soft inside her helmet.

An image was burned into her mind, the lop-eared, hairy face of Mop at the viewport on the bridge, his head jerking with silent urgency as he barked his alarm at being alone on a ship moving off into space.

"Erin?"

"I don't know."

"She was not under her own power."

"No. We'd have felt the force of the flux drive."

"What?"

She took a deep breath. She had just over three hours to live, plus ten minutes on the suit's reserve air, and she was thinking more about a frightened, lonely little dog than about her own predicament. She shook her head. "Let's take a walk," she said.

For *Mother* did not leave under her own power.

"As it happens," Dent said, "I have nothing else to do."

The chemically activated jets which gave some degree of maneuverability to a suited spacemen had limited capacity. Dent's vain attempt to catch *Mother* had almost exhausted his fuel. They crawled from point to point, aided somewhat by the small amount of artificial gravity generated by the tiny flux units that powered the suits. The asteroid was a large one, perhaps a quarter of a mile in diameter. A half hour's air was used up before they reached a point that allowed a view of the side of the asteroid away from *Mother*'s former position.

Erin leapt up onto a large protrusion, missed her footing, fell slowly, arms windmilling. The fall saved her life, for as she fell a slash of light passed over her head.

"Take cover," she ordered, her voice calm in spite of the fact that she'd just been narrowly missed by a lethal beam from a saffer. As she landed lightly on her feet and bounced, her own weapon was in her gloved hand. To her right, at a distance she estimated at about two hundred feet, although distances were deceiving on the sharply curved and uneven surface, she saw movement. Her reaction was the result of training. She brought the saffer beam down from above the head of the space-suited man who had fired on her and saw the sizzle of death as the figure was knocked backward by the force.

"Behind you," Denton yelped.

She whirled. Rock disintegrated beside her as she slipped to her left, swinging the saffer in a horizontal arc to cut the legs out from under a second assailant. As the integrity of the attacker's suit was breached, she saw a fine mist of blood and fluids spew out to dissipate into the vacuum of space.

"My God," Dent said in disbelief, "they were trying to kill us."

"Bet your sweet ass," Erin said, swiveling in the stiff suit, examining the shadowy, rocky landscape carefully. There was no further movement. She edged forward and there was a ship, anchored to the asteroid by her field at a point directly opposite *Mother*'s former perch. Denton crawled to lie beside her.

"Mining vessel," he said.

"Probably has laser cannon."

"But why?"

"Gold," she said.

"But there's enough for everyone," Dent said.

"They didn't think so."

"They wanted to kill us so that they could have all of the gold?" Dent asked.

"What else?"

"I can't believe that," he said. "No one ship can possibly mine the whole belt."

"Believe it."

"In real life men don't kill for gold. That happens only in holo-dramas."

"Bullshit," she said.

"How many in her crew?" he asked, nodding his head inside the helmet to indicate the sleek ship.

"Four, usually. She's a fleet type scout. I don't know what was done to her during her conversion to a mining vessel. I doubt if they made *more* crew space. Four men could work the equipment around the clock.''

"They used their generator to negate *Mother*'s field?''

"What else?'' she asked. "A Mule's generator is powerful, but that was a military ship before her conversion. With *Mother*'s generator on low, just enough to keep us on the rock, one quick surge of power with the mining ship's field in reverse would send *Mother* off into space.''

"They had to know, then, that we were not aboard.''

"They knew.''

"Then they know we're here.''

"Yes, but now we know *they're* here,'' she said grimly. Denton swallowed. Two men were dead.

"Next thing to do is get you a weapon,'' she said, starting to crawl toward the crumpled form of the man whose legs had been cut away. Denton reached the body first, bent to take the saffer from a gloved hand, gasped.

"It's a woman,'' he said.

"So it is,'' Erin said, looking at the ruined face and wisps of blonde hair behind the clear mask.

"A woman.''

"Not a very well trained woman,'' Erin said.

"And you are,'' he said bitterly.

"Better thank God that I am.''

He was silent.

"All right, people,'' Erin said, looking at the ship. "Where are you?''

As if in answer, rock shattered in eerie silence so close to Denton's head that he rolled away in panic. Erin's eyes followed the lance of the saffer beam to a shadowed alcove between two rocky protrusions. She saw movement.

"There are two of them,'' she said.

"Where?''

She pointed.

"What are we going to do?'' Denton asked.

"I think it might be a good idea if we kill them before they kill us.''

"Maybe we can talk to them.''

"Go ahead. Step forth in peace,'' she said.

He was silent.

"In less than two hours we've got to be aboard that ship," she said.

"I think those two over there might have something to say about that."

"Probably." She looked around, nodded to herself. The attackers had already shown themselves to be unskilled, even a bit stupid, but, as Denton had pointed out, not too many people went around murdering others these days. A certain lack of experience had been evidenced by the attackers, which was fortunate for Erin Elizabeth Kenner and Denton Gale.

"What I'm going to do," she said, "is jet off behind that rise over there. I want you to keep up a fire on their position. Keep their attention on you."

"I've never fired at a person."

"I think now is the time to start."

"Let's try to contact them by radio."

"Listen, damn it," she said, "I want you to lay down a covering fire on them *now.*"

Denton's saffer sent a beam of concentrated energy that shattered rock and caused a stir of movement in the shadows. Erin pushed the jet controls and shot upward and outward at a shallow angle. Every muscle was tensed as she waited for fire to lance into her body, but then she was in the protection of the rocks and could relax her sphincters. Denton was firing at roughly five second intervals. She took a survey of the terrain and lifted off once more. From the rear, she soared over the concealed position of the unknown enemy. An overhanging ledge protected them. She fired as she moved forward, seeking a point where her beam could lance under the overhang. The two suited figures looked up, saw her. One of them leapt into the open and took a two-handed stance, his saffer aimed directly at her. She pushed a button to activate a jet to turn her so that she could fire at the man in the open, hit the wrong one, sent herself spinning. She was an easy target, spinning around suspended just above the two would-be killers.

"Denton," she cried out.

Fire lanced out from Denton's position. The man who had been drawing a bead on her burned. She corrected her spin, aimed her weapon downward only to see Dent use the last of his jet fuel to put himself in firing position. The fourth man died while he was trying to get situated to shoot at Erin.

"Hold your fire," she sent to Dent. "They're dead."

Denton was standing quite still, saffer dangling from his gloved hand. One of the dead was a brown-haired woman and it was evident that he was greatly affected by the knowledge that he had killed her. Erin saw that his eyes were wide, that his lips were trembling.

"You did well," she said. "You saved my life."

"I never killed anyone before."

"Do you think I make a habit of it?"

"You were so cool, so unconcerned."

"You couldn't have driven a nail up my anus with a sledge hammer," she said.

"You are so damned dainty."

"Thank you, love." She moved away, turned back. "If you're ready to quit bleeding over those bastards who tried to kill both of us—"

They approached the ship from her stern, moving with great caution. The last hundred yards was in the open. She bled half of her jet propellant into Dent's suit. Side by side, they soared to the cover of the ship's flux mount.

"What if there's someone inside?" Denton asked, as they moved slowly and carefully toward the outer lock.

Erin didn't answer. She examined the lock.

"No way we'll figure the combination," she said.

The suit's air timer showed that she had thirty-seven minutes before going on reserve. She lifted her saffer.

"If the inner hatch is open you'll get explosive decompression," Denton warned.

"Yep," she said, narrowing the beam to a pinpoint cutting frequency. Metal gave off gases that quickly disappeared into the merciless vacuum of space. A rush of air through the hole that she'd cut in the hatch scattered the residue left from the cutting operation. "The inner hatch was closed," she said.

In the air lock she turned as the outer hatch slid shut, stuffed the hole where the lock had been with a cloth used to wipe dust off the glass of her helmet.

"Here goes," she said, putting her hand on the air control. Denton lifted his gloved hand and tried unsuccessfully to cross his fingers. Air hissed into the lock. The makeshift patch held, although, as the lock filled, escaping air made a whistling noise.

The inner hatch opened. Erin, weapon at the ready, stepped into the suit closet. It was empty. She opened a door cautiously and moved into a corridor.

"Well, you're back," Gordon Plough said.

Erin whirled. A uniformed man was standing in a doorway, a saffer dangling from his right hand. Erin's arm moved only slightly.

Gordon Plough died before he had time to understand that his plan had not worked, at least not for him. He had one nanosecond of puzzlement as to why one of his own crew was lifting a saffer at him.

"Damn, Erin," Dent protested.

"Look in his right hand," Erin said harshly.

Denton walked to the dead man, saw the weapon in his hand, swallowed, looked away quickly. Erin made a quick check of the rest of the ship. There were permanent quarters for four crew members and a temporary setup for another. Five in all. All of them accounted for with four dead outside on the surface of the asteroid and one in the corridor.

Erin approached the computer, a first generation Unicloud, not state of the art but years newer than *Mother*'s old Century Series. There were files for the usual star charts. The ship's papers gave her the name, the *Murdoch Miner,* and told her that the ship was registered on Haven in the name of the Haven Refining Company, the firm that had bought her first cargo of ore. She got a mental picture of Murdoch Plough, tall, self-centered. So, she thought, he hadn't taken it so lightly after all when X&A put the strong arm on him and forced him to pay a fair price for her gold.

"Well, I guess that's it," Denton said. "I guess it's back to the nearest civilized planet to call—" He shook his head. "Who do you call? You can't call the nearest policeman."

"X&A," she said. "The Service handles any crime in

space.'' She was pushing buttons. ''Time enough for that later. Right now we've got to find *Mother.*''

''Oh, hell, poor Mop,'' he said. ''I'll bet he thinks we've deserted him for sure.''

She lifted ship. The *Miner* was much more agile than the old Mule. She circled past the asteroid and headed out into the big empty roughly on the vector followed by *Mother.* The *Miner's* state of the art detectors had the Mule on screen within seconds. After that it was a matter of closing with *Mother,* of sending Denton out into the void again.

''Put *Mother* down where she was when it all started,'' she told Dent.

''And you?'' His voice was slightly distorted by space as it came from *Mother* by radio.

''Beside you,'' she said.

She refilled her suit's tanks, left the outer hatch of the *Miner* open when she left her. ''How's Mr. Mop?'' she asked, as she stood on the bare rock.

''I think he was happy to see me.''

''I need your help out here, Dent.''

''All right. Let me get suited up.''

''I wouldn't ask, but I can't do it all alone.''

He emerged from *Mother* into full sun that glared off his suit. She was already moving one of the bodies toward the *Miner.* ''Bring the woman,'' she told him.

An hour and a half later they had put all four bodies, two men and two women, aboard the *Miner* to join the body of the man Erin had killed aboard ship.

''What are you going to do?'' Denton asked. ''Lock onto her and take her back to the nearest U.P. planet?''

They were standing near the mining ship with the crowded core star fields gleaming harshly over them. Starlight reflected off the treated glass of their helmets. Erin took a deep breath. ''Why did we come out here, Dent?''

''Am I supposed to answer?''

''I wish you would.''

''For gold.''

''For how much gold?''

''For enough so that neither one of us would ever have to worry about money again.''

"Have we gathered that much gold?"

"Nope," he said. "But listen, Erin—"

"Why did they—" she moved her gloved hand in the direction of the *Miner*—"come out here?"

"For gold."

"And they were perfectly willing to kill us to get it. All of it."

"Where are you going with this, Erin?"

"Do you have any idea what sort of red tape we'd have to go through if we show up on Haven or some other U.P. planet with five dead people?" He shook his head. "I'll tell you this. You'd be old and gray before you finished filling in forms, being tested to see if you were telling the truth, and answering questions. I don't have time for that. I didn't ask these people to follow us out here and try to kill us."

"I don't think I'm going to like this," Dent said.

"I'm ex-X&A, and I'd still be put through the wringer," she said. "I've paid my dues. I spent six years on *Rimfire*. I don't want to spend two years explaining to a board of inquiry how we got lucky enough to kill five people who were trying to kill us."

"What do you have in mind?" he asked doubtfully.

"I'm going to go aboard and program a timed blink into that computer," she said, and her eyes turned toward the nearest sun, an atomic furnace that would swallow the *Murdoch Miner* and her dead easily and with finality.

"I don't know, Erin. We're walking the line by not reporting Old Smiley and the other bones. I'm not sure I want to go that far across the line."

"Then just go on back to *Mother* and tell Mop I'll be along shortly and I'll take care of it. Your conscience will be clear."

He grunted once, twice, shook his head. "No," he said, "you've done enough. You took charge. You saved our lives. You wait here."

He disappeared into the bowels of the ship. A few minutes later Erin's hair tried to stand on end as the blink generator was activated. Denton came hurrying out of the air lock as if he were being pursued by the ghosts of the *Miner*'s dead.

"Thirty minutes," he said. "Plenty of time for us to get back to *Mother* and get the hell out of here."

They bounced and jetted their way back to the ship in silence. When the inner air lock hatch opened, Mr. Mop went wild with joy on seeing them both, walking on his rear legs, gnawing on them playfully. Erin picked him up and scratched his belly. Dent went on through to the bridge and soon *Mother* lifted away.

"It just occurred to me," she said, "that they might have left some trace of their presence on the asteroid."

"Not to worry," he said, positioning *Mother* so that they could see the *Miner* on her rocky perch. He checked his watch. "About—now," he said.

The *Miner* and the asteroid winked out of existence. *Mother*'s sensors followed the blink. The mass of ship and rock continued to exist for one brief moment in the corona of the nearest star before being broken down into basic subatomic building blocks.

Neither of them felt like working. Erin checked *Mother*'s orbit, made sure that she was clear of any strays from the belt, said, "I'm going to bed."

"Drink first?"

She shook her head in negation, went to her quarters, showered, put on a lacy nightgown and threw herself down onto the bed. The elation of victory over dangerous odds was gone. The stimulation of facing deadly danger had left her drained. A storm of melancholy submerged her in guilt. She slept.

She awoke with Mop pawing at her hand and making begging noises. "What? What?" she asked. Mop leapt to the floor and ran to the door, which she'd left ajar so that he could perform his duty of keeping an eye on both her and Denton. He whined and ran back to the bed, jumped up, pawed at her leg, ran to the door. Fear came to her.

"Something wrong, partner?" she asked, as she ran out onto the bridge.

Dent was sprawled in the control chair, head thrown back, mouth open. He was snoring. Mop leaped up into his lap and whined.

"He's just asleep," Erin whispered. Mop pawed at

Denton's lax hand. There was a strong smell of brandy. "And a little drunk," she said.

Denton said, "You're wrong, lady."

"It talks," she said.

"I'm more'n a little bit drunk."

"Good for you."

He opened his eyes. They were red, as if he'd been weeping.

"Come on," she said, "I'll help you get into your bed."

"Let's go fin' some more people to kill," he mumbled.

"Denton—"

" 'Cause you seemed to enjoy it."

"You and the horse you rode in on," she said, turning to go back to her cabin.

"I killed me a woman and I killed me a man," he said, "an' 'en I scooped 'em up and put 'em in their little ole spaceship and zapped 'em into a sun."

She turned. Huge tears were running down his cheeks. She went back to him, put her hands on his face. "Would you rather it had been you and me?"

"Me? Maybe. You?" He looked at her with eyes that wouldn't quite focus. "Never you, Erin. Never you. Beautiful Erin."

She took his arm. "Come on, buddy. You're going beddy-bye."

"Pretty Erin," he mumbled, leaning on her shoulder.

She knew that she could never hoist him onto his elevated bunk. She guided him to her bed. He fell onto his back and dragged her with him so that she landed atop him.

"Had to do it," he said. "Had to kill 'em. They woulda killed my Erin."

"Hush," she said. "Go to sleep."

His eyes opened wide. "I never killed anyone before."

"Hush. I know."

"It hurts."

"I know."

"I didn't want to kill them."

She kissed him lightly on the lips. He tasted of brandy. "I know."

"Did you want to kill them?"

"No," she said.

"Do 'at again."

"What?"

"This," he said, pulling her face to him. He did not kiss like a drunk. His arms *were* strong. She did not resist as he rolled her onto her back and let his hands discover that her nightgown fell away with a simple tug at a tie around her neck. She helped him undress, for she, too, had faced death and had delivered death, had seen the color of blood and had smelled the odor as it gave an entirely new dimension to the recycled air aboard the *Murdoch Miner*.

But there was more involved than the age-old desire of a man and a woman to affirm that, after being near death, they were alive. After the first cooling of mutual passion she lay with her head on his shoulder and watched him sleep. When he moved in the middle of the night she, too, awakened quickly. When he whispered his love to her, she could almost form the words to answer him.

Dent was awake and about the next morning before Mr. Mop decided that it was high time for Erin to get out of bed. Mop licked her nose and made urging noises in his throat. Erin groaned, sat up, reached for the cover, for she was nude. Then she remembered and made a disgusted face. She went directly to the shower.

Denton was eating breakfast when she went onto the bridge. He didn't speak, but his eyes were questioning.

For a moment her face was grim, and then she remembered the taste of him, the feel of him, the goodness of being in his arms. No, she could not regret what had happened.

"Hi," she said.

"Hi, yourself."

She went to him, kissed him.

"You're not angry," he said.

"Should I be?"

"I wasn't sure. Your bed. I remember you said that you thought a bed was as personal as underwear."

"I'm very careful about lending my underwear," she said. "I'm even more picky about sharing my body."

His face turned red. She laughed.

"Erin, I—"

"If you apologize, I'll slug you," she said.

"But—"

"Hush," she said, closing his mouth with hers.

Mop, wanting to get into the play, leapt onto Denton's lap, stood on his rear legs, and tried to lick them both in the face.

"Now look, you hairy little monster," Denton said, "you can sleep on my bed and sit in my lap, but when it comes to sharing my girl with you—"

CHAPTER NINE

Once again they had made love. Mop, who had been banished to a spot under the bed, waited until all was still to sneak quietly to lie at Erin's feet with his head against her leg. She patted her hand on a spot by her side and the little dog came to snuggle there, sighing in contentment as she let her hand rest lightly on him.

A living ship in space is never silent. Servomechanisms hum quietly. Relays and thermocouples click as they do their work vigilantly. The life-support system mutters contentedly to itself.

The sounds were familiar, so much a part of life that Erin didn't notice them until the hums, the clicks, the muttering ceased to be mechanical and seemed to become a confused babble of voices. She stiffened. Mop, feeling the change in her, lifted his head.

"It's all right," she whispered. "I'm just getting a bit space happy."

It was time to find a nice deposit of a certain yellow metal, top off *Mother*'s cargo, and drain the big generator while making blinks as fast as they could be punched into the computer. She wanted to be past the Dead Worlds before laying by to charge. She longed to be near human populations on civilized planets where sleek, converted military spaceships did not sneak up and disgorge killers.

She could not understand the words, but the voices were there. She told herself that it was all in her mind, pulled Mop to her, and hugged him. Denton slept on, making a soft little buzzing noise. Was it censure she sensed in the garbled voices? She angrily rejected it. She had defended

her life. She had killed only to keep from being killed.
The voices faded.

"Space happy," she whispered to Mop.

Aside from the comforting, familiar little sounds made
by *Mother*'s housekeeping, it was quiet. Erin closed her
eyes and tried to go back to sleep, but her lids flew open
when Mop suddenly stiffened and came to his feet.

"What?" she asked.

He jumped down from the bed, ran to the door, and
scratched. With chills chasing each other up and down her
spine, Erin pulled on a robe and opened the door to the
bridge. Lights came on. A quick check of critical instruments showed that *Mother* and the computer were healthy.

"What?" she asked. Mop ran here and there as if looking for something. "You're scaring me, you little poof."

She sat in the control chair and ran a quick systems
check. Everything was humming along nicely. Feeling very
foolish, she activated *Mother*'s rather primitive biological
sensors. Cold, empty space seemed to laugh at her as the
sensors registered—nothing, blankness, the void.

Before going to bed they had positioned *Mother* over a
good vein of ore in solid rock. She went to the mining
room and began working. With luck, three more days of
digging would fill the ship's cargo areas. She could feel
the slight vibrations as the biter scraped against rock. No
more voices. Mop had climbed from her lap to a space
just behind the controls for the mining equipment. Now
and then he opened one eye to watch the movement of her
hand.

When the vein of gold-carrying ore was exhausted, she
looked at the clock. She'd been at it for eight hours. It
was almost time for the scheduled work period to begin.
She secured the equipment, went back to the cabin. Denton slept on as she showered and dried herself. She reached
for a nightgown, shrugged. The need for modesty was
gone. Thoughts of man and woman together heated her as
she knelt on the bed and looked at his sleeping face. She
smiled as she noted that the light coverlet was tented over
his manhood. She eased herself under the sheet and moved
with stealth to position herself, eased down, down, sighing.

She sat very still for a long time before he turned his head to one side and made a sound in his throat. She began to move, put her hands on his shoulders, shuddered with pleasure as he awakened and thrust upward.

After a timeless period of fusion she lay beside him, pleasantly expended, warm, core-soft.

"I was having the damnedest dream," he said.

"Umm."

"There was this city, this fairyland city, and people were flying in panic and screaming—"

"Running away?"

"Flying," he said.

"As in, like, birds?"

"Yep."

She shivered, remembering the voices.

"And I was there and not there, because at the same time I was in a great room, like a courtroom but more magnificent, and someone was saying that defiance of the law leads to ruin."

"Ah, guilt feelings," she said.

"As you are fond of saying, you bet your sweet ass." He held her close.

"Two more days," she said. She thought it best not to admit that she, too, had experienced remorse.

"And how many more trips after that?"

"Well, if you want to be poor, with only a million or so, we can turn the whole thing over to X&A when we get to Haven with this load."

"Haven?"

She knew the intent of his question. The ship that they had blinked into the sun had been a Haven ship. "It would look suspicious, since I sold my first load there, if I went anywhere else."

He nodded. "All right. But I've never been a good liar, Erin."

She brushed his thick hair back from his forehead tenderly. "I don't think anyone will question us. If Murdoch Plough sent that ship after us, he wouldn't dare ask questions, for that would be admitting that he knew his men tried to kill us."

"As always, you're probably right," he said.

''But let's not make that decision right now. We've got a few weeks of travel before we get to Haven.''

He held her close and was quiet for a long time before he said, ''They had golden skin.''

''Who?''

''The people in the dream.''

''They were suntanned?''

''Bronzed. Golden.''

''Make up your mind.''

''I wonder what caused it.''

''What?''

''The blowup. Whatever it was that shattered a planet.''

She shivered again, remembering Mop's actions and her own feeling that there was something out there in the asteroid belt.

''Did they know? In my dream the sky was fire. I could sense the fear.'' He shook his head. ''Wow. To know that you're going to die—''

''Everyone knows *that.*''

''Yeah, we all know we're going to die someday. But to know that you're going to die in a matter of—what? Seconds? Minutes? Hours? Days? How much warning did they have? And to know that not only are you going to die but everyone you know, everyone you love, and everyone you don't know, and everyone you hate is going to die with you. Family, friends, lovers, children, the young, the old—'' He sighed. ''Pets? And every material thing is going to perish with you. Total destruction.''

''You're being very negative,'' she said, trying to sound as if she were teasing but not succeeding totally.

''Yep.'' He squeezed her. ''Time to get up and about, lazybones.''

''You get up. I just put in eight hours on the miner.''

''Huh?''

''Couldn't sleep.''

''So you *were* bothered.''

''I'm not totally insensitive.''

''No. Sorry.'' He slapped her playfully on the rump. Mop bounced up on the bed to get in on the fun. ''Toes, Mop,'' Denton said, removing the coverlet from Erin's feet. ''Get those toes.''

Mop attacked Erin's bare toes, gnawing carefully. He was a gentle little dog. Erin squealed. Denton held her legs down.

"Toes," he kept saying as Mop, stubby tail going in ecstatic circles, was urged on to greater efforts by Erin's laughing protest.

Mop supervised from his usual perch on the console as Erin lifted the ship and started the search for one more deposit of the yellow metal. Several times the sensors gave heavy metal readings.

"Since this is the last one," she said, "let's make it good."

She set the detectors to the density of sedimentary rock of the type that had yielded pure gold in placer deposits. In such rock fossilized bones were found. Hours went by. They eased past hundreds of oddly shaped asteroids of the most common types. Most of the smooth-skinned rocks registered iron, and their contours seemed to indicate that they had solidified in cold space. Core material. The living heart of a planet, molten, fiery, bursting into the black emptiness through the fragile, solid crust, scattering the debris that had been a world.

More than once the computer sang out that the sensors had found stone of the desired consistency with gold deposits near the surface, but for some reason that Erin did not try to explain, even to herself, she was not satisfied. Perhaps, since the next people to see the belt would be the crew of an X&A ship, she just wanted to explore as much of the belt as possible.

Deep inside the tumbling, crowded belt the sensors located the largest slab of sedimentary rock they had seen. There were solid indications of gold. Erin ran an additional check, setting the sensors to detect the minerals present in fossil bone. Denton raised his eyebrows when the indicators registered a strong presence.

"Are we mining or bone hunting?" he asked.

"Little bit of both?"

"Might as well," he said.

There was a perfect landing place directly atop the strongest readings for heavy metals. Erin locked *Mother* to the rock and stabilized the tumble. There was one final task to be performed before beginning mining operations. She put a slow spin on the entire asteroid so that once every hour *Mother*'s detectors could scan all of the spaces separating her from the neighbors. Twice now danger had crept up on the ship's blind side. It would not happen again.

Heavy gold nuggets had collected in a pocket. They had a rich, pure color. To the relief of both of them the work went on with riches being accumulated in the cargo space without the distraction of encountering fossilized humanoid remains.

"That's it," Dent said. The nugget pocket had been very productive. He swung the loader back into its pod after dumping one last load of gold-flecked sand into the cargo space. "Unless you want to pile some ore under your bunk."

"I'm not quite that greedy," she said.

He checked the clock. "We can be back on the established blink routes in half an hour."

She nodded. She was toying with the sensor controls, zeroing in on an area that gave the readings of fossilized organic material. "Dent?"

"I don't think I want to hear this."

"Just look."

He checked the sensor gauges. "Ummm. Big."

"Bigger than anything we've seen."

He shrugged. "All right."

She used the remote panel to lift ship just far enough off the rock to move a few feet to the right. She used the biter carefully to nibble away the rock, postponing the time when they would have to climb into suits and go extravehicular. When the sensors showed only a thin layer of stone over fossil, she employed the laser and exposed a dome of grayish material.

"Looks like another skull," Denton said.

"I'm afraid so."

"It was your crazy idea," he said.

"You don't have to go with me," she said.

"No, I don't have to." He leaned to kiss her on the cheek. "But I will because you have such splendidly proportioned mammary glands."

"Hands off," she said, as he fondled her breasts.

"I can play with your bosom if I want to," he said.

"It's my bosom."

"If that's the way you're going to be, then you'll have to marry me," he said. "In fact, as captain of this ship you can marry us and then what's mine is yours and vice-versa."

"Not my body," she said.

"Just half of it," he said, putting both hands on her left breast, which was slightly larger than the right. "I'll take this half."

"I don't think you quite understand the legal concept of community property," she said, pressing his hand against her breast. "And besides, it's not play time."

"Anything I hate it's a bossy female captain," he said, moving off toward the suit closet.

"You *never* get used to it," she said, as they stood outside on barren rock.

Dent led the way into the rather cramped space under the ship. He started using his hand-held laser at one end of the trench. She worked around the skull, freeing it from its encasing stone to look down into rock-clogged eye sockets.

"Erin, come have a look at this," Denton said.

There was something in his voice that caused her to look over her shoulder. The horizon was quite near. The rock burned with light, and beyond the rim there was the star-swarmed fabric of emptiness. She bent to let the glare of her helmet light merge with Denton's.

He had carefully cut the matrix away from the upper surface of small bones. She did not at first understand the reason for his awe.

"They're still articulated," he said.

The small bones, several of them, made up what was, obviously, a foot. The short joints of toes were in perfect position. She squatted, something that took some doing in the suit, and ran her fingers over the fossil bones.

"Cartilage would have decayed long before it could be fossilized," he said. "But look closely here, where I've cleared away the rock from the joints of the toes."

A grayish connection existed between the separate

bones. She shook her head and stood. Denton used his laser and began to expose a long femur, working upward toward the hip joint. Erin watched in fascination as the joint was exposed, articulated to the hipbone by ball and socket. And then the pelvic saddle was bared.

"Female," she said.

"Big lady," he said.

She went back to work, cutting away matrix along the shoulders, down one arm. All joints were intact. She had planned to simply free the bones from the rock that had held them for countless millennia, but the surprisingly intact condition of the fossil skeleton altered her plans. They used the mining laser to cut a deep trench around the entire deposit, then, after careful measurements and searchings, undercut the oblong, coffin shaped area of rock atop of which the skeleton was exposed like some ancient carving in bas relief.

Weight, of course, was no problem in space. Inertia was another thing. It wouldn't do to let a few tons of rock bang *Mother* even at a very low rate of speed. Erin went aboard, greeted a wildly enthusiastic Mop—once again his humans had come back, had not, after all, deserted him, joy, joy—and moved the ship from atop the trench.

Back outside with Dent, she said, "Slow, easy," as they impelled the slab containing the fossil bones into motion. Erin used the jets of her suit to stop the upward movement, then, together, they eased the slab over a flat area, horsed it to a stop, lowered it to the surface.

It was necessary to go aboard ship to renew the air in the suits. Air recycling equipment had not yet been successfully miniaturized to fit inside a unit as small as a flexsuit, but *Mother*'s recycler took care of the stale, oxygen depleted air in the tanks and soon Erin and Dent were back at work, carefully cutting away matrix to reduce the bulk and weight of the slab but leaving enough of the encasing stone to hold the bones in their perfect alignment with each other.

After some tricky adjustments the slab was suspended above the surface and Erin was working underneath, blowing away stone from the back of the skeleton.

"She must have been lying atop something," Erin said.

Denton came to stand beside her. He rolled the slab to let the skeleton lie on its side. "Easier to work this way."

"Smart ass," she said, wondering why she hadn't thought of that.

Lying along the skeleton's back, there were long, delicate bones unlike any they had seen. Smaller bones, somewhat like ribs, radiated away from the long ones; and the longer bones were one atop the other next to the figure's back.

"What the hell?" Denton asked. "Did she fall on an animal or something?"

"I think we'd better leave this mess here at the back alone," she said.

"You're planning to take this thing with us?" Denton asked.

"I think we'd better."

"She's been here a long, long time. I think she'd wait for an X&A ship."

Erin was reluctant to try to explain that it was absolutely vital to put the fossil skeleton aboard *Mother*. She couldn't have told him why, she just knew that it had to be done.

"Let's melt away a few more pounds of rock," she said. "But be careful."

Only the surface of the long, curving, graceful bones that reached down to the skeleton's knees had been exposed. The slab had been reduced to mummiform shape. To trim its bulk further, Erin worked around the neck and shoulders. The arm bones lay at the figure's side. There was a curious, rather massive protrusion from the back side of each shoulder blade. She used the laser carefully, hoping to detach the humanoid skeleton from the bones of the life-form that had lain under it. But the protrusions from the shoulder blades were fossil bone that formed a ball and socket joint much like the hip joint, and from that joint the long, delicate bones swept outward in a graceful ellipse.

"Dent," she whispered.

He heard, for he had been standing directly behind her, watching as she cut away the matrix to expose two features of the humanoid skeleton that were definitely nonhuman. First, and most obvious, the long, delicate bones connected to the skeleton's shoulders by ball and socket joints could have had only one purpose. Second, a broad, solid bone extending across the skeleton's back was perforated with small holes where tendons had once been connected. The solid plane of the back formed a foundation for connecting muscles to power the leaflike formations extending downward from the shoulders.

"Wings," Erin whispered.

"Yep," Dent said.

"The arts and crafts colonies of Delos make them," Erin said. "They're patterned after the old illustrations in The Book."

Denton nodded inside his helmet. There was, of course, only one "The Book." The Bible. The only book of Old Earth literature that had survived the exodus into space.

"Angels," Erin said. "They make angels on Delos. They wear long robes and they have beautiful, long hair and—"

"And wings," Dent said. "But before you start calling her Gabriel, tell me how, if she's an angel, she got here." He spread his hands, taking in the small asteroid, the tumbling, crowded belt that arched off into the blackness, the glare of the core stars. "And angels don't die, Erin."

"No. I'm being silly."

"Look, let's leave her here. Let's get to Haven as fast as we can and let the heavy thinkers at X&A figure it out."

"She's so lonely," Erin said.

"Come on, Erin. She might have been lonely once. She's not now."

"We can't just leave her here like this."

Dent sighed. "All right, whatever it takes to get you aboard and moving toward Haven."

There was still considerable weight to be put into motion, to be guided into the air lock, which became very crowded with two live, suited human beings and one very dead whatever it was. Mop took one look at the thing that his buddies pushed carefully out of the air lock and retreated, barking with high-pitched intensity.

"Hush," Erin said.

"Minds well," Denton said, as Mop barked more excitedly than ever.

They had decided that there was only one place to carry the skeleton. Her mass—that's the way both of them were thinking, her, not it—had to be secured and the only place with floor space large enough to lay the mummiform slab flat was in the gym. That meant moving her through the bridge where one slip could smash the force of a few hundred pounds of inertial motion into delicate instrument panels. They secured the skeleton's slab with lines so that if it got away from them—they had to cut off the ship's artificial gravity in order to move the weight—the lines would halt the motion before the slab damaged something vital.

The job was accomplished with only minor abrasions to Dent's arm, which became caught between the slab and the door frame as they floated the skeleton into the gym. Dent welded eyes to the metal deck and lashed the slab securely. Mop watched the operation with clearly expressed doubt, and from a distance, sitting with his head extended, making his neck look longer.

Erin wasted no time in programming the ship's generator to blink them toward the U.P. sector. In quick order, *Mother* leapt to and past the sac in which swam the Dead Worlds. The last blink was on an established blink route.

Mother lay beside a blink beacon, her generator drawing charge from the nearest stars. Her crew were celebrating, having a special meal with wine. The activity of the generator produced a not unpleasant tingle in the air, a deeply buried perception of dynamic energy.

Mop wasn't particularly fond of the charging period. It tended to make his hair stand up, and, being a rather hairy, silky little dog, when his hair tried to stand up he looked rather bedraggled. He sat at Erin's feet, politely accepting a taste of people food now and then, but not being demanding about it. Denton had selected soft music to form a warm, bland background. Neither he nor Erin felt especially talkative. Both seemed content to smile as eye contact was made, to touch hands now and then across the little table.

Erin selected a nice tidbit and, not taking her eyes off

Dent's, held it down for Mop. When her offering was not seized immediately, she turned her head. Mop was seated at the closed door to the gym, his hair standing up oddly, a low growl issuing from his throat.

"Hey," Erin said. "Want a nibble?"

Mop ignored her. She had never heard him growl in just that manner. She felt a shiver of dread, for there was definite warning in Mops' stance, in his steady, low growling. She walked to the gym door and opened it. Dent saw her freeze. He sprang to his feet and went to look over her shoulder.

The metal deck was littered with rock particles. The encasing shell of matrix material had shattered away from the skeleton, leaving each fossil bone free of encumbrance. The accretion inside the skull cavity had been expelled. The eye sockets were empty, black. And, most unnerving of all, the wing bones that had been folded under the body were spread out on either side in a graceful sweep.

"I am not liking this," Erin said.

"What the hell?" Dent asked, moving forward to kneel beside the skeleton.

Mop, refusing to enter the gym, sat outside the door, growling steadily.

"Let's get out of here," Erin said, tugging on Denton's arm.

"You talked me into it," he said.

She locked the door, went to the console, and activated the communicator. Dent looked over her shoulder as she sent a blinkstat to the beacon beside which the ship rested. It was directed to Captain Julie Roberts of the U.P.S. *Rimfire*. Over Erin's name, the number of the originating blink beacon, and the route that *Mother* would be following to Haven it said: "Imperative you come immediately."

To that message Erin added one word, a word that would have meaning only for Julie Roberts and the female officers aboard *Rimfire*.

During the long and boring circumnavigation of the galaxy there'd been lots of time for girl talk, and not even the captain was above such diversions. One dreamy-eyed little ensign had voiced a reverie about finding a race of perfect men on some undiscovered planet on the opposite side of the galaxy, men who would know how to treat a woman, men who were tender and romantic, polite and considerate, and very skilled in the erotic arts. The ensign's dream became a sort of "in" joke among the female officers. They knew, of course, that *Rimfire*'s mission was to lay a blink route around the periphery of the galaxy, but they all agreed that it would be fine with them if Rimfire also found what one wag called F.R.A.N.K., the Faultlessly Romantic Alien Nooky Knocker.

Before the end of the trip the acronym F.R.A.N.K. had come to mean any alien, not just a romantic male.

And so Erin's message read: "Imperative you come immediately. F.R.A.N.K."

A blinkstat was next to nothing traveling through nothingness instantaneously. The small generators in the blink beacons relayed the message along the way without pause and before *Mother*'s generator was charged the stat had gone to X&A Headquarters on Xanthos to be relayed outward along *Rimfire*'s known route into an unexplored area of the galaxy.

"Will she come?" Denton asked, eyebrows raised in amazement.

"She'll come," Erin said.

"Secret code?"

She laughed. She didn't feel like laughing, for she could remember with more detail than she liked the way the skeleton had shed the matrix rock, the way the wings had been repositioned. She told him the meaning of F.R.A.N.K.

"I guess she'll come, then," he said. "You told her you'd found an alien. The question is, when?"

"I doubt seriously if she'll be able to meet us before we get to Haven."

"What would you say," he asked, "if I suggested that we drop back to DW I and deposit our friend in there on the surface in a safe place?"

"Ah," she said, "she makes you a little uneasy, too."

"A little? Hah." He grinned. "Of course, we can say that it was an effect of blinking, or the charge in the air that caused all the rock to peel off of her."

We can say that, I guess.''

"I know that she's been dead for only God know how long," Denton said. "My reason tells me that she's not even organic material anymore, that she's nothing but stone, but I seem to have a low threshold for terror."

"I think Mop would agree with you," she said.

Mop was sitting in front of the gym door, making that eerie, warning sound deep in his throat.

"Maybe we'd better go see what *she's* doing in there now," Denton said.

"You go," Erin said, only half-joking.

Denton went to the door. "What's old Miss Bones doing in there, Mop?" he asked, as he opened the door.

Mop yelped and went scrambling backward to hide under the console. Erin felt a thrill of pure fear. Before her eyes, Denton Gale ceased to exist. A red spray lashed at her face stingingly as Dent exploded. She opened her mouth to scream. A red mist clouded the viewport, beaded the glass of instruments, colored every surface on the bridge.

Erin's scream did not make it past the original thought impulse before she, too, was annihilated, erupting into molecule-sized particles that dispersed themselves on the metal walls, deck, and ceiling of the bridge and further coated instruments and surfaces.

Under the console, protected from the damp spray, a little dog cowered in abject fright.

CHAPTER TEN

Captain Julie Roberts never wore *Rimfire*'s favorite duty uniform, shorts, overblouse, and hose. She was a private person. No one aboard her ship knew that under her service slacks she had a pair of legs that would stand comparison with those of any young woman in the crew. Her tailored tunic did not, however, completely conceal the fact that she was a well endowed woman. She wore her dark hair at optimum Service length so that it clung to her head in natural, kinky curls. She did not always wear a hat, but no member of the crew had ever seen her when her face was not perfectly done with skillfully applied, understated makeup.

The captain did not always keep regular hours, did not pull a definitely timed watch. She just came and went, and the very unpredictability of her schedule kept the crew always on the alert. As it happened, Captain Roberts was asleep and Lieutenant Ursulina Wade was on bridge watch when Erin Kenner's blinkstat caught up with *Rimfire*.

The big ship was motionless in space, waiting for her generator to charge. She had covered the assigned area of search, laid new blink beacons to an area of the galaxy where there were no life zone planets, but where she had charted a few gas giants, a hot planet with an atmosphere of toxic chemicals, and one barren near-sun globe of rock that might offer mining possibilities after the proper exploration.

Ursulina, known to her fellow officers as Ursy, had matured since she had dreamed openly of finding the perfect man on an alien planet in the first months of *Rimfire*'s circumnavigation. She had not given up her dream, even if two periods of experimentation with a handsome married officer named Jack Burnish and a young man fresh out of the Academy had proven to be a bit disappointing, but she had learned to keep her fantasies to herself.

When she took Erin Kenner's blinkstat off the machine and read it, she flushed, thinking that someone was bringing up an old joke that had lost its humor. But the stat had come through a host of beacons on its way to *Rimfire*. Ursy remembered Erin Kenner well. She had tried to pattern herself after Erin, for Erin had been an excellent officer. Apparently, since she'd enjoyed two promotions since Erin quit the service, she had succeeded.

Now Ursy faced a decision. The "Captain's Status" board indicated that Julie Roberts was sleeping. The captain did not like to be awakened without very good cause. Ursy read the message again. "Imperative" was a pretty strong word, but the "F.R.A.N.K." was even stronger. She pulled herself up, punched the captain's communicator, and waited.

"Speak," the captain's voice said.

"Captain, there is a blinkstat that, in my opinion, requires your immediate attention."

"Send it to my cabin."

Ursy called the navigator from his cubbyhole and told him to take the watch. It wasn't that she couldn't entrust the message to someone else, it was just that she wanted to see the captain's face when the captain read it. She knocked on the captain's door. To her surprise Julie Roberts was not fully dressed, but was bundled into a furry, white robe.

The captain nodded in answer to Ursy's greeting and held out her hand. "Did you back-check the blink routes?" the captain asked after a quick glance at the stat.

"No, ma'am."

"This message could have originated on board. Some wag having a little joke?"

"I'll go check immediately, ma'am."

"It would have saved time had you checked first."

"Yes, ma'am."

"Never mind. Go back to the bridge. I'll check it myself."

In a quarter hour the captain was on the bridge. She sat down at the computer and punched in a long series of numbers. Ursy looked over her shoulder as the viewer showed the route of Erin Kenner's stat. A long line extended back from *Rimfire*'s position to a point opposite the U.P. main worlds, then inward to Xanthos. From Xanthos the line led toward the core and terminated at a blink beacon near the Dead World sac.

"Lieutenant," the captain asked, "what does this message mean to you?"

"I think, ma'am, that Erin has found something, ah, well, something alien."

"And why does she contact me instead of X&A Central?"

"Erin admired you very much, Captain. I think if she were in some kind of trouble she'd call on you first."

"Trouble?"

"The same question came to me, ma'am," Ursy said. "A ship could blink in to Erin's position from one of the U.P. planets much quicker than *Rimfire* can get there. But I think Erin would call on you in any emergency, Captain."

Julie thought for a few moments. She and Erin Kenner had enjoyed a good relationship, as much of a friendship as could exist between a junior officer and the ship's captain. Once or twice she'd heard Erin complain about Service red tape and the ground-bound commandos at X&A Central on Xanthos. It was understandable for a field officer, a woman who had spent six years aboard *Rimfire* without seeing a human face other than those in the ship's crew, to have a mild case of distrust for headquarters types.

One thing was sure. Erin Kenner was not the hysterical type, not the type to send out false alarms. There was, of course, doubt in Julie Roberts' mind that Erin had found something alien. But the stat had originated quite near a spot in the galaxy that, if one dwelt upon it, could give one nightmares.

"Ursy, this stat is to be kept between me and thee," Julie said.

"Yes, ma'am. We're going, then?"

"Well, hell, Ursy, you've been looking for the Faultlessly Romantic Alien Nooky Knocker for years. Would you want to miss this opportunity?"

"Ma'am," Ursy said seriously, "I'm not sure that Erin is qualified to judge whether or not she's found F.R.A.N.K. I'm not so sure that I agree with her taste in men."

Julie Roberts did not answer, although she was aware that both Erin and Ursy had fallen for the smooth line of Jack Burnish.

"Shall I program a blink, Captain? We're ninety percent charged."

"Blink away, Lieutenant," Julie said. "Have navigation figure us the shortest route to Haven. Erin should be there well ahead of us."

Minutes later, *Rimfire* shimmered and disappeared to emerge into normal space light-years down the route toward home.

CHAPTER ELEVEN

She lashed out blindly toward movement and, although her reaction was a defensive one, stemming from the knowledge that she was weakened, her blow was catastrophically harmful to fragile flesh and blood entities. She realized that she'd made a mistake even as she struck and was taking readings and measurements to rectify her hasty action even as the two bio-masses were being disassembled into fragments no larger than molecules.

She feared that she had been too slow, for she had been confused by the fossilized evidence of her long agony. As she preserved physical patterns down to and below the cellular level, she was surprised by the complexity of the entities. That degree of intricacy in intelligence was unexpected. As she began to loose the psychological bonds of the nightmares of frozen eternity, she came to respect what the two entities had been.

It was pleasing to her to find that there was still another biosystem at hand, an entity of passive receptiveness that was available for use as a data bank. She made certain decisions, took action. That done, she allowed herself a respite.

The fossil bones were, of course, useless to her. They were a curiosity, nothing more. Once she had shed them, once she had broken free of the constraining layers of stone, she was finished with that remnant of her former self.

As she rested, she explored these new surroundings. Although the race that had constructed the thing of metals and artificial materials was familiar in form—she had seen two of them and there were images of many others contained in the electronic mind of the machines—their thought patterns and lifestyles were totally alien to her. They were quite primitive, having to depend on an artificial hard shell of protection against the vacuum of space and having to use electronics and machines to draw the power of movement from the stars, but the way in which they had compensated for their shortcomings was ingenious.

The computer interested her. She explored it, had some difficulty understanding how it retrieved specific data from an electronically charged chamber filled with a dense cloud of aerated acid. Even though the computer had a greater capacity for logic than the minds of the beings who called themselves man, or humans, it was quite limited and had no ability to originate thought.

She examined the small biosystem that had been hiding under a chair. Interesting. Relatively large brain capacity for its size, but of very low intelligence, operating, in fact, largely on the instinctive level.

She was very weak. She wished for a companion with whom to share a joke: "I'm afraid that I'm feeling *very* insubstantial at the moment."

It amused her to assemble the scattered organic matter to form a composite of the originals. She did so because she was, or had been, accustomed to carrying more mass than was represented by either the male or the female man. She considered placing the genitalia of the two entities in opposition, but she had other things to do. She could experiment with the pathetic little emotions of man later.

To her pleasure, she gained vitality as she formed a body and extended herself into it to feel two hearts beating, to experience the flow of blood and to wonder at the little secretions and acquisitions of some rather clever organs and glands. She became distracted for a period of time as she experimented with the release of certain chemicals into the large brain which she had assembled from the cells of both the male and the female, but she soon tired of such childish gratification. As she built and formed the large body, gathering the scattered material carefully, painstakingly, the little one—she discovered by reviewing the images stored in the machines that they called it a dog—made an irritating noise and bared tiny, white teeth.

"You are brave enough," she said, using the words of man. The harshness of her voice sent the little dog cringing away to hide under a chair. She did some modifications on the voice box and practiced speech until the dog peered fearfully out from the shadows to see who it was who was calling him so softly and so caringly.

Mop quickly saw that it wasn't one of his humans who was calling. It was a large thing that smelled familiar but was quite frightening in its bulk.

It took a while to customize the body to her liking. She noted that the dog had his own food and water dispensers and that now and then he went into another room to sleep on a rumpled bed. Once she had her body adjusted for comfort and utility, she spent a few days gathering as much knowledge as there was available about the curious culture and lifestyle of man. She was ready to leave the limited confines of the ship and venture into the wider universe. She willed transfer to a rather pretty world that the men called Delos. Nothing happened. The ability to move instantly to any spot in the galaxy was gone from her. She accepted that lack along with the loss of her own physical form. She reentered the available body and cranked up its systems again. It seemed that she was to be confined, at least for the moment, to the ship. Since her body was only flesh and blood, it would not survive in the vacuum of space.

Something had gone wrong in the indeterminable period of time since she had been locked away in the cooling core material of a destroyed world. She examined herself minutely and found that she had lost many abilities. She would simply have to make the best of what was left.

Perhaps these *men* had developed materials and techniques that would help her regain the magnitude that had once been hers. She spent more time with the materials in the ship's library and resigned herself to the fact that she would have to travel about in a man-made spaceship and imitate the mechanical and electronic structures of man in order to accomplish her desires.

She soon discovered that there was not quite enough

written or recorded material aboard ship to tell her everything she wanted to know about the blink drive. Moreover, the men had been secure in their knowledge of ship's operations and had not included a basic manual in the library. The knowledge which she needed to operate the ship safely was not included in the material in the library. With her powers so diminished, she didn't want to chance being stranded in space, perhaps to drift for more eternities.

She divided the organic matter in her large body into the two original units and lifted the female entity from her repository in the dog's skull and inserted her into her own frame.

CHAPTER TWELVE

Murdoch Plough, owner of the Haven Refining Company, leapt to his feet in shock when his secretary announced that Miss Erin Kenner was asking to see him. His face first drained itself of blood, so that he was quite pale, but by the time he had recovered himself enough to tell the secretary to send Miss Kenner in he was feeling flushed and feverish. Erin Kenner's presence on Haven presented possibilities that Plough was not quite ready to face. He tried to tell himself that there could be alternate explanations for his not having heard from his brother and the crew of four whom he had sent to replace Erin Kenner and the man she'd picked up on New Earth as possessors of the source of the richest gold ore he'd ever seen.

Plough was still musing about the unpleasant possibilities when the Kenner woman and a man about her own age entered the room. He had received no messages from his brother since Kenner's *Mother Lode* left the main United Planets blink beacon range and headed toward the core.

Seeing the woman brought an uneasy smile to his large, square face. She was a looker, all right. As he glanced toward her helper or lover or whatever the hell Denton Gale was, he felt a little easier about his brother, because there was no way that these two pussies could have survived had Brother Gordon and his crew isolated them on a mining planet somewhere off the established blink routes.

"Well, Miss Kenner," he said. "Have your brought a representative of X&A with you this trip?" It still rankled

Plough that the woman had pulled influence on him, forcing him to pay premium prices for her ore.

"Mr. Gale is my associate," the Kenner woman said flatly.

"What can I do for you?" Plough asked, walking around his desk to shake Denton Gale's hand.

"We have a load of ore," Kenner said.

"Ah, excellent, excellent," Plough said, wiping his hand on his trouser leg. Denton Gale's hand was cold and damp. "However, Miss Kenner, I'm afraid that the market has fallen slightly since you were last here."

"We have a load of ore," Kenner said.

Plough looked at her a bit more closely. She was looking straight at him, but there was an oddness in her eyes, as if they were focused beyond his face.

He named a price lower than the price he'd offered her originally for her first load.

"We will take the proceeds in U.P. credits," Gale said.

"Sure, sure," Plough said. "I'll deposit the amount in your account, Miss Kenner."

"We will take the proceeds in U.P. credits," Gale repeated.

"You mean in cash?"

There was a moment of hesitation until Kenner said, in that flat, wooden voice, "We will take the proceeds in cash."

"That's a lot of paper," Plough said. "Is your load as heavy as the last one?"

Neither Gale nor Kenner spoke.

"Well," Plough said, "I'll have my men move your ship over to the loading ramp."

"I will move the ship," Kenner said, turning to lead Gale out of the office.

Plough followed them into the reception area, watched them walk stiffly out of the office. "That broad act a little odd to you?" he asked the secretary.

"I didn't notice, honey." the secretary said. Since her prime duty to her employer was of a private nature, she tended to be a bit casual when she and Plough were alone.

Plough watched the *Mother Lode* lift and move laterally to the ramp. Soon some very rich ore was rattling down the conveyor belts toward the smelters. Kenner and Gale stayed aboard the ship. Plough went to the communication room and placed a call to Haven X&A, expressed concern about an overdue Haven Refining Company mining ship, was told that there'd been no communication from the *Murdoch Miner.*

"If you will give us the projected route of the ship, sir," the X&A operator said, "we will begin a trace."

"No, no, thank you," Plough said. "I'm probably being needlessly concerned. "I'll get back to you."

The *Mother Lode* sat beside the loading ramp through the smelting operation. Neither Kenner nor Gale left her until Plough called to tell them that he had the money in United Planets credits. Gale came to the office and accepted the large bag of credits without a word. Plough kept waiting for an irate call from X&A complaining that he was cheating an ex-X&A officer, but nothing happened.

When Gale left the office, Plough was just behind him. As the *Mother Lode* lifted ship, she was followed by Murdoch Plough's own private yacht, a converted fleet light destroyer armed with some weapons that were legal for a deep space miner that often entered unexplored areas and with some armament that would have landed Plough in deep trouble if his yacht were ever inspected by X&A.

To Plough's surprise the *Mother Lode* did not leave Haven immediately. She orbited halfway around the world and landed at the spaceport on the other continent. Plough didn't like the idea of taking his heavily and illegally armed ship into a landing other than at his own home port where there were no interplanetary customs offices and no X&A station. But he wanted to know what Kenner was up to, so he went down from orbit in a launch.

The *Mother Lode* was taking on cargo. It was fairly simple for Plough to find out that Kenner was buying a rather odd assortment of materials, calling in her orders from the ship, paying on delivery in cash. All he had to do was intercept the delivery vehicles and hand out a couple of credits and he knew that a wide array of chemicals and electronic equipment were being loaded into the *Mother Lode*'s cargo bins.

The most puzzling thing was that while the equipment

and materials were being loaded, the mining equipment was being gutted from the *Mother Lode*. It looked as if Kenner and Gale intended leaving the almost new and very expensive equipment sitting out in the weather on the pad beside the ship, but when Kenner called Control for permission to lift ship she was asked—Plough was tuned into the control frequency—her intentions in regard to the discarded equipment. When she hesitated, Control told her that the machines would have to be removed from the pad before the *Mother Lode* could be given clearance.

Plough shook his head as the Kenner woman babbled on to Control, asking really stupid questions until she was finally told that Control didn't care what she did with the equipment just as long as it was removed from port property. Plough felt faint when a couple of hundred thousand credits worth of perfectly good mining machinery was given to the port's waste removal service, but he didn't have time to make an effort to salvage it, because Control was giving the *Mother Lode* lift clearance. He took the launch back to his yacht and was ready to follow when Kenner's ship reached orbit and blinked away. He had come to the conclusion that something had happened to his little brother. He wasn't worried. Knowing Gordon, the *Murdoch Miner* was probably cruising around a couple of hundred light-years away from where she was supposed to have followed Kenner's ship, with Gordon wondering how the hell to find his way home.

As the *Mother Lode* used her big generator to make multiple blinks before recharging, Plough was happy that he had a converted military ship with a generator to match the capacity of the Mule. He had a good crew, six of them, four women and two men. They had been with him for a long time, and he had taken care of them as he built his business from one antiquated mining ship to a fleet and then to bigger and better things. More than once the crew had obeyed his orders without question when there was gain to be had in seizing a rich mining location that had been discovered by others, but Plough had not jumped a claim or disappeared isolated miners in the far outback of space for a long time. It had taken the unbelievably rich deposits being mined by Erin Kenner to arouse his instinct

for avarice enough to lure him away from the comfort he
had built on Haven.

He knew he had goofed in sending his younger brother
to do whatever it took to gain access to Kenner's mines;
but now he had left the comfort of his office and the charms
of no less than three mistresses to make up for his mistake.
He wasn't too unhappy about it because in that last load
of ore there'd been an almost incredible richness of pure
nuggets mixed in with the veined rock. With a source like
Kenner's mine, he'd be able to buy Haven, if he wanted
to, but most likely he'd accumulate so much money that
he could have power on any planet in the system. With the
proper amounts of money it wouldn't be difficult to find a
more pleasant spot than Haven.

For a while it looked as if Kenner's mine was in the
Dead World sac, but the *Mother Lode* had merely paused
for charging and when her generator was ready she blinked
onward.

Plough brought his yacht back into normal space at a
safe distance and saw the *Mother Lode* lying near an asteroid belt that formed a ring around a good G-class sun
at approximately one astronomical unit of distance, the
usual position for a life zone planet. To be sure he was at
the right place, he put his sensors to work. He had the
latest equipment, state of the art, and from outside the ring
he was able to locate a dozen asteroids showing pleasingly
large gold and platinum deposits. This *was* the place. He
told his crew to get ready for some work. The converted
light destroyer had huge cargo spaces. The load of ore he'd
take back to Haven would make him a very rich man.
First, however, there was a little chore to be done.

Plough himself took the controls and maneuvered the
yacht among the tumbling asteroids until he was within
laser range of the *Mother Lode.* He considered using a
computer guided torpedo, but that would have been over-
kill. It would simply blow the Mule into bits, and would
leave enough scrap metal floating around in space so that
if someone—like an X&A explorer—stumbled onto it the
particles could be identified as having come from a Mule.
Simple logic led him to arrive at the same solution for
getting rid of a spaceship completely as both his brother

and Erin Kenner had. He would hole the hull of the *Mother Lode* with a laser. Explosive decompression would take care of Kenner and Gale, leaving the ship intact. Then he'd use his generator to boost the *Mother Lode* into the sun and no one would ever be able to say what had become of her.

He positioned the yacht to bring a laser cannon to bear, sighted in on the viewport on the control bridge, ordered the laser's power to be turned on. There was a sinister sizzling sound as the weapon built toward destruction force.

Plough was calm. Getting rid of Kenner and Gale and their ship was going to be almost too easy.

CHAPTER THIRTEEN

Haven was a lightly populated planet composed mostly of scrublands and deserts. Her two principal land masses were of similar size and were on opposing sides of the globe in the northern hemisphere. So alike were the continents that their weather patterns were similar. Alpine ranges on the western edges lifted the moisture-laden ocean air to cooling heights so that a narrow band of rain forest faced the sea. On the eastern side of the mountains, on both continents, arid conditions prevailed, scrub giving way to the sand wastes and barren rock of the deserts that extended two thousand miles to the semi-arid west coast.

Throughout the cruel deserts, where, in summer, the daytime temperatures reached one hundred and twenty degrees, were the camps and digs of miners and prospectors. Haven, having little agricultural land to offer, compensated for that lack by being rich in utile ores such as iron, manganese, copper, bauxite, and a good representation of trace minerals, in short, most of the metallic raw materials that were necessary to build and expand a civilization that had spread from one very old and rather small planet, New Earth, to encompass a degree of arc that, on charts, seemed impressive.

A new feature appeared in Haven's skies, for *Rimfire* was that large, her surfaces that reflective. When she went into orbit she became, to those on the surface, a fast moving star, and the scattered seekers of metallic riches turned their faces upward.

In Haven's two large cities word spread rapidly that the biggest and most complex spacecraft ever constructed was orbiting over Haven. The territorial governors of both continents were on hand when *Rimfire* requested landing instructions at East Havenport for the *Captain's Gig*. The launch was directed to the governor's own pad where Lieutenant Ursy Wade landed her after a spectacularly swift forty-five degree approach that flattened dramatically at the last possible second to allow the gig to contact the pad without so much as a jar.

Ursy ran out the gig's boarding stairs before the dignitaries could approach the ship. A grimy worker standing on the edge of the pad behind the baffles said, "Welcome to Haven, babe."

"Thank you," Ursy said.

"After you get through messin' 'round with the H.M.F.I.C., I'll be glad to show you the sights."

"I appreciate that," Ursy said, holding back a smile.

"What did he say?" Julie Roberts asked from behind Ursy.

"He tried to hit on me," Ursy said.

"I am aware of that," Julie said icily. "What were those initials? H.M.F.—"

"Don't ask, ma'am," Ursy said.

"I just did."

"Ask him," Ursy said, pointing to the governor as the dignitaries reached the pad. "I'll give you a hint. H.M.F.I.C. Head mother in charge. Supply the middle initial from your knowledge of old English ma'am."

"I see," Julie said, even more icily. "Thank you, Lieutenant."

Julie stepped forward, stood in the hatch at stiff attention, saluted, said, "Captain Julie Roberts, X&A Expo ship *Rimfire*, sir. I thank you for the hospitality of your world."

Ursy took advantage of the movement to slip away, descending to the pad via a cargo chute and walking away with the bulk of the ship hiding her from the crowd. Captain Roberts descended and stood in the chill wind while the H.M.F.I.C. of East Haven took turns with his West Haven counterpart in praising X&A, Captain Julie Roberts, the *Rimfire,* and the United Planets in general. Each of them managed to get in lengthy commercials for Haven which, Julie heard with some skepticism, was a garden planet waiting to be cultivated, lacking only a few billion credits from X&A's terraforming fund.

Julie politely turned down an offer of a guided tour of the scenic deserts from both H.M.F.I.C.s, stating that *Rimfire* was at Haven on Service business, and that her stay would be quite brief.

"I'm sure," said his Honor, the governor of East Haven, "that you'll want to give your crew liberty. You'll find the accommodations in East Haven City to be quite—"

"Gentlemen," Julie interrupted, "I wish I could. My crew deserves it." She mentally crossed her fingers for she had a *good* crew who deserved *more* than East Haven City. "However, there is a possibility that *Rimfire* will be passing Haven on her return trip and if time allows I will most certainly consider your kind invitation."

His Honor tried to smile, but the thought of losing the opportunity to have several hundred members of *Rimfire*'s crew turned loose with good U.P. credits in his town turned the attempt into a rather sickly smirk.

Ursy Wade entered East Haven Control, saluted the guard on duty, requested to see the officer in charge, stated her business, and very quickly had a copy of the port's log showing that the *Mother Lode*, Erin Kenner's ship, had paid two visits to Haven, one that had been terminated quickly after a brief stay only weeks previously. East Havenport wasn't the busiest place in the U.P. sector by any means. Two full years of recorded comings and goings were recorded on one Compuleaf so that when Ursy fed the data into the ship's Unicloud it took only three or four "page turnings" to check every ship that had been in Haven's sector in that length of time.

Julie Roberts joined Ursy in the computer room and nodded as Ursy pointed out the two visits of Erin's Mule to Haven.

"You'll note, Cap'n, that she did not file a flight plan in either instance," Ursy said.

"Not all that unusual," Julie said. It was prudent for a ship's captain to file a complete plan of his intended blink routes with the control tower at his point of departure, but since it was, after all, a free galaxy, such practical wisdom could not be mandated by law.

"She wasn't the only one who didn't file a flight plan," Ursy said. "This private yacht that left right behind her the last time didn't register her destination, either."

Julie took note of the name of the yacht, *Murdoch's Plough*.

"It seems, ma'am, that she would have waited," Ursy ventured.

"Yes, it does."

"Unless she expected us to make for the blink beacon from which she sent the message," Ursy said.

"That's way to hell and gone toward the core," Julie said.

"A few blinks."

"Start making them, Lieutenant," Julie said. "And her reasons for this had better be good. If she's jacking us around on a wild goose chase, I'll boot her ass right up between her shoulder blades."

Ursy smiled to herself. It was seldom that Captain Roberts resorted to spacehand vulgarity. That she had done so indicated that she was more than a little bit: 1. Angry. 2. Concerned. 3. Tired. Maybe just a little bit of all three, Ursy thought, as she went to the control bridge and gave orders to the navigation team.

CHAPTER FOURTEEN

The history of man was in the process of being rewritten. New and often humbling discoveries were being made on the planet where the race had originated. Some called Old Earth Man's Graveyard, for billions of the Old Ones had perished there in a cataclysm of nuclear fire.

With the Old Ones had died their cities and a way of life—one hesitated to call it a civilization or a culture in view of its end—that had covered a world which had once had more habitable land area than any planet in the U.P. sector.

There were acrimonious debates among scientists and historians about the length of time that had passed following the holocaust before an Old Earth Healer named Rack used the substance and life of a Power Giver to travel to Earth's moon in search of clean, breathable air. There were those who said the mutations that produced the New Ones in their several varieties, Healer, Power Giver, Far Seer, and Keeper, would have required millions of years. In opposition to this view were those who practiced the prevalent religion of the United Planets sector, a creed based on the one piece of Old Earth literature that had survived the Exodus.

The mutants, said these later scholars, had developed as a result of divine intervention within no more than four generations. As proof they cited Old Earth's poisoned ecosphere. Only mutants could have survived the radiation that enveloped the Earth following the war; so God, they said, preserved that which He had created in His own image by making rapid changes in the race.

By the time that Rack the Healer made his epic bio-powered voyage from Earth to the Moon, Earth's atmosphere had become so toxic and, with the death of the microorganisms in the seas, so depleted of oxygen, that not even the mutated New Ones could have survived had they not been removed to more suitable planets after an X&A ship found Rack the Healer dying on the Moon, holding his love in his scaly arms.

The Post-Holocaust history of Old Earth resided in the fleshy data banks of the idiot savant Keepers, accessible only to the Far Seer who had cared for his Keeper since her birth. The Pre-Holocaust record of mankind was a poisoned layer of crust on a devastated planet with the evidence consisting of scraps of stone, metal, and the artifacts of an advanced technological culture. The history of Modern Man, man of the United Planets, began on Terra II, called New Earth.

There were men and women who specialized in each area of man's history, and a few who tried to assimilate the three separate branches into a logical whole. The most favored overall view was that man had evolved very slowly on Old Earth, sharing ancestors with a variety of other life-forms known to U.P. science from the scanty fossil records that had been accumulated since the reunion of the two racial branches.

U.P. man, in his copious numbers, traced his ancestry to a very few men and women, perhaps less than a hundred, who survived a decades-long space voyage in a primitive sub-light, rocket-propelled spaceship to make a disastrous crash landing on New Earth.

The colonists, most historians agreed, escaped Old Earth just before the final fury of war left billions dead. There was also agreement that the Exodus had been poorly planned, for, apparently, the accumulated wisdom of mankind had been contained in the bowels of a computer aboard the spaceship, to be lost completely when the crash destroyed all means of providing electrical power. There had been only one book aboard, an ornate presentation copy of The King James Bible, the Old and New Testaments.

Fortunately for the future of the race, scientists aboard

the ship were able to use the ship's laboratory to produce test-tube specimens of the domestic animals upon which mankind depended so heavily, for man was to find that while Old Earth had been a teeming stew of life, with life-forms filling all available niches in the ecosphere, animal life on even the most fertile of planets other than Old Earth was severely limited.

The Tigian planets had their grass eaters and one carnivore, the Tigian tiger. Other than the Tigian varieties of life, man had encountered a few reptiles and some birds. Thus, from the beginning of U.P. history, it had been up to man, himself, to seed his newly discovered planets with life.

On New Earth and—when the race struggled back into space on the spoils of yet another fruitful planet—throughout the inhabited worlds, one found food animals, cattle, and domestic fowl. Man the practical had provided the frozen seeds of milk cows and herd bulls which produced beef animals, for egg laying chickens and for ducks to be roasted. He had brought with him from Old Earth hundreds of varieties of plant seeds, fruits, vegetables, trees for lumber, shade, and shelter, crops of the fields, and the rose and other flowering things whose only purpose was to add beauty. Space-going man could have his wheaten cereal with milk and sugar, could sear a steak over charcoal briquettes made from an Old Earth oak, could start his day with a ham and egg breakfast. Man had his bread and his beer, and he marveled at how little things had changed during the thousands of years since the Few had left Old Earth on a roaring column of fire. For scientists wearing hot suits and breathing bottled air dug from the ruins of a vast museum on Old Earth ancient clay tablets that spoke of bread and beer; and on a scorched desert where once a mighty river had run they found, near one of Old Earth's greatest enigmas—a series of vast pyramids constructed of huge stones—drawings preserved in underground rooms that showed oddly dressed men hunting ducks with hand weapons, men harvesting grain, men herding long-horned cattle.

Yes, practical man had sent the colony ship into space with her storage bins filled with the fruits of the Earth and

the frozen seed of Earth's useful animals. But then man
had always been efficient and ingenious. That he was not
a creature of cold logic only, however, was illustrated by
the fact that from New Earth there spread throughout the
growing U.P. sector dozens of breeds of dogs and cats,
for man had ceased being practical when faced with living
without his pets. He had brought with him poodles and
St. Bernards, greyhounds and terriers, sheep dogs and
hounds, working breeds and miniature breeds in all their
amusing varieties; and a few misguided masochists had
insisted on bringing along Persian and Maltese and Sia-
mese and Abyssinian and tabby and calico and plain old
alley—cats.

When self-styled philosophers and those who were
called social scientists—social theorists would have been
more accurate—dwelt on man's character, his ability to
destroy himself and Old Earth with nuclear war was balanced by his love affair with his dog.

A race that could form so perfect a symbiosis with what
most said was a lesser species—although an argument
could be joined there—could not be all bad. A race of
people who could weep bitter tears over one dead dog
lying in the dust while accepting the destruction of entire
planets in the Zede war was rather puzzling, but then no
one had ever accused man of having understandable mo-
tivations. Man told himself, well, by God, we really *can't*
be all bad when our dogs are so devoted to us.

The dog. He is content to pattern his entire existence
around his human. He has long since sacrificed his native
survival instincts and when he is lost or abandoned he is
helpless, for in giving his total devotion to his human he
has left himself totally dependent. He lives for the sound
of his human's voice, the touch of his human's hand. He
makes his human chuckle with his enthusiasm as he treats
a hundred foot walk to the mailbox with the same excited
anticipation as a hunt in the meadow or a walk on the
beach. He asks little. Food and water, attention and affec-
tion. He will forgive the cruelest of treatment.

And when he is heartbroken, he is one of the most piti-
able things in the universe.

Mr. Mop was heartbroken. He was a little dog, but not

as small, at seven pounds, as some of his breed, the York-shire terrier. He was of the drop-ear variety, or at least mostly of that sort, since neither John Kenner, his original human, nor Erin Kenner, whom he adopted after John Kenner's death, trimmed the abundant hair that weighted his ears and left him able to lift the left one only in mo-ments of great excitement, such as when his human said, "Let's go." He had a sharp muzzle and a fine beard that shaded down into gray from the long, blond hair on top of his head. He was a silverback, the hair on his back lustrous and silver-gray, and the sweeping fall of hair that touched the floor all around, except under his chin, was golden brown. His stub of a tail trailed a long tendril of hair as it pointed proudly upward and blended in with the hair of his body when he was feeling sorry for himself, as he now was all the time, every day, every waking minute.

He had been abandoned. He had been forgotten. He was being ignored. His humans, Erin and Dent, were there, and a Mule wasn't that big inside. There were times when Mop had to scoot away to keep from being stepped on as his humans went about their work. They were there, but they weren't there.

Mop didn't go hungry, although he was a little off his feed. All he had to do for food and water was to push buttons that had been designed for his feet, but he couldn't push a button and make Dent say, "Hey, Mop, what's up?" He couldn't push a button to make Erin stoop down to pick him up and cradle him in the crook of her arm and rub his chest and belly. He couldn't even make them talk to him, couldn't elicit one word from either of them. They just worked and worked and paid absolutely no attention to a lonely little dog.

He had tried everything. Time and again he had ap-proached Erin, put his head on the deck between his front paws, hoisted his rear into the air in his look-at-me-I'm-charming pose, wiggled his tailbone in a frantic circle, and made pleading little noises. Time and again he had used his special little growl that had always paid off in attention from Dent. They didn't even speak to tell him to get out of the way. They just swept him aside with an arm or a foot, and it was breaking his heart.

Any decent, dog-loving human being would have felt a stab of empathy for the little dog as he moped around with his usually ebullient tail tucked between his legs. He was a portrait of dejection, a canine magnet for maudlin sympathy. He was man's best friend betrayed, a subject for poets, a source for fountains of sentimental tears. Mankind, because his relationship with his dogs went back beyond the parameters of recorded time, would have looked at little Mop the Dog and said, "Shame, shame," to his humans, for they looked quite normal as they worked almost around the clock to construct a maze of electronic webs and connectors and generating fields in the cabin that had once housed the mining equipment.

At that time no one, not even Erin Kenner, who, at times, was closer to Mop the Dog than Mop could suspect, would have had any inkling that the fate of man, the race, the swarming billions, rested with one hairy little dog who pouted under the control room chair wondering why his humans were mad at him.

CHAPTER FIFTEEN

Murdoch Plough had not bothered to be stealthy in bringing his yacht into laser range of the *Mother Lode*. Once he had assured himself that the Kenner woman had, indeed, brought him to the source of her gold it didn't matter whether or not she and her friend knew that they were not alone in the belt. Neither of them was going to live long enough to be a problem.

The *Plough* was threading her way among the drifting asteroids in the open, so there was no reason why the *Mother Lode*'s sensors had not spotted her. Plough ordered readiness on the laser canon but held off giving the order to fire. He had a question or two for Erin Kenner. He activated the radio and said, *"Mother Lode,* I have you on visual. Come in."

The background sound of a deep space communicator was not exactly static, was not even noticeably audible. It was more a subconscious awareness of unfathomed distance and blank nothingness. Not even a man like Murdoch Plough was immune to the penetrating loneliness that was embodied in the hissing silence. He said, "Erin Kenner, I want to talk to you."

He knew that unless things had gone totally awry aboard the Mule the computer's monitor systems would alert Kenner and Gale to a radio call.

"Now come on, Miss Kenner," Plough said. "I've got a pair of fleet standard lasers trained on you. I want some answers."

* * *

Mop the dog heard little bells and responded excitedly, running to the room where Erin and Denton were working to tell them, "Hey, someone's coming."

Mop's reaction to the call-incoming alert was conditioned by the fact that John Kenner, while overhauling the *Lode,* had made the radio alert the same as the doorbell in his home. Before John Kenner died, Mop had come to know a few friends such as Denton Gale and the sound of the doorbell meant either that one of his friends was paying a visit, in which case he'd get a cheerful greeting and some pats and rubs, or that there was a stranger at the door against whom John had to be warned. John had programmed the doorbell sound into the computer's alert system so that each time someone hailed the *Lode* by radio Mop would have a little excitement. And, although Mop was an exceptional little dog, handsome, personable, considerate, and highly intelligent, he never got over wondering why, when the doorbell rang aboard ship, no one ever came in.

It really didn't matter, however, that the *Mother Lode* was way to hell and gone out in deep space, the bell had rung and it was Mop's duty to tell his humans that something important was happening.

The problem was that they ignored him. He ran around in circles, barking, his stub of a tail going at flank speed, but Erin and Dent kept their heads down over some piece of equipment that was growing like a cancer in what had been *Mother*'s mining control. He ran up to Erin and pressed his nose against the calf of her leg, a signal he used often to say, "Hey, I'm down here." She didn't even glance down. Frustrated, Mop ran to stand on his hind legs and put his forepaws on Dent's knee. Dent's head remained bent over his work.

She had to look into the female's mind to understand why the dog was exhibiting behavior she had not witnessed before.

"Someone is calling us on the radio," Erin said, not in words but in thought.

She let her senses burst out of the body, through the metal hulls, and there was a thrill of elation. Ever since leaving the planet of men, Haven, she'd been regretting not having brought along a supply of basic biological building blocks. She could only assume that her long imprisonment had diminished her capacity for reason, at least temporarily. Now there were seven of the men at close range, not riches in way of material, but more than triple that which she had available aboard the *Mother Lode*.

She willed. Her will was, of course, obeyed.

"This is the *Mother Lode*," a female voice said.

"Miss Kenner?" Plough asked.

"I am Erin Kenner."

"You know who I am."

"Yes." The voice was without modulation, almost as flat and mechanical as that of a computer. "I know who you are."

"Good," Plough said. "You heard me say I have two laser cannon on you."

"I heard."

"Not that I intend using them, of course," Plough said, with a forced laugh. "It's just that I want to be sure I have your attention. Now listen. I sent a ship out here. I want to know what happened to it."

"It was annihilated in the nearest star," the robotic voice said.

"Holy—" Plough was stunned. "Repeat, please?"

"We set the generator to blink the ship into the corona of the sun," the voice said.

"Gaaaaawd damn," Plough said, then punched the sender. "And the people on her?"

"They were dead before the ship went into the sun."

"Stand ready to fire," Plough said.

She was probing. She could feel the minds of the five men aboard the *Plough*, but once again she was frustrated. Once she could have enforced her slightest whim on such minds from far greater distances. Now she was unable to break past the red haze of anger that she felt emanating from the mind of Murdoch Plough.

That there was danger was evident. She knew something about the weapon the men called a laser, for there had been lasers aboard to be used in mining. A quick probe of the mind of the female who was manning fire control on the *Plough* gave her an image of the *Mother*'s hull with a sizable hole, quite large enough to send all of *Mother*'s air blasting out into the vacuum. That would be quite damaging to the bio-masses she controlled, and quite inconvenient to her, for, since she was incapable of independent movement in space, she would, at best, be left floating. At worst, she would be tossed into the nuclear fire of the sun if she did not leave *Mother* before those who were approaching carried out their intentions.

She caused the female voice to be sent to the man who threatened. "We need to talk, Plough."

"All I want to know is how you managed to kill my brother and four other people," Plough said.

One tendril of her extension crept past the barriers and she saw a mind filled with anger, knew that the man fully intended to lance holes in the hulls of the *Mother Lode*. And then she found the weakness and began to influence the entire entity through his memory of Erin Kenner's ash blonde hair, sea green eyes, and her very feminine body.

"There is gold enough for both of us," Erin Kenner's voice was saying, and there'd been a change in tone. Plough couldn't help but notice. The flatness was gone, replaced by a breathy quality. "We can work together. We would be very good together."

Plough felt himself stir inside. She wasn't talking about mining gold. One part of him was laughing at the clumsy attempt to change his mind about killing Kenner and Gale. But need was growing in him, a desire more powerful, more debilitating, than anything he'd ever experienced. He had to swallow to prevent the suddenly stimulated flow of saliva from overflowing. He sniffed, for the mucus membranes in his nasal passages were becoming engorged, too.

"I will bring my ship alongside," Erin Kenner said.

"Boss, what the hell's going on?" one of Plough's crew asked.

"I'll handle this," Plough said.

"I am ready," said the woman at the weapons control panel.

"Hold your fire," Plough ordered. "Secure lasers."

He *was* the boss. He was obeyed, although the crew members exchanged looks with each other and one of the women whispered, "Who the hell does that broad think she's kidding?" For to those not being affected by the She, the female voice coming over the radio was a burlesque of seduction, a bit out of some comedy routine.

"I must see you, quickly," Erin said. "I am moving ship. My lock is, of course, X&A standard."

"Same here," Plough said. He felt an urgency that caused his teeth to chatter. In his mind was a picture of Erin Kenner nude. He'd never seen her nude, of course, but the vision was as real as the Mule class ship that was fluxing slowly to come alongside the *Plough*.

"Boss, I don't like this," one of the crewmen said, as Erin Kenner's voice made suggestive remarks that would have made a horny teenager laugh.

"Shut up," Plough said. "Let's see what the broad's up to."

Plough punched orders to the air lock control. The two ship swam side by side. The members of the *Plough*'s crew fingered weapons as the distance closed and the clang of contact echoed throughout the ship. Plough checked instruments. Pressure in both ships was equal, X&A standard. There was a hiss of air into the *Plough*'s lock.

"Just stay alert," Plough ordered his crew. He left the bridge and ran to the lock. He saw Erin Kenner standing in the hatch of the *Mother Lode*. Her ash blonde hair brushed her shoulders, her sea green eyes gleamed in invitation. She was wearing Service shorts, tunic, and hose. Wings extended outward from her shoulders.

"Wha—"

The question was never finished. Murdoch Plough's mouth remained open. He froze as he stood, feet apart, arms hanging at his sides, and then slowly sank to the deck. Behind him, on the bridge of the *Plough,* the six members of the crew became vegetables, retaining only enough brain function to power the basic life functions of their bodies.

* * *

The She had no use for the life force of the seven men. She wanted only the basic bio-matter. She was tired of being limited to the mass of the two men of the *Mother Lode*. She directed the female body to carry her on a tour of the converted destroyer. She was unimpressed by the luxury of the living quarters, but was pleased to find that the ship had additional generators to power her weapons system. She would be able to use that power when the time came to undo the disaster that had happened in a time so remote that not even she knew how to date the event.

Satisfied with the new source of working materials, she went back to the gym aboard the *Mother Lode* and picked up the skull that the female man called Old Smiley. Old Smiley was a male. His bulk had been great when he was whole and alive. It would take more than two units of her new bio-material to form him. She concentrated and a glow of light seemed to emanate from the skull. Aside from that, there was nothing. The only force detectable came from her own resources. Hope that had grown failed and in a moment of pique she shattered Old Smiley into dust. The ship's filter system, detecting the source of the air pollution, caused her further irritation by closing off the gym and starting noisy suction to clean the air.

She looked at the fossil skeleton on the deck. Although it was large, there was a delicacy about it. The wing bones, perfectly preserved, formed a graceful curve.

She had been exceedingly beautiful.

The suddenly realized knowledge of how much she had lost brought rage and sent a surge of fever through the human body, causing muscles to jerk spasmodically. She felt her limitations as lances of pain, knew a hate that threatened to damage the delicate brain cells of the human female. She sensed fear and pain, controlled her emotion, took out her frustration by destroying the fossilized reminders of her shame.

The life-support system of the *Mother Lode* felt the electronic equivalent of panic and called in all of the mechanical reserves to combat the huge dust cloud that filled the gym.

The She watched the miasma being absorbed and filtered. She was calm again. She sent her extensions searching outward, sensed, at some distance, a feeble, comatose presence locked away as she, herself, had been bound. Perhaps, soon, she would no longer be alone. In the meantime there was work to be done.

CHAPTER SIXTEEN

"I know, I know," Erin said. "I know. I know."

There was a feeling of misty sadness. Her eyes would not work properly. She was looking at a very limited monochromatic world from the height of her ankles. There was a layer of fuzzy obstruction that obscured even that view.

She lifted her eyes and saw a vaguely humanoid thing of nightmare proportions. There was something familiar about the face. Naked flesh had embarrassing but eerily distorted shapes.

She was aware of fear, of dread. "Ohhh," she moaned in sympathy, but there was no sound.

There was no pain. There was no feeling. The impressions she registered seemed not to come from her own senses. There was a smell. Distinctive smells. Not long ago Denton had walked past the captain's chair in his stocking feet, leaving his own particular scent. From her place she saw herself walk past. Was that actually the way she smelled? Musk and perfume?

"It's all right," she said, not knowing why, but with a soothing tone to her voice, a tone heard by no one, for there was no sound.

Eons or seconds later she seemed to be more aware. "Hey," she said, and this time she knew that she was talking to a frightened little dog cowering under the console. "It's all right, little buddy."

She said the words, but they did not issue forth from her lips. She did not understand how she knew that Mop was hiding, and that he was sad. It wasn't because she was seeing him. She knew that eons or seconds before

she'd been feeling sympathy for Mop. He had been so
frightened. And the hair that fell down in front of his eyes
interfered with his vision. She would, next time she gave
him a bath, trim his bangs. It was bad enough to see the
world in shades of one color without having part of it
dimmed by a curtain of hair in front of one's eyes.

"Mop?" The word was a scream of shock and pain, for
she was looking upward through the fringes of hair, seeing
herself and Denton moving about woodenly. She was
looking out onto a limited world through the eyes of the
dog, knowing his sadness, his fright. He was so lonely.

Madness. One part of her was screaming mindlessly as
she parroted words dictated to her by someone else, knowing on one level that Murdoch Plough was cheating her,
paying her much less than her load of gold ore was worth,
but unable to break the bonds that held her so tightly, her
every action controlled, only the deep, deep down part of
her mind free to voice protest and shock.

Everything was blended into one jigsaw mosaic. There
were moment of clarity, but most of the time she was
floating mindlessly in a sea of confused images and
thoughts and feelings.

She was bending over a work table constructing a circuit
board of impossible intricacy, working with a glue gun,
the tip of which had been attenuated to incredible small-
ness. The opening was too minute to allow passage of the
material, but the glue itself had been altered into smaller
molecules.

She had no sense of time or continuity. Mixed in with
the work that she did not comprehend were seven dead
people, including Murdoch Plough. She was so alone, no
contact, no Denton, only memories of their closeness that
had come—astonishing storms of regret—too late, too late.
And poor Mop, as alone as she, able to see his humans
but not being given a word, a touch.

Like her, Mop was unable to understand what had happened, and his drooping tail seemed more lamentable to
her than her own feeling of hazy unreality until she saw
with her own eyes but with another's vision the brain dead
bodies of Murdoch Plough and his crew and then was

looking into the empty eye sockets of Old Smiley only to face a storm of fire that threatened to consume her.

The helpless rage that she felt, she who controlled where Erin's eyes looked, what Erin's hands did, burned away some of the mist from Erin's mind. She had been dead. She remembered the instant of terrible pain. She remembered how it had felt—dull, incomplete, somnolent—to be a prisoner inside the tiny skull of Mop the dog.

"Denton?"

She saw the skeleton burst into dust motes, just as she and Denton had shattered into oblivion. The violence of it cleared her mind for a moment.

"Who are you?"

She was heard. Just as the thing that was in command of her eyes saw Mop's pathetic little efforts to gain the attention of his Erin, so did *it* hear her question. And just as Mop was ignored, she was ignored.

"Damn you, who are you?" She was beneath notice, nothing more than a tool.

"I am not something to be used and discarded," she screamed with righteous anger. She had the attention of the thing. She felt a slight twisting of her mind that was something more than pain.

Once again she was looking at the world from Mop's eyes. After the shock of adjustment she felt good, for she knew that she had annoyed it, whatever it was. She was banished. She was coiled in a very small place. Her nose— no, Mop's nose—brought to her the scent of a molecular bonding machine at work. She, or her body, was working side by side with Denton.

She was getting used to seeing a one color world with a myopic lack of clarity. The mining equipment had been removed. The room that had housed the controls and Denton's quarters was almost filled with an electronic constructions of amazing complexity.

"Mop," she whispered, the word existing only in awareness, "let's go have a look."

Mop stayed as he was, curled into a ball, his nose tucked into the hair on his hind leg. She could feel his melancholy, but he could not be made aware that she—or some part of her—was closer than he knew. She called out. She talked to him softly. She sent waves of love toward him in an effort to get his attention, to make contact, but he merely lifted his head, looking up at the two humans bent over the workbench, and sighed.

When she was allowed into her body, she had a sense that she was being told, "There, now behave yourself."

"You and the horse you rode in on," she said, but the words didn't reach her lips.

Erin knew, somehow, that the work was finished. There was no direct communication from the thing that held her prisoner in her own body, but she knew that the creature had accomplished whatever needed to be done.

The order was to activate *Mother*'s sensors. The instruments were set to search for heavy metal. Erin readjusted for the mineral content of fossilized bone. *Mother* was still attached, lock to lock, to Murdoch Plough's yacht. That made maneuvering a bit more difficult as Erin, under orders, searched the belt with all sensors on high, moving the two ships forward along the vector of the orbiting belt until, days later, there was a signal indicating a mass of fossilized material of a bulk surpassing the skeleton that Erin and Dent had found.

To land *Mother* required disengaging from the *Plough*. The yacht was parked a few hundred yards away from the asteroid onto which *Mother* settled.

"We have no mining equipment," Erin said.

But they had hand weapons, saffers.

Once again Erin was in a flexsuit alone in the big empty, but her mind was not her own to be used in philosophical musings. She did not give way to the usual awe, but moved purposefully toward the spot indicated by *Mother*'s sensors. She directed the saffer toward the rock and began to blast it away. It didn't matter if the embedded fossils were damaged. It was only necessary to remove the burden of rock from them.

Gradually she exposed the gray stone that had once been living bone. And there was something else. She reached down a gloved hand and shook it loose from the shattered small bones of a hand. It was the only item she'd seen in the belt that indicated the work of intelligence. It was a beautifully cut yellow diamond of perhaps ten carats. She tucked it away in a pocket on the outside of her flexsuit and realized with a thrill that she had taken an independent action, had made movements that were not dictated by the thing that controlled her. She turned to face the ship, lifted the saffer. Yes, she could use the weapon, if she chose, against the ship. It was only a hand weapon, and it would have taken quite some time for the beam to cut through *Mother*'s hull, and all she would have accomplished was death for herself and for Mop and Denton.

As if to make up for the lapse, she was dominated so thoroughly that thought became a haze and she worked mechanically to free the skeleton from the rock and to move it as she and Dent had moved the first one, the bones still attached to a thin slab of rock, into *Mother*'s air lock.

The She blasted away the remaining matrix rock, causing the filtering system to panic again and leaving the broken skeleton lying in disarray on the deck of the gym. Her attention was diverted from the intelligence that she dominated. Erin saw the disjointed bones move as if of their own accord.

The She gathered herself, prepared for what would surely be a strike when he was first released from the prison of eternity. It came, and because he was confused and weak it was easily countered, and then she was holding him close and whispering to him. He ceased his struggles and listened. A soundless laugh was an expression of sheer delight from him. The She joined in, for she was no longer alone.

An observer of the actions of her own body, Erin was on Murdoch Plough's yacht. The thing's method of reassembly of the available materials was not as messy as it had been in the first instance, when she'd felt the presence of Erin and Denton and lashed out. First the five breathing bodies were placed in a heap. This task was accomplished by Erin and Denton. In the process of moving the bodies all of their clothing was removed. Erin cringed at being forced to inflict the indignity on the victims, even if they were nothing more than breathing corpses.

Denton had taken on a new role, for the other creature was there. The She no longer occupied both human bodies. Together the aliens melted the bio-mass into a red-tinged, pulsating glob held together by their joint force.

Once again, with the original creature's attention focused elsewhere, Erin was a careful observer as the mass was separated. One bulk was larger. Slowly the two masses began to take form.

He stood a full seven feet high. His form was that of an idealized man except for the wings, huge, graceful wings that folded neatly against his back. She was grace in motion, beauty incarnate. She was tall, slim, shapely. Her skin had the color and smoothness of old silk. Her wings, smaller than his, formed lovely lines along her shoulders and back. Her golden hair gleamed with a light of its own. Her eyes were the blue of a desert sky.

Erin was alone. For the first time in an eternity she could feel, see, hear, smell with her own organs. There was constraint, for when she decided instantly to take advantage of their preoccupation and backed toward the air locks connecting the two ships with the idea of getting her saffer from the flexsuit, she ran into an unseen barrier and could not move further.

"You are useful but not indispensable," the alien said inside Erin's head.

"You noticed me," Erin said. An image flashed into her mind—the way Mop touched his nose so softly, so gently to the back of her leg to say, "Hey, Erin, I'm down here." She felt shame and anger. She was not some lesser being. She would never again be guilty of trying to attract the alien's attention just to say, "Look, you bitch, I'm here." If she ever again tried to attract her captor's attention it would be to deliver a message of much more import and effectiveness.

Without forming words the creature gave orders. Erin and Denton left the *Plough*, went aboard *Mother*. Mop stuck his head out from under Erin's bed when she went to her cabin. With tears in her eyes, Erin knelt and said, "Come on, little buddy."

Mop leaped into her arms with a yelp of pure joy. He forgot his usual politeness, surged upward to lick her face.

He squirmed in bliss as she tucked him in the crook of her arm and rubbed his chest and belly.

Dent was standing over them. Mop wriggled free of Erin's grasp and leapt up onto Dent's leg and received a greeting from his second most favorite human.

"And I was feeling sorry for him," Erin said. "Here we are facing God knows what and instead of trying to think of something to do about it we're both petting a hairy little dog."

"Erin," Denton said, and the sound of a human voice after months of silence was sweet, "what in hell is going on? Who and what are those things?"

Erin rose. Mop leapt onto the bed and stood on his rear legs. After months of being ignored he hadn't had enough loving.

"They're old," Erin said. It was difficult to form thoughts about her. Erin had observed her in action, had seen her power, her easily aroused rage. "She's able to manipulate matter. I don't know how potent her ability to destroy is—"

"I felt it and saw it in action," Dent said. "She's one mean mother, and I'd guess that he's as bad."

Erin was forming a thought that frightened her. She tried to keep it from being born, lest the alien hear, or feel, or sense, or do whatever it was that she did to get inside Erin's head and take over. She said, "Look at this room. Isn't it a mess? Give me a hand to clean it up."

"This is no time—"

She put her finger to her lips to indicate silence, tapped her temple with one finger. "The whole ship needs a cleaning," she said. "Give me a hand with this spread."

Denton moved to the other side of the bed and helped her smooth the sheets and pull up the spread. She continued to chatter on inanely, but she made motions with her hands, motions that he understood. He nodded and looked toward the door.

"I'm going out onto the bridge," Erin said. "There's some picking up to do."

Denton held his breath. He stood in the door to Erin's quarters, Mop in his arms. Erin picked up papers and put them into the disposer, moving ever closer to the control panel. With one glance over her shoulder she jabbed her fingers toward the air lock controls to close the lock and separate *Mother* from *Murdoch's Plough*. Just before the tip of her finger touched the button she felt the fires of a sun burst inside of her. She screamed once before the agony overcame her and left her to sink limply to the deck.

CHAPTER SEVENTEEN

The electro-gravitational field aboard the *Mother Lode* was so powerful that Erin's ash blonde hair formed a huge, fair-colored, three-dimensional halo around her head as she bent over the controls in the room where the beings had built the electronic thing that, for lack of a name supplied by them, Erin had come to think of as the Amplifier.

They, in all of their grace and beauty, stood motionless, hand in hand, their lovely faces blank of all expression, their entire force directed into the fields of power bursting outward from the two ships that were locked side to side. The military strength blink generators of both vessels contributed their eerie powers to the Amplifier.

Erin's semiautonomy made it possible for her to try to analyze what was happening. The vastly complicated electronic construction that had been assembled by her hands, and by Dent's hands, produced no force of its own. However, the fields of power, will, force—choose a word—that came from the aliens, combined with the power of the blink generators, caused things to happen in the belt.

The distances involved were measured in astronomical units. One astronomical unit equaled the average radius of the orbit of New Earth around the sun. Two astronomical units away from the *Mother Lode,* on the other side of the sun far removed from New Earth, the asteroids in the belt became agitated. Some slowed. Others increased their speed. Orbital stability was no more. Masses of rocks smashed together and rebounded only to be drawn into a chaos of new collisions.

Erin could only guess at the intensity of the immense

surges of power flowing outward from the Amplifier, but the effect was awesome. Asteroids were accelerated to a significant fraction of the speed of light to crunch into the growing mass with cosmic force. The darkness of space was brightened by the flares of impact.

In an incredibly short time the entire belt was in frantic motion, asteroids flashing past the position of the two ships to their rendezvous with the accumulating mass that was beginning to take on a roughly globular shape even with perhaps no more than ten percent of the debris in the belt congregated.

It was tiring work. Sweat poured down into Erin's eyes. Mop, seated on the control console, was uneasy, for the powerful field made him look quite odd, with all of his blond-brown, silky hair standing up straight. Even the beings tired, and the strain on the two blink generators drained them quickly so that recharging was necessary.

"My God, they are beautiful," Denton said, as he lifted his head to gaze at them. They were still side by side, hand in hand, larger than life. Their magnificent, graceful wings were partly open to show the gossamer film that connected the sweeping curves of the bones.

A smile came to Erin's face, for they were wonderful. Her eyes stung with tears engendered by sheer beauty, but then her reason returned and she wiped away the telltale moisture while making a genuine effort to rekindle the hate she felt for the thing that held her prisoner in her own body.

Ah, but it was difficult to hate, for the being's face glowed with her loveliness, and her stance was so proud, so proud. Erin jerked her eyes away. The strong field of power was fading. Her scalp tingled as her hair fell into place.

She turned to Denton. "So now we know," she said.

He nodded, knowing that she was talking about the purpose of the Amplifier. On the opposite side of the orbital ring a moon-sized body swam in the darkness.

"Poses some questions, doesn't it?" Denton asked.

She nodded, glanced toward them. "I think we can go now."

She rose, picked up the Mop, who flung himself into

position in the crook of her arm to have his chest rubbed. She nodded to them. They took no notice. Dent followed her out of the room. No overt permission had been given. They were above the ordinary little matter of day to day existence for the humans, but *they* had recognized the necessity for mere men to eat, rest, and perform bodily functions, all of which Dent and Erin did in the next hour. Erin had a shower and let the fragrant, dry wind evaporate the moisture from her skin.

Dent was already in bed when she came out. His eyes were closed. She knew how he felt, for her limbs were leaden. They had not been overly generous in allowing sleep time. She eased into bed so as not to wake him. He sighed in his sleep, turned, put one arm around her. It was the first time since he had opened the door to the gym only to vaporize into a red mist that he had touched her. Reminded of what she had found with Dent, and then had lost, she wept quietly.

She awoke with a sense of pleasure that became, as she swam up from deepest sleep, Dent's caress. She moaned in protest, but, after all, was she so tired? Her body said no as his lips found hers demandingly. She moaned again, but in a different tone. His hands were exploring her.

"Ouch," she said, wincing away from him.

"You thought he was beautiful," Dent said.

"What?" The alien was the last thing she wanted to think about at that moment. Once before she had thought that she was in love—with Jack Burnish aboard *Rimfire*—but after that first night in Denton Gale's arm she had realized that she had never known the meaning of love until she was alone with Dent near the core of the galaxy.

"His magnificent body," Dent said. "You liked it."

"Hey, Dent—"

"No need to be coy. Tell me what you would like for him to do to you."

"Get out of here," she said, pushing on his shoulders.

His hands became cruel clamps bearing down on her shoulders.

"You're hurting me, Dent."

"Then do as I tell you."

"I don't understand," she said, trying to push him away.

"You wanted him."

"Dent?" She lifted her head, looked into his eyes, felt her blood surge in fear, for in Dent's face was the slackness that she had come to associate with control by one of them. She knew, then, that the alien was there, that he'd pushed Dent back into the prison recess somewhere, that Dent was helpless, perhaps looking on to see him with his hand touching Erin's soft breast.

"Yes, I am Dent. But you wanted him. Tell me."

She started a prayer in her secret mind and felt a sheet of pain as he punished her. His hand twisted and she screamed in sudden agony.

"Tell me," he said.

"Yes, it is true," she whispered, for, although he had done no visible damage, the twist of his iron fingers had sent a lance of pain throughout her entire body. "I wanted him. I thought he was beautiful."

He became gentle, but when she fell silent he hurt her in a very intimate area, a hurt that caused her to shudder and jerk in anguish until he stopped long enough for her to continue. She struggled for words to speak of his beauty. She became incoherent, for he was using her and although it was Denton's familiar, beloved body, she knew revulsion, felt that ultimate insult that only a woman can know when she is taken against her will.

She found that she could keep him from administering pain by saying, "Yes, yes, yes," by moaning as if she were in ecstasy, by doing something she had never done before, pretending to enjoy being used.

When she thought it was over, it had just begun.

"He found that to be quite unsatisfactory," he said. "We must try again."

And this time she felt him entering into her mind as well as her body, so that he saw her revulsion and punished her. He knew how to find the most sensitive spots on her body, and he used the strength of Denton Gale's hands and fingers, combined with shocking force, heat, and lances of pure pain that originated in his own mind. And that mind became open to her, for the pain he gave her stimulated him and urged him on to strenuous moves. It seemed to excite him to force her to look into his mind and be driven to the brink of insanity by the cesspool of cruelty she saw there, evil so bottomless, so infinite that she could absorb only a fraction of his affliction before loathing and terror caused her mind to go blank to all but the hurt he was giving her.

Surely, she thought, I will die.

But she did not.

She lay on the bed beside the exhausted body of Denton with her limbs trembling, her breath coming in short, frantic gasps. She was afraid to move, afraid that he would return, or that movement would bring back the excruciating agony that he had inflicted. She closed her eyes and lay very, very still.

"Erin?"

She tensed, jerked away from Dent's hand.

"Erin, it's me."

She opened her eyes. Dent was weeping.

"Don't," she said.

"He made sure that I was aware."

"Damn him."

"Oh, God—" He clasped her to him and his strong, young body shuddered with his sobs.

"Don't, Dent. Please don't."

"I couldn't do a thing. Nothing. I could only watch, and hear you begging him to—"

"Do you still think they're beautiful?"

It worked. His sobs halted. He sniffed. "The thing is, I don't know what to do."

"I don't either," she said. "We can't fight them. They're too powerful."

"And they are weakened by having lost their own world."

"Did you understand that from him?"

"Yes."

"And what they're doing is recreating their world?"

"Yes."

"Will they do it in seven days?" she asked, then clutched at Denton's hand. "Believe me, I'm not trying to be sacrilegious, not now."

"I know. But this wasn't heaven that was destroyed, Erin."

"If it was, then the preachers have been telling us lies all of our lives," she agreed, shuddering as she remembered the enjoyment that he got from her pain and from her screams for mercy.

"If they're angels—"

"No," she said. "They're not. They may look like the angels that the craftsmen make on Delos, and like some of the illustrations from that old Bible, but there is nothing divine about them."

"Do you remember my telling you about my dream, where the world was about to be destroyed and the people were flying around trying to think of a way to escape the cataclysm?"

"Yes. The people in your dream were like them?"

"Yes and no. Alike in form, but not in malevolence." He cradled her in his arms, kissed her cheek. "There was something I didn't tell you about that dream, because, quite frankly, it scared the hell out of me. It seemed so real. After I saw the people with wings flying around in panic and it was all over, I woke up and *then* I heard a voice say, 'Leave them to their rest and go from here.' "

"Now you tell me," she said.

"I should have told you," he said. "But would it have made any difference?"

She snuggled close, fighting the revulsion she felt, for it was Dent's arms around her, not his.

"No," she said. "I had gold fever. I would have laughed at you."

They were both silent for a long time.

"Dent?"

"Ummm."

"You know that they'll never let us go."

"I've been trying not to think about that."

"They'll use us to make a body for another one of them. They killed Plough and his crew without the slightest hesitation. They need us, at the moment, to do the work aboard ship. When they don't need us anymore, they'll take the life out of us and toss it away just as they did with those on the Plough ship."

He squeezed her, kissed her. She did not answer his kiss, for her mind was elsewhere.

"Now and then," she said, "when she's concentrating on something else, she relaxes her control over me. If the time ever comes when I can take advantage of it, be ready."

He did not speak. He held her close, so close that it was difficult for her to breathe and she sensed that he was terribly afraid not of the danger of becoming nothing, but of losing her. She'd never known such sweetness. What she felt for Dent and what he felt for her in return was worth fighting for.

"All right, you gormless mother," she said to herself, directing all of her hate toward the alien female. "All right." And even though her reason told her the situation was hopeless, that she and Dent were helpless in the power of the two winged things, she was, after all, human, a product of a race that could find hope while standing on the brink of the grave.

CHAPTER EIGHTEEN

The stats from X&A Headquarters on Xanthos caught up with *Rimfire* as she was leaving Haven. The inquiries were politely worded, or at least as courteously stated as could be expected when the admirals on Xanthos became aware that the prime exploratory ship on X&A service had been diverted from her priority mission of opening up a new section of the galaxy.

Messages left *Rimfire* traveling on two paths, one back to Xanthos and one along the blink route given to Captain Julie Roberts by Erin Kenner's blinkstat, the one that had invoked the magic letters, F.R.A.N.K. The messages to Xanthos were answered. The stats sent toward the swarming splendor of the core worlds were not.

Julie Roberts knew that she was risking a lot on her personal assessment of Erin Kenner. She wasn't exactly betting her command and her career that Erin would not have evoked the ultimate dread of space-going mankind, xenophobia, without good cause; but if it turned out that she had taken *Rimfire* on a spook chase her status as the fair-haired, A-number-one, up-and-coming, sure-admiral-to-be would be eroded, perhaps enough to allow a couple of her male competitors to jump over her on the promotion list. You were allowed a few goofs as a junior officer, but when you reached the rank of captain you were playing a sudden death game. One serious mistake and you found yourself benched, navigating a desk back on Xanthos.

The series of coded stats to Xanthos did not fully explain Julie's reasons for *Rimfire*'s diversion toward the Dead Worlds and the radiation storms of the core. While the big ship was charging her generator in the Dead Worlds sac, drawing power from the stars that looked down unfeelingly on those devastated planets that were still capable of giving even the bravest human nightmares, Julie had her communications officer send one last stat to headquarters.

"On the authority of the captain," the stat read, "U.P.S. *Rimfire* will depart established blink routes at beacon D.W. 476 to pursue the basic purpose of the Service."

The captain of an exploration ship had the authority to make decisions in the field, for there were times when he would be at distances so great that even blinkstat contact with higher officials was inadequate, times when, indeed, he would be cut off completely, with no blink routes behind him to carry communications. That was not the case with *Rimfire*, at least not at the moment, but the authority of the ship's captain was still paramount, even when the leeway of a ship's captain to make independent decisions was being stretched to the breaking point, as Julie was doing.

Not even in code would Julie state that she was chasing aliens, but the admirals on Xanthos could take two meanings from her message. They could read it with a slight chill, assuming *Rimfire* had some reason to suspect the presence of heretofore unknown intelligent life, or they could guess that somehow *Rimfire* had knowledge of a life zone planet in the dense star fields toward the core.

The twofold basic purpose of the Service was embodied in its name, The United Planets Department of Exploration and Alien Search. The two functions were usually considered as one, although, for the most part, when laying new blink routes into formerly unexplored areas, a ship's primary interest was in looking for new planets suitable for habitation by man. However, when an X&A ship ventured into the unknown she went armed. Even though the idea was not always in the forefront, there was always the possibility that the race that had pulverized the surface of a score of planets and killed some of them from the inside out, leaving once molten cores cold, would be encountered in their own haunts, or that the planet killers would come sweeping in from vast, intergalactic distances with weapons flaring.

While it was true that in the thousands of years that man had been in space, traversing distances measured in light-years and parsecs, he had not encountered intelligence, he had found traumatic evidence that intelligence had existed.

As *Rimfire* drifted in space, charging, she looked out—with her advanced instruments, on twenty worlds that had once flowered, had, according to the meager evidence that survived, harbored intelligent life. And the expedition to the colliding galaxies in Cygnus had brought back, salvaged from a radiation-scarred, heat-battered but still functioning beacon in space, a manuscript that told of the death of two advanced races.

From the earliest known writings of man, the Bible, that one piece of man's early history that had survived the Exodus from Old Earth, to the musings of modern philosophers and teachers, it was agreed that there was evil in the world, system, galaxy, universe, and that there was good.

Interestingly enough, the only living, overt evil known to man was the evil that men do. Although man had not committed mass murder since that most horrendous example of all, destruction of worlds during the Zede War, individual men still killed, and raped, and maimed, and coveted the property of others. Man was accustomed to that evil, and was in the process, it was hoped, of erasing the dark side of the human psyche.

The galaxy itself, most thinking men felt, was neither good nor evil, but was simply intolerant of the weak flesh and blood of man except on those rare, miraculous havens called life zone planets, and neutral to his presence. When a man died in space because his ship blended with an object during the state of semi-nonexistence of a blink, or when a miner miscalculated and was trapped outside to die of oxygen deprivation in his flexsuit, the galaxy paid no heed. There was personal loss to the dead and to the survivors when a man died by accident in space, but there was no real evil involved.

Of course, there was the age-old evil of which the Bible spoke. Everyone read the Bible at one time or another, for it was classically beautiful, the premier example of the one language that had reached space from Old Earth, but, although God lived—it was just too inane to think that the universe, and life in all of its complexity, was a cosmic accident—Satan had fallen out of favor. Hell had lost its fury, its pale fires dimmed into nothing more than a feeble reflection of the nuclear fire of a sun. Man knew the hell of war, and of tyrannical distances, and the weight of threat offered by nighttime skies with glimmers of light coming all the way from eternity. Compared to the deadly gravitational pull of a black hole the old boogeyman's power was puny.

True evil was that miasma of almost superstitious dread that was associated with the Dead Worlds. Evil embodied was represented in the abstract by those, whoever they had been, who had destroyed worlds so completely that not one single artifact had survived or could be reassembled from the tiny fragments of fabricated things, alloys that did not occur in nature, everlasting plastics, all that remained of what had been, obviously, a highly technological culture.

Evil was the stranger. Evil was alien.

In Julie Roberts' time, scholars were just beginning to understand, based on the archaeological digs on Old Earth, that man had brought with him into space the one evil that had, more than any other single cause, made the home planet a perpetual war zone. Fear of the stranger had been, it seemed, a primordial defect in man. The murderer, Cain, had departed from the Garden of Eden to take a wife from an unknown people who, it was inferred, were evil. Fear of the stranger had grown into tribalism, and then nationalism, and then nuclear ruin.

Once and only once in post Exodus times had that age-old defect in man surfaced and grown strong enough to cause man to revert to the barbarism of war. The belligerent nationalism of the Zede subsystem and the personal ambition of a charismatic leader had led to the destruction of worlds. In the long run, the loss of planets possessed of sweet water and clean air was the tragedy of war that was remembered. It was impossible for the mind to conceive of the instant death of hundreds of millions of people. But a life zone planet was the galaxy's most precious commodity.

Considering man's history, his own talent for destruction, his knowledge that at times the universe shivered and blood flowed because of man's nature, he was quite ready to accept, even embrace, an unseen, frightening, almost omnipotent enemy—the alien. The Planet Killers.

There were thinkers who said, but usually in still, small voices, that the Planet Killers had done more to advance science and technology than any other single factor, for even the most humane of local politicians knew the best way to unify a community was to present it with a challenge from the outside world. Therefore, the best way to unify a people, and to cause them to make sacrifices and the most prodigious efforts, was to supply them with a common enemy.

The several hundred worlds of the United Planets sector had their boogeyman. The Planet Killers.

Thus, when the captain of the *Rimfire* departed station and blinked parsecs away from the zone she was supposed to be charting, she got away with it because the admirals on Xanthos were as aware of the common but unseen enemy as anyone. They couldn't believe that the Planet Killers were there, just next door in a manner of speaking to the Dead Worlds, but Captain Roberts' cryptic message had hinted that she had knowledge that she did not want to transmit even by coded stat. For the time being, the admirals would assume that Roberts had good reason for altering her orders. The chilling coincidence that Captain Roberts was taking *Rimfire* into the sac of the Dead Worlds wrinkled many a brow back on Xanthos and caused the Chief of Staff to put the fleet on medium grade alert.

As *Rimfire* blinked past the sac and to the end of the established blink routes, she was X&A in action. She went armed. Her crew was alert, and ready, and, perhaps, just a little bit nervous, for Julie Roberts told them while the ship lay charging in the sac:

"Tomorrow we will leave the blink routes and venture once again into the unknown. I have heard your questions as to why we are here in this part of the galaxy. I have been made familiar with a few of your speculations. Most of them are wrong.

"We are not here to make a new study of the Dead Worlds. This must be obvious to you since we have blinked past the sac.

"I have always believed in being as honest as possible with you. Therefore, I am going to tell you that we are here because an alarm has been raised by a former officer of the Service."

She read Erin Kenner's blinkstat.

"If there are those among you who are too new to the *Rimfire* to be familiar with the acronym used by Lieutenant Kenner, I will explain."

Poised on the dividing line between the explored and the unknown, *Rimfire* was the largest spaceship ever built. She represented the highest achievement of United Planets man. She carried in her crew scientists and experts in all fields. Her weapons were state of the art. She carried more firepower, up to and including planet busters, than the entire Zede fleet that, a thousand years in the past, had threatened the stability of the populated areas of the galaxy. She represented the power of the race of man at his most potent, and she tiptoed into the uncharted core zone, sending out impulses ahead of her, not trusting the temporary blink beacons laid down by the *Mother Lode*, checking out each jump in advance.

Her weapons systems were on standby. Her crew was in condition yellow, just short of battle stations, for space was wide and dark, and there were millions of stars and planetary systems that had not yet been explored, and Erin Kenner had said "F.R.A.N.K."

There were those who thought that calling all aliens F.R.A.N.K. was a little bit too precious, even before one spelled out the words indicated by the initials. But as *Rimfire* blinked her slow and cautious way deeper into the core, F.R.A.N.K. ceased to be cutesy and quaint and came to mean just one thing.

"There are strangers here. Beware."

The big ship had to charge again. She lay amid the gleam of the core near a tandem system of suns that revolved around each other. Her instruments searched out the dimensions of the relatively uncrowded area around the twin suns and found that one of the stars had a planetary family. There were two parched and barren small planets near the sun that had spawned planets, a couple of gas giants, and. . . .

"The captain's presence is requested in the observatory," Ursy Wade said into the communicator.

Julie Roberts was inspecting the weapons control room when the call came. She said, "Carry on," and marched to the observatory.

Ursy Wade was bending over the shoulder of the technician who was operating the ship's optics. She straightened, nodded, motioned the captain to take her place. Julie looked down over the operator's shoulder to the large screen.

One of the most beautiful sights in the universe, at least to a being who is composed of flesh and blood and has a large percentage of water in his makeup, is a water planet, a planet in the life zone of a star, a living world that gleams blue from space, blue because of her oceans, blue because of an abundance of that precious substance that is necessary to all life as man knows it. Water.

"Ummmmm huh," Julie said, for there on the screen swam a blue planet with green and brown land areas and fleecy areas of clouds and polar icecaps. "Oh, yes," she whispered, and then, "Scan results?"

"Negative on all, Cap'n," the tech said. "Negative on electromagnetic radiations. Negative on life signals."

"Distance?"

"Point-nine b.m."

Julie nodded. *Rimfire* was almost one billion miles from the pretty, blue planet. It would take some damned sophisticated equipment to detect her at that distance.

"Keep on it," she said. She motioned to Ursy and they left the observatory together.

On the bridge Julie slumped into the captain's chair, chin in hand. Ursy brought up the blue planet on the bridge screens.

"Get me communications," Julie said. And when the signal was answered, "Service, emergency, and hailing frequencies. Send just this: *Erin. Respond.* Send it five times, thirty seconds apart.''

She put her feet up on the console. Worn places in the service gray paint showed that she was not the only one who assumed that relaxed position while on watch.

''Keep checking with the observatory,'' she told Ursy. ''Take her in on flux, slow, and keep all eyes on the planet.''

''Aye, aye,'' Ursy said, punching cruise orders into the computer.

Minutes later communications said, ''No answer, Captain.''

''Thank you,'' Julie said.

''I really expected her to answer,'' Ursy said.

Julie Roberts felt a tickling, crawling feeling on the back of her neck.

''I wonder why Erin didn't wait for us on Haven,'' Ursy said. ''Do you suppose she's down there somewhere the planet?''

''You tell me,'' Julie said. ''What I'm wondering is why she'd fool around mining a few million dollars worth of gold when the prize money for finding a life zone planet would make her one of the richest women in the U.P.''

''I hadn't thought of that,'' Ursy said.

Julie pushed the communicator with her toe. ''Observatory.''

''Aye, Captain.''

''Scan results?''

''Still negative on everything.''

''Combustion products?''

''Not quite near enough yet for that, Cap'n.''

''Let me know,'' Julie said.

So far there was no sign of life on the planet. There were no electromagnetic waves such as those created by the broadcast of sound, image, or power. There were no life signals such as would emanate from large groupings of biological life. If there was only scattered and nontechnologically advanced life on the planet, the ship's instruments would pick up combustion's products when she was near enough. Smoke from fossil fuel would be significant and would cause her to go into a program of approach that had been used only once before, when an X&A ship had rediscovered Old Earth and moved very, very carefully toward contact with what was thought to be an alien people. Widely scattered, small sources of wood smoke could mean a less advanced people.

There was nothing to do but wait.

"I'll be in my quarters, Ursy. I am available."

"Yes, ma'am."

No one had mentioned it as yet, at least not on the bridge, but Ursy was smiling because she knew that the whole crew stood to gain from the discovery of a water world. Since exploration was their job, the Service people wouldn't receive the rights and payments that went to a civilian who found a good world, but there'd be a small monetary bonus and, best of all, liberty time added to that which had accrued. Ursy's favorite place to spend liberty was on her home planet, Tigian III, where the waters of the lake on which her parents lived were virgin pure and teeming with the meanest and best tasting fish on any U.P. world. Finding a water world would mean an extra month there when *Rimfire* went back to Xanthos for routine servicing.

CHAPTER NINETEEN

As the work aboard the *Mother Lode* continued, Erin and Denton were locked into an exhausting routine. They were part of the Amplifier. They were only given time to sleep a few hours. In order to eat they had to snatch a bite on the run. A sense of urgency emanated from the two beautiful, winged entities as the titanic force of their will combined with the power from the generator and was funneled through the Amplifier to send the tumbling asteroids of the belt crashing into one growing mass.

Time was meaningless. Erin saw the chronometer as she passed through the bridge, but hours, days, weeks, all were the same. While there was charge in *Mother*'s generator she worked, and while she was working the control was tight, causing her to function mechanically, making independent thought difficult.

While the generator was charging, both Erin and Dent fell into bed, spent. Talking required energy and the aliens were demanding more than the human body was equipped to give over a long period of time. Even thought was an effort, but after sleep, alone in Erin's quarters, dreading the next period of work, they could cling together and wonder.

The winged beings were making a world. With the power of the stars and their own will they were reassembling the destroyed planet piece by piece. At first, swarming masses of asteroids had crashed together in roiling, splintering violence. Now, after a period of time, the accumulated mass was larger and the available material was thinning out. Even at accelerated speeds that were significant fractions of the speed of light it took time to move an asteroid along an orbital path that measured millions of miles in circumference.

They were growing more and more intolerant. No longer were they oblivious to mere men. Even in the numbed state of helplessness that was existence under the control of the female alien, Erin began to sense that they were becoming more and more angry. Punishment in the form of mental pain that blacked out all existence for a period of time came for the smallest infraction, for looking up from the work, for an errant thought.

Following one sleep period, while the generator was still charging and Erin and Dent were in the captain's cabin nervously awaiting the summons to return to the workroom, Dent said, "They are not divine."

Erin just shook her head, too weary to play the game of conjecture about them.

"They're going to fail, Erin, and when they do they'll be mad as hell." He put his hand on her shoulder and turned her to face him. "In a lot of ways they're ignorant, or naive. Or maybe what was done to them, having to spend only God knows how long imprisoned in rock, drove them just a bit insane. First of all, there's not enough material to form a planet of the same size as the original. When it was shattered, large chunks were propelled out of the sun's gravity well, or, at best, sent off on errant orbits, like comets. *They're* going to find that the planet they're building will be considerably smaller, maybe too small to hold an atmosphere."

Erin nodded.

"They're not God," Dent said. "They have the ability to fling the broken pieces together. Natural forces may or may not heat the core, but what then?"

"They're pretty amazing," Erin said. "They can totally disassemble a living thing and put it back together in the same form or in an altered form."

"But that is not creation," Dent said. "That's my whole point. Maybe they can form a planet. Maybe, over a few million years, natural forces will cause vulcanicity. Maybe they can even accelerate the process. Since they can dismantle a living thing and use the cells or molecules or

whatever for building blocks, maybe they can even manipulate nonorganic materials. Maybe they can break oxygen
and hydrogen loose from the rocks and combine them to
make water—''

''I think I know what you're saying,'' Erin said. ''They
haven't performed any act of creation. To form their bodies they had to have the material from Plough and his
crew.''

''So even if they can make a world and give it oxygen
and water—''

''They can't make a blade of grass.''

''And before a planet is habitable there must be vegetation,'' Dent said.

''How much of his thoughts do you pick up?'' Erin
asked.

''He gets a little careless at times. He's a horny bas-
tard.''

She shuddered, remembering his ruthless attentions.

''He sees in his mind a sort of paradise, empty except
for the two of them. There's lush vegetation but no animal
life. Apparently they don't eat.''

''Have you noticed that they're losing weight?''

He nodded. ''They don't eat, but their bodies are made of
flesh and blood. That's another reason why I feel that they
might be a little bit insane. Otherwise they'd have to see that
they're using up the material that forms their bodies.''

Mop, who had been sleeping at their feet, decided that
it was time for him to get some attention. Erin rubbed his
silky ears. He flopped onto his back with a contented sigh
and she rubbed his chest and belly.

''What's going to happen then?'' Erin asked.

''I think when they realize that they're going to fail in
their attempt to recreate their world, they'll start looking
for a world that has already been made.''

She shuddered again.

''Can you imagine them loose on a populated planet?''

''If *Mother* had a self-destruct button, I might think of
pushing it,'' she said.

Dent held her close, for the mere thought of her death
devastated him.

However, he had entertained similar thoughts.

* * *

They could use the power of the generator and their wills to break out oxygen and hydrogen from the rock. And they did it in mighty floods that quickly filled huge basins to form oceans. The power of the sun condensed water and there was weather.

But under the rains the sterile rock glistened and endured. The process of erosion would be one for the ages. Soil formation was a thing of the far future. The waters of the blue oceans were unfruitful.

They looked down on their work and fretted. They sent thunderbolts of pure power to shatter unyielding mountains, but there was no life.

She vented some of her frustration on Erin, jerking her from her body to put her in storage inside the small skull of Mop the dog. The transition was no longer shocking. Man is a very adaptable animal. Erin used such times to try to make her little buddy aware that he was not alone in that odd little brain of his, that he had an unwilling but well-meaning guest.

Life was so simple for Mr. Mop. He ate. He slept. He coaxed his humans into playing with him, or petting him. He did not have headaches, acid stomach, stiff limbs, or sore muscles. He went through the day with his stub of a tail pointed jauntily high, a barometer of his spirits. He had come to accept that now and then his humans were not available. He knew that Erin was not at home in her body at the moment. Of course, he could not think in those terms, he was just aware that it would be useless to try to attract Erin's attention as she made jerky, robotic movements at the control console of the Amplifier.

"I'm here, Mop," Erin was saying. "Listen to me, you hairy little rascal."

She tried various ways of getting Mop's attention. With great intensity she envisioned juicy, meaty tidbits of people food. Mop put his nose between his paws, twitched one ear, and took a little nap. When he awoke, she went back to the work of trying to break through into his doggy consciousness. Nothing worked. In mock anger she said, "May the fleas of a thousand camels infest you." She didn't mean it, of course, she was just frustrated at being unable to have any effect at all on Mop's behavior.

Mop lifted his left rear leg and scratched energetically. He squirmed, began to scratch with the other leg.

"Hey," Erin said. "I didn't mean it, buddy. You don't have fleas."

He continued scratching. She reviewed what had happened. Mop was getting a bit frantic, scratching and biting, and Erin knew that the sanitary measures taken before *Mother* left New Earth made it impossible for the dog to have fleas.

What had she done?

She talked to the dog, told him he didn't have fleas. Mop whimpered and scratched as if he were being eaten alive.

She said angrily, "What in hell did I do?"

His left ear twitched.

"I am angry with you," she stormed. "I have told you that you do not have fleas. Now stop that scratching."

Mop gave his right ear one final little twitch with his hind leg and sank down onto the deck.

Anger. Or pretended anger. Anger penetrated the barrier. She experimented. "I want water," she said angrily.

Mop rose, stretched, went to press the button that gave him fresh water.

"I want food," Erin grated.

Mop ate. He was a champion button pusher. Although he was color blind, he knew which button to push for water, which for his regular food, and he knew that pushing the botton for his milk bone worked no more than twice a day.

"It's all right, baby," she said, still talking as if she were angry. "It's all right. Go lie down."

Mop looked around in puzzlement, seeking Erin.

"I'm here," she yelled at him.

His stubby tail did a few circles as he turned all the way around, looking for her. He padded to the workroom and saw her there at the console, jumped into her lap, climbed up behind the controls and looked at her with his deep, brown eyes, saw the blankness in her face that meant she would not talk to him.

"Over here, Mop," Dent called.

Mop jumped to the deck, leapt into Dent's lap and onto the console. Dent managed to pat him once before the male alien sent a wave of pain, his way of saying, "Leave the dog alone and concentrate on your work."

"It's all right, boy," Dent whispered. "She'll be back."

The communicator rang. John Kenner's doorbell sound indicated that a radio call was being received. Mop bounced to the deck and announced that someone was at the door, barking excitedly.

"No, no," Erin shouted at him, because they were becoming annoyed by the noise.

The doorbell sounded again thirty seconds later. Mop, seeing that neither Erin or Dent was doing anything about it, barked hysterically. That might be one of his friends at the door.

"Mop, Mop, shut up," Erin yelled, in real fear that they would do harm to Mop. But, although Mr. Mop was usually a very gentlemanly little dog, when there was an alarm to be sounded he did his duty.

On the third sounding of the doorbell—*Rimfire*'s communications officer had been ordered to broadcast the call to the *Mother Lode* several times at thirty second intervals—the female alien turned, let her lovely emerald eyes rest on the excited Mop for a moment before sending a small wave of force that hurled Mop out of the room and sent him sliding across the deck of the bridge to bang painfully into the pedestal of the command chair. He yelped just once and then crawled under the console, shivering in fright.

Erin forgot to speak with mock anger as she tried to comfort him, but then, as she turned her attention to The She, her anger was real, causing Mop to quit licking his bruised leg and lift both ears in alarm.

"You bitch," Erin screamed, "you bloody, mothering bitch."

If pure hate could have killed, the alien would have died at that instant.

It was the wave of enmity sent by Erin that made The She inquire about the irritating sounds issuing from the communications system. The male alien got the information from Dent's mind, sent Dent to activate the communicator, listened to the message from the *Rimfire*.

He did not have to voice questions. He merely willed that Dent answer.

"Rimfire is a large spaceship," Dent said. "She has several hundred people aboard." He went on and on, giving all of the information he had. Dent told the alien what he knew about the armament of an X&A explorer. There was no possibility of holding back anything. He had merely to command and Denton had no choice but to obey. Had he been able to resist, the alien could have gone directly into Denton's mind to find the answers.

The aliens had become totally contemptuous of the presence of the humans. The He didn't bother to close off his thoughts as he said to The She, "The new ship will be useful."

"Captain to the bridge," the communicator said, waking Julie Roberts from a dream of childhood in which she had been feeling such a sense of love and warm security that, on losing it, she looked at the plain walls of her cabin and shivered. She went to the bridge. Lieutenant Ursulina Wade was on watch again.

"Ursy, if you're going to make a habit of waking me every time you have the duty—" Julie said.

"Sorry, Captain," Ursy said. "I thought you'd like to see these." She punched buttons and brought up detailed photographs of the surface of the planet which *Rimfire* was approaching.

"Well, hell," Julie said, for the planet was raw. There was water and an atmosphere rich in oxygen, but barren, incredibly sharp and rugged mountains touched torrent-raining clouds and mighty rivers spread over the rock surface. There was no green.

"Some days there just ain't no fish," Ursy said.

"Yep," Julie said.

"If the air is good, there'll be mining stations. And she'll be a good source of water if anyone ever finds a planet nearby that has soil but not much water."

"You're a little ray of sunshine," Julie said.

"She's negative in all areas of detection down to earthworm size," Ursy said.

"I can see why, but we'll have to check the seas."

"I've laid out an orbit, Captain," Ursy said, bringing up measurements on the screen. "Close enough to take good readings for metals and minerals and to send down the scouts for air and water samples."

"Very well," Julie said. "Do you mind, Lieutenant, if I go back to bed now?"

"Not at all, ma'am," Ursy said. "Have a nice rest."

Julie didn't bother to undress. She had slept for four hours. She punched up coffee and sipped moodily as she considered the implications of the current situation. Even if the planet that Erin Kenner had led her to was not a Class A Habitable world, it was a world, and it did have water and atmosphere. If it was the source of Erin's gold, it wouldn't be a complete washout. She'd squeak through without a reprimand, but the admirals wouldn't be happy.

"Damn it, Erin, where are you?" she said aloud.

It wasn't likely that *Rimfire* would find F.R.A.N.K. on a planet that wouldn't support a mouse. But if Erin wasn't on the planet, where was she? The temporary blink beacons from the *Mother Lode* ended here, at the orbit of that blue planet. It didn't add up. Erin Kenner was not irresponsible, not easily excited. Erin was, in Julie Roberts' opinion, one of the last people to bring *Rimfire* several thousand parsecs on a spook chase.

She finished her coffee, paced the deck. She was moving toward the communicator to give orders to make a thorough surface search with scanners set to detect the presence of a small spaceship, Mule class, when she heard Ursy's voice to the communicator again.

"Captain to the bridge. Captain to the bridge."

Julie patted an errant lock of hair into place and walked to the bridge. Ursy was grinning.

"You did it again," Julie said.

"We've found her, ma'am," Ursy said, motioning toward a viewer.

At first the shape of the image on the screen did not make sense, and then Julie realized that what she was seeing was two ships, a squarish Mule and a sleek converted fleet destroyer lying side by side, air locks joined.

"I assume you have tried radio contact?" Julie asked.

"Yes, ma'am. Negative."

"Readings?"

"Life readings. Four entities of roughly humanoid bulk, and one very small one, in the area of five pounds."

"Roughly humanoid?" Julie asked.

"Two of them are quite large. One of them weighs in the neighborhood of four hundred pounds."

Ursy's eyes were wide, her cheeks a bit pale. Julie nodded, knowing what the lieutenant was thinking.

"Did you double-check those readings?"

"Affirmative, ma'am." Ursy was being very formal. It helped her to control her excitement, but then the agitation broke through. "It's F.R.A.N.K., Captain, sure as hell."

CHAPTER TWENTY

Although Mop learned quickly, it was very hard for him to keep silent when the doorbell that John Kenner had installed to indicate an incoming radio call rang again and again. Muffled "murfs" rumbled in his throat. He sought out Erin and Dent, stood on his hind legs to put his forepaws on their legs. Once he lost control and barked, risking the anger of the thing that had hurt him by throwing him across the deck. Erin scooped him up and closed his mouth with her hand, saying, "Shush, shush."

The big X&A explorer was picked up by the *Mother Lode*'s instruments when she was still several astronomical units distant.

Erin and Denton had been left to their own thoughts ever since *Rimfire* had announced her presence near the core by her first attempts to contact them. The aliens had closed themselves off mentally and physically. Erin and Dent stayed mainly in Erin's cabin. It was a relief not to have every move directed by an alien will, but the relative freedom served to make the knowledge of their helplessness even more bitter. Once, after several hours of non-interference from them, Erin went out onto the bridge and actually had the communicator on before a wave of pain swept through her. Compared to The She's usual efforts, the pain was not severe. It was as if the alien was so preoccupied with other, more important matters that she couldn't really be bothered to render more than a token punishment to Erin for her attempt to warn *Rimfire*. However, as Erin sent the mental order to her finger to activate the communicator, partial paralysis came with the pain and she backed slowly away toward her cabin.

"We must do something," Erin whispered.

Denton, too, had been trying to think of some way to evade the control of the two winged beings. "I know," he said, "but. . . ." He spread his hands.

He didn't have to say more. She'd been over the same things time and time again. Although she could not feel the alien's control at times, it was there, as she'd proven again by her attempt to use the communicator. Even if her macabre fantasy of using a nonexistent self-destruct button to disintegrate *Mother* and *everything* aboard her had been possible Erin would not have been able to push the button, for The She knew Erin's every thought, every impulse. Still Erin considered means of killing the aliens, or, at least, means of destroying their flesh and blood bodies, and it gave her pause to realize that she was thinking murderous thought about them without being punished.

Her service hand weapon was in its holster on her flexsuit. It was capable, given time, of burning a hole in *Mother*'s stout, double hulls. If the mining laser had not been left on Haven and if she could have jury-rigged some way to turn it on *Mother*, then some serious holing would have resulted.

But if a frog had a glass ass, it wouldn't jump but once.

Civilized man didn't think about ways to accomplish his own death along with the destruction of his spaceship. He considered ways of bringing about the death of others, if it become necessary. He went armed. *Rimfire,* in addition to having the best long-range detection equipment in the U.P. sector, was also the most powerfully armed spaceship ever built. With the weapons aboard her, she could make rubble of a world and—although it had never been tried—in the unlikely event that it was ever vital to the continued well-being of mankind, she could make a sun pretty sick.

Man was a deadly species, and that made him pretty cocky, so confident in his own ability to meet any challenge that he didn't plan for defeat. Thus there was no self-destruct button aboard the *Mother Lode,* nor aboard any ship of the fleet, for that matter. There were no explosives on a Mule turned miner, no heavy weapons that could be turned against herself. Perhaps that was why Erin was able to imagine—because it was basically impossible—destroying *Mother*. She had never actually come face-to-face with death. The statistical risks she had faced during her just over thirty years of life had been small. As she'd once told Dent, everyone knows that he's going to die—someday. But since U.P. man had earned—by good nutrition, medical advances, and the elimination of most of the diseases, malfunctions, and to a large extent even the accidents that had once plagued the race—the lifespan mentioned in the Old Bible in Genesis 6:3, she had lived only one quarter of her allotted span and to her the concept of death was still an abstract idea. Not even in her current situation could she believe that she was going to die.

So she indulged in idle speculations about how to overcome them, and felt guilt—for it was possible to concede that others might die—at doing nothing while men and women she knew were coming ever closer to being within reach of two things who had absolutely no regard for human life.

She was letting the precious minutes spend themselves and she was doing nothing but lying on the bed with Dent's arm around her *wishing* that there was something she could do. She wept. Mop, with that canine instinct that knows when a beloved human is in stress, came to snuggle up to her side and licked her elbow just once, politely, as if to say, "Hey, Erin, I'm here and I'm sorry you're unhappy."

She slept. When she awoke to the alien's summons she knew it was too late to help her former shipmates in *Rimfire*. No longer capable of independent thought or action she went to the bridge and activated the communicator.

Mop, having seen the slack look come over Erin's face, followed her out of the cabin and darted under the console and curled up into a hairy ball to wait for Erin to be Erin again.

"*Rimfire, Rimfire,* this is the *Mother Lode.*"

The answer was immediate, telling Erin—and The She who dominated her—that *Rimfire* had been keeping a constant communications watch.

"Rimfire, I am Erin Kenner. I want to speak with Captain Julie Roberts."

"Wait one, *Mother Lode.*"

Erin's trapped mind was writhing, struggling, but it was to no avail.

"Hello, Erin," Julie Roberts' voice said. "We have you on visual. What is your situation in regard to the converted destroyer?"

Erin's voice was without inflection as she answered. "We claim salvage. The destroyer has been converted to private use. We found her abandoned and derelict."

"Her registration?" Julie Roberts was looking at the mobile graphs of a voice analyzer. Erin's words were being compared to her voiceprint from *Rimfire*'s files.

"There is ninety-eight percent correlation," a technician said while Julie waited for Erin to answer.

"She sounds almost as if she were under the influence of a drug," Ursy Wade said.

"The ship is registered to the Haven Refining Company, of the planet Haven," Erin said.

"Her name?" Julie asked.

"Murdoch's Plough," Erin said.

"That's the ship that followed the *Mother Lode* when she lifted off from Haven," Ursy said.

Julie nodded grimly. Her eyes squinted in thought before she pressed the send button and spoke again. "Erin, it's nice to hear your voice. We got your stat that mentioned Ursy Wade's as yet to be met friend. Explain, please."

There was a long pause. Aboard the *Mother Lode* it took the alien thirty seconds to dig out of Erin's mind that the "yet to be met friend" was an entity named Frank. Then Erin said, "I'm afraid Ursy will be very disappointed. We discovered some fossil bones, that's all. They're humanoid and very interesting."

"Cap'n," Ursy said, "If that's Erin Kenner speaking, there's something wrong with her."

"There is a certain oddness in her voice," Julie agreed. "I think it's time we got down to business." She pushed the send button. "Erin, our life sensors show four entities on your ship."

With sudden anger, The She caused Erin to turn off the communicator. To Erin's surprise, she was addressed directly, not in words but in thoughts.

"They can detect *our* presence?" the alien asked.

For the first time since she'd seen Denton explode into a red mist Erin knew hope. Could she, after all, hide at least some of her thoughts from her captor?

"Yes," she said. She started to add that *Rimfire* could also determine the body weight of any living thing and that, therefore, those aboard the X&A ship were well aware that the two extra entities aboard *Mother* were considerably larger than life, but she buried the thought and the alien did not detect it.

"Tell them," the alien ordered, "that you took on two extra spacehands on Haven."

"Yes," Erin said, trying to hide her elation, for now she knew that the alien could not see everything that she was thinking. She relayed the lie to *Rimfire*.

"Okay, Erin, fine," Julie Roberts said. "Look, it's been a long time since we've had the pleasure of your company. I'm going to come over in the gig and bring a couple of your old friends."

"Like a dozen fully armed space marines?" Ursy asked.

"No," the alien had Erin say. Then, quickly, "Denton and I will come aboard *Rimfire*."

"Not bloody likely," Ursy muttered, earning a raised eyebrow from Julie as the captain pushed the transmit button.

"It will be good to see you," Julie said.

"We'll use the gig from the *Plough*," Erin said.

"We'll take you at lockport forward two," Julie said. "*Rimfire* out."

"Captain," Ursy protested, "is it a good idea to give *them* access to the ship?"

"What do we know, Ursy?" Julie asked. "We know that there are two extra life-forms on that Mule, one of which weighs about twice as much as a very healthy professional athlete. I don't think *they* can sneak into the air lock with Erin and this Denton Gale without our notice, do you?"

"No, ma'am," Ursy said. "It's just—"

"It's just that maybe, we're face-to-face with a living alien," Julie said. "I don't think we should act like people in a low budget space opera and assume that all aliens are bad guys."

"They're not being very straightforward with us," Ursy said.

"How do you judge when an alien intelligence is being friendly?" Julie asked. "Unless you give them a chance to show their intentions."

"According to Erin, or whoever that is over there on the Mule, that converted destroyer was deserted. That means something happened to four or more people."

"Take it easy, Lieutenant," Julie said.

"I guess I'm just a bit nervous," Ursy said.

Julie laughed. "And you're the one who dreams about F.R.A.N.K."

"Used to," Ursy said. "I've decided that I'd settle for a less than perfect ordinary human man."

"Captain," said the rating who was monitoring the ship's detection systems, "there's a small boat leaving the destroyer's air lock."

"She's in a hurry," Julie said, touching her fingertips to her cheek. "Ursy, tell the medical officer to stand by. We'll sanitize our visitors while they're in the lock."

"I'd like to order interior scans and ultrashock," Ursy said.

Julie hesitated. It wasn't really hospitable to submit guests to having their innards examined and to bombard them with unpleasant vibrations that sought out and killed any bacteria or virus that was not normal to the human body. Before the ultrashock technique was perfected, the treatment killed all of the necessary bacteria in the stomach, causing some inconvenience and discomfort for a while, but now those benign microorganisms were spared. The process was just unpleasant for a couple of minutes.

"Permission granted," Julie said.

"Yeah, I know," Ursy grinned. "You're thinking that I'm being too uptight, that a four hundred pound F.R.A.N.K. couldn't hitchhike into the ship with Erin and Gale."

"I'm thinking, Lieutenant, that your suggestion was a very good one," Julie said. "Carry on."

Although Mop had made it a practice to stay out of reach when his humans were being odd, when he saw them leave *Mother* and go aboard the larger ship he had to follow. Then Erin and Dent were getting into a small vessel and it was obvious that they were going to *go*. Going was one of Mop's greatest joys. He jumped up and scratched the side of the gig, barking. He was ignored. The hatch started to close. He sat down, lifted his bearded muzzle, and howled his sadness at being left behind.

The She started to quiet the dog with a surge of force, but then she felt Erin's thoughts forming.

What Erin was feeling was anger, rage mixed with the fear that she would hurt Mop badly.

She lowered herself once again to make direct communication with the subject entity.

"Julie Roberts would know that I wouldn't leave Mop here all alone," Erin said.

Anger. Anger had helped her make contact with Mop while she was being "stored" in Mop's little skull. Anger apparently hazed over some of her thoughts, hid them from the alien. Julie Roberts had no way of knowing that Erin even had a dog.

Mop leapt up excitedly as Erin opened the hatch. She lifted him into the gig. He raced around in great joy, managed to give Denton a big kiss right on the mouth. Denton didn't even lift his hand to wipe it off.

Lieutenant Ursulina Wade was in the ship's sick bay with the chief medical officer, a graying sub-captain who had a lot of questions about just what the hell was going on.

"You know, Lieutenant," the doctor said, "that being shocked free of germs is damned uncomfortable. We do it to every poor son-of-a-bitch who goes into space for the first time. Are you sure this is necessary?"

"Captain's orders, sir," Ursy said.

A low signal tone came from the ship's com-system. The doctor said, "What's that?"

While it was true that a medical sub-captain outranked a field lieutenant on paper, officers like Ursy Wade looked upon non-operational ranks with condescending tolerance. "How long you been aboard, Doctor?"

"Long enough to give up trying to figure out what the hell all your cute little bells and whistles mean," he said.

"The signal tone means that our guests are arriving," Ursy said.

The small shock of the gig's lock making contact vibrated through the deck under Ursy's feet. She activated the air lock viewers. Erin Kenner stepped through the lock first and, on seeing her face, Ursy frowned in thought. It was Erin, all right, but she looked as if she were sedated. The young man who followed her into the *Rimfire*'s lock had the same vacuous expression on his face. Only the third occupant of the lock, a small, blond-headed dog, seemed to have any animation. The dog shivered when *Rimfire*'s outer hatch clanged shut and stood on his hind legs, begging Erin to pick him up.

"Well, Lieutenant, shall I zap the poor bastards now?" the doctor asked.

"Zap away," Ursy said, turning on the sound pickups.

She heard the little dog yipe in surprise when the ultrashock hit him. He leapt into the air and turned one hundred and eighty degrees to see what had attacked him from the rear and then, perhaps remembering that he'd felt the odd sensations before, stood quivering.

"They-are-using-ultrashock," Erin Kenner said without expression. "It-is-normal-procedure."

"Who is she explaining it to?" the doctor asked. "You don't get into space without having been cleaned out with ultrashock."

CHAPTER TWENTY-ONE

It was not the female alien who panicked when the reinforced ultrasonic vibrations began to beat against her. *She* heard and felt Erin Kenner's explanation. Denton Gale was a member of a class of people who had not been, despite the assertion of the chief medical officer aboard *Rimfire*, cleaned out inside by ultrashock before going into space. Before joining Erin in *Mother Lode,* Dent's one venture into space had been aboard a passenger liner, and paying customers on passenger liners did not have to undergo the discomfort of ultrashock.

The feeling of being internally electrified came as a surprise to Denton Gale, and to the male alien, since he could not extract from Denton's mind knowledge that it did not have. The ultrashock was, of course, harmless to humans—and to little dogs, for that matter. It was in standard use throughout the United Planets sector as both a cure and a prevention of disease, and it was deadly to unwanted invaders of the human body as the originating machine changed frequencies at the rate of several times per second.

The He and The She were alien to the bodies they inhabited. They were not microlife, not cells gone bad nor virus, but they were alien and the vibrations of the ultrashock threatened to break their attachment to the minds of their two carriers.

The female, able to take warning from Erin's knowledge of the treatment, braced herself and clung to Erin, knowing that the force that was battering her would cease quickly. The male felt threatened and, as was his nature, lashed out. His anger sought the mind that was directing the attack against him.

The medical sub-captain made an odd sound in his throat. Ursy Wade felt lightning flash through her and looked quickly to see if the ultrashock machine had shorted out or blown up. She couldn't breathe. Stabs of pain went horizontally and vertically throughout her entire body. She saw the doctor sink to the floor, saw the flesh begin to melt from his bones. His face fell away before he contacted the floor, leaving a partially exposed skull from which two eyeballs, looking as if they were twice normal size, stared out.

Ursy tried to scream, but no sound came. She fought the pain and reached for the control panel just vacated by the doctor. Her hand hit the ultrashock lever and that saved her life, for the alien, about to lose his grasp on the living thing to which he had attached himself, was seeking relief, striking out at the next nearest living being. His full force of deadly will was being turned toward Ursy. When he felt the battering force cease, he pulled back. That give Ursy a moment. She gasped in a breath and her fingers flew over the control console. *Rimfire*'s systems obeyed. Several things happened with a speed that left the aliens in the air lock raging.

While it was true that space-going man did not spend time and resources providing himself with ways to commit suicide and destroy his ship, he had given considerable thought to completing the second stated intent of X&A's mission, the finding of alien life. Alien life did not necessarily have to be intelligent life, nor did it have to be of interest. The first explorers to encounter a Tigian tiger had learned as much, while discovering that an alien animal might have little respect for human life.

The lock to which Julie Roberts had directed the gig from *Murdoch's Plough* was the capture and hold lock. It had been designed to imprison a beast as strong and as fierce as a Tigian tiger and, at least in theory, things that strained the imagination, up to and including what many scientists thought to be a definite possibility, a life-form consisting of pure force.

Ursy Wade had seen a shipmate die a horrendous death, with his flesh melting away from his bones. Her fingers were given extra urgency by the feeling that her own flesh was beginning to slip. She hit the "Secure All" switch on the control panel. Doors of durasteel clanged closed at the inner hatch. The air in the corridor outside the lock sizzled and hissed as incredible power was drawn from the ship's Blink generator to be concentrated in the intricate webbings of circuitry installed between the triple bulkheads of the air lock and create a field of force that would have withstood the direct strike of a lightning bolt.

The female alien felt the presence of the force field too late. The lash of her anger, at an intensity that would have vaporized more than half of the *Rimfire*'s crew, was absorbed by the field. The male joined her in an effort to smash the walls of their prison.

"Enough," she said. She was weeping in frustration, for once she had possessed the power to reduce the entire ship to its constituent subatomic particles.

"Rest," he said. "We will need our energy later."

"I want a med-crew here, now," Ursy Wade ordered. She was trembling. Her limbs were weak. Her eyes ached.

On the deck, the doctor's blood was pooling. The air filters had cranked up to remove the meaty smell of it. The door burst open and a med-tech skidded to a halt. The doctor had fallen onto his back. His white skull peered out from sagging folds of bloody flesh.

"Captain," Ursy said into the communicator. "I have activated 'Secure All.' "

"I'll be right there," Julie Roberts said.

"May I suggest 'Full Alert'?" Ursy said. "We've got us some bad mothers here."

Within five seconds she heard the ship's speakers sounding "Alert-Interior." She'd heard the signal in drills, but never had she thought, not even in her wildest nightmares, that anything threatening could gain access to *Rimfire*'s interior.

Julie Roberts ran into the room where the med-team was examining the doctor and where Ursy was glued to the viewers showing the interior of the air lock. Julie saw Erin Kenner and a handsome young stud standing almost at attention, faces blank of emotion. Her heart gained a beat in sympathy when she saw the little dog cowering at Erin's feet, looking up pleadingly.

"Put me on," she told Ursy, pointing to the communicator. "All ship."

Ursy flipped switches, gave central communications an order, nodded to the captain, who said, "Now hear this. We have secured in air lock forward two an unknown force. To the eye it looks as if the lock is occupied by a man and woman, the woman being ex-lieutenant Erin Kenner, who served aboard this vessel in the recent past. Neither Kenner nor the man is armed. However, there has been one casualty of a particularly violent nature. My orders to you are to be alert, to stay at your stations."

Since *Rimfire* was on Full Alert, the airtight doors that isolated her various compartments were already closed.

"Since we are dealing with an unknown killing force that penetrated the bulkheads of lock forward two before the force field could be activated, my orders are this. Should Erin Kenner or her companion escape the security of lock forward two, all force is authorized to destroy them. Stand by for visuals."

Ursy's fingers flew. The blank faces of Erin and Dent were shown on all viewers throughout *Rimfire*.

"Now hear this," Julie said, still talking to the entire crew. "We intend, at this time, to try to make contact with the occupants of the air lock. I will leave the audio and visual channels open so that you may see and hear what happens."

She nodded to Ursy, said, "Put me through to them."

"You're on," Ursy said.

"Erin?" Julie said softly.

Erin Kenner slowly turned her eyes toward the speaker at the top of the lock's inner hatch.

"Erin, do you hear me?"

"I hear you," Erin said in a flat, unmodulated voice.

"Erin, we know you are not alone in the lock."

"Yes. Denton Gale, my friend, is with me," Erin said

woodenly, as the alien directed, for the being was still searching frantically for a way out.

"And there are others, Erin," Julie said.

There was a visible flash of force that seemed to emanate from Erin's eyes. Julie jerked backward in spite of herself, then recovered.

"It would be just about as easy to penetrate the force field that surrounds you as it would be to escape the gravitational pull of a black hole," Julie said calmly.

The alien ceased her attempt to break through to the arrogant human.

"We know you are there," Julie said. "Can we talk? We might discover that we have common ground. You live. We live. We are both creatures of intelligence."

The She laughed through Erin's lips. The sound was sarcastic, brittle.

"I think I detect a certain arrogance," Ursy Wade said, keeping the communicator open. "But think about this, sweetie. You're the one who's got her ass locked up inside durasteel walls and a force field, not us. So who the hell is the most intelligent?"

The alien stormed.

Mop crawled away to cringe against the bulkhead at the back of the lock. Both Erin and Dent swayed with the force of the blast of anger and frustration.

"Look at baby," Ursy said, "someone licked the red off her candy."

A scream of pure anguish howled from Erin Kenner's lips and then all was quiet.

"Since our detection instruments show two living bodies aboard the *Mother Lode,*" Julie Roberts said, "I assume that you are present—" She paused, rolled her eyes at Ursy. "How do you say this?'

"They're present only in spirit?" Ursy said.

"We are here," the alien said, speaking with Erin's lips, but without hesitation, emphasizing the word, "here."

"Who are you?" Julie asked.

"You would not understand."

"Let me try," Julie said.

"*I* am—"

"You're right," Ursy said, breaking into a rolling sound that continued on for long, long seconds, "we don't understand. Is that a name or a confession?"

The She was thinking more clearly. They had been robbed of the full extent of their greatness, but not by mental pygmies like the arrogant humans. While it was true that they were unable to break the field of force and the durasteel walls that enclosed them, there were other means of taking charge.

"My name is Legion," she said.

"Sounds vaguely familiar," Ursy said, casting a look at Julie.

"I am Captain Julie Roberts of the United Planets X&A ship U.P.S. *Rimfire*. I am fully empowered by my government to make contact with you and to discuss mutual concerns. We cannot forgive the fact that you have killed one of us, but we are open to discussion."

As her voice came from Erin's lips, there was no hesitation, no lack of modulation. It was a strong but pleasant voice with a husky contralto range. "We have misjudged you," she said. "We will compensate you for the loss of one of your crew members."

"I don't think compensation is the question," Julie said. "The problem is, how do we carry on a peaceful dialogue?"

"Now that we understand you better," the alien said, "there will be no more conflict between us. You may lower your force field."

"No, no," Erin screamed from her place of imprisonment, and so strong was her hate that her lips moved before the alien silenced her with a burst of mental pain. The movement of Erin's lips was not lost on Ursy Wade.

"Erin?" she whispered. "Erin, are you there?"

"I'm here," Erin tried to say, against the pain that the alien was giving her. "Don't let them into the ship."

She spoke directly, and silently, to Erin. "I have been more than patient. One more outburst and I will—"

Erin did not understand the word that she used, but the meaning was made clear by the menace in her voice.

Ursy cut off the communicator for a moment. "When

she suggested that we lower the force field, I saw Erin's lips move. She said, 'No, no.' ''

"I saw," Julie said. "I don't think we'll lower the force field."

Ursy activated the communicator again.

"We have reason to believe that you have taken control of a woman who is our friend," Julie said. "You are not, you who are now conversing with me, Erin Kenner, and yet you speak with her lips."

"We did not want to alarm you by coming to you in our own form," the alien said.

"Well, I'm not too easily alarmed," Julie said, "but I don't quite cotton to the idea that you can take over Erin's body."

"She has not been harmed," the alien said. "Help us and she and the man will be as they were."

"How can we help you?" Julie asked.

"Lower your force field and we will talk of what we can do to mutually help each other."

The med-team was carrying the doctor away. Julie looked directly down into the exposed bones of the man's skull. "I think not," she said. "Perhaps we will be able to talk more successfully if you return to your own forms and release Erin Kenner and her friend."

There was a long pause as the alien carried on an interior dialogue with Erin.

"She is trying to trick us," the alien said. When we are away from the *Rimfire* in the gig, she will fire on us."

"No," Erin said. "She will keep her word."

"You must convince her to lower the force field."

"I can't," Erin said. "And I wouldn't if I could."

Actually, the conversation, as such, was not in words. The She probed forcefully, seeking answers deep in Erin's mind. She found Erin's wall of anger and hate and could not penetrate it, but was not concerned, for she felt human emotions to be a sign of racial weakness and, in her superiority, she could not imagine that Erin's "inferior" mind had depths beyond the protective anger. She found what she wanted to find, Erin's memories of Julie Roberts.

"Truly," the female told the male, communicating on another level, "the men have a peculiarity. They think that it is honorable to keep their word, even to—'' she laughed—''an enemy who will destroy them. We will let her set the terms and then we will wait for the one opening we need.''

''There are hundred of life units on this ship,'' he said. ''They will be very useful when it is time to make our world fruitful.''

She gave him the equivalent of an affirmative nod. Life was life. It could be converted into any form, including but not limited to flowers, trees, waving fields of grass.

She spoke through Erin's lips. ''We will do as you say, Captain Julie Roberts. We will return to our ships and regain our own forms.''

''Any display of force once you are disengaged from our air lock will be met by overwhelming destruction. I don't know exactly what you are, but I doubt if you can survive laser disintegration.''

''There will be no force,'' she said. They could survive laser blasts, but in their present state they would be left to float in space without means of movement. No, they would not initiate force.

''Go into the gig,'' Julie said. ''We will cast you off. When you have reached the *Mother Lode,* you will assume your own form and release Erin Kenner and Denton Gale. Is that agreed?''

''Agreed'' she said.

''Then we will talk,'' Julie said.

''Agreed,'' she said.

''Don't let them go,'' Erin tried to say. ''Don't—don't—''

The She was annoyed, but she had found the Erin entity to be useful. She was not yet finished with it. She exerted minor will and Erin was looking up at herself and Dent from a height of inches.

Dent went into the gig. When Erin followed, Mop started after her. Erin thundered her anger and ordered Mop to sit. The little dog, confused, delayed just long enough for the outer hatch to close.

''They've left the dog,'' Ursy said.

''So I see.''

''With one of them inside?''

Julie mused for a moment. ''I think it would be best to evacuate the lock.''

''Ah, the poor little thing,'' Ursy said. To evacuate the lock meant death for the dog as his body was blown into the vacuum of space. ''We can't do that.''

''No, I guess not,'' Julie said. ''But until we're sure he's nothing more than a flop-eared little dog, he's going to stay there behind the force field.''

Mop, left all alone, lifted his muzzle and howled.

The gig left *Rimfire's* lock and fluxed toward the two joined ships that formed one small star as they reflected sunlight.

Julie Roberts punched a number and was answered by *Rimfire's* technical officer, Jack Burnish. ''Jack, any findings about our recent visitors?''

''Mainly a feeling of awe,'' Burnish said. ''What force can go through three layers of durasteel without damaging them and kill a man?''

Burnish's action station was in a tight little room filled with monitors and controls for *Rimfire's* massive array of sensors and detectors.

''I can tell you one thing,'' Burnish went on. ''There were two of them. We had a good chance to work on them while they were in the lock. We got emanations originating from the brains of Kenner and Gale in three totally alien ranges. The human thought patterns were almost undetectable, overpowered by the alien presence.''

''Jack,'' Ursy asked, ''can you be sure there were only two of them?''

''I wouldn't bet my hat and ass on it,'' Jack said, ''but we had three separate indications of a powerful force from the man and the woman.''

''None from the dog?'' Ursy asked.

''Nope.''

''Are you still monitoring?'' Ursy asked.

''We see a very confused and sad little pooch,'' Burnish said.

Ursy turned off the communicator. Mop was still howling brokenheartedly. ''Julie—'' Ursy said, spreading her hands in supplication.

"No," Julie said.

Ursy turned up the volume of the sound. Mop's mournful howl echoed in the room.

The female alien would have called it weakness, and, had she suspected that the humans could be so foolishly sentimental, she would have tried to take advantage of the flaw in the racial character.

Julie Roberts looked at the sad little dog, all alone in the barren air lock, and said, "Let Jack and his little gang of geniuses observe him for a while, and then—"

Ursy grinned.

When the inner hatch of the air lock hissed open, Mop's good ear stood up with interest. He saw a woman in uniform. The woman knelt and held out one hand, saying, "Hey, fella. Hi. How ya doin'?"

Mop had always been a gregarious dog. He'd only met one human he didn't like, but his recent experiences with the aliens aboard the *Mother Lode* had colored his natural friendliness with suspicion.

Ursy moved forward, talking soothingly. Mop advanced cautiously, sniffed at Ursy's fingers, decided to risk it and let Ursy wiggle her fingertips on the top of his head. He decided that Ursy smelled good and—although he tensed and was a bit nervous—let her pick him up. She rubbed him and talked softly. He gave her hand one gentle, polite little lick and, with a sigh, threw himself onto his back in the crook of her arm, exposing his chest and belly for a little rub.

Julie Roberts was on the bridge. The gig carrying Erin Kenner and Denton Gale and *them* was disappearing through the access port of the converted destroyer. She saw Ursy come onto the bridge with the little dog in her arms, but her attention was on the viewers and the radio.

The duty ratings on the bridge took turns getting acquainted with Mop. He was polite, offering his paw to be shook, getting in a little lick now and then.

Ursy took her watch position at the weapons control panel. Mop sat at her feet, looking up with his hopeful, brown eyes. She reached down and put him in her lap. After a while he stepped gingerly up onto the console, found a small area that was blank of buttons and keys and levers, sighed, and curled up for a little practice nap.

"Captain," a rating said in an edgy voice, "the generator on the Mule has just been activated on flux."

"Weapons, stand by," Julie ordered.

Ursy clicked off the fail-safes for *Rimfire*'s battery of laser cannon.

The *Mother Lode* slowly separated from the converted destroyer.

"Weapons ready," Ursy said.

"Stand by," Julie ordered.

A melodic tone indicated the activation of *Rimfire*'s radio receiver. The strong contralto voice came from the speakers. "We have done as we agreed," the alien said. "We are now ready to talk."

"I'm pleased that you have decided to be peaceful," Julie sent. "If you will allow Erin Kenner and Denton Gale to contact me—"

"Those you mention," the alien said, "are aboard the vessel called *Murdoch's Plough*. However, it will be some time before either of them can speak. I hasten to inform you that they are unharmed, but it will be a few hours before they recover from the non-damaging mental trauma of being, once more, separate entities."

"Until then," Julie said, "we have nothing to discuss. You can, however, demonstrate your good will by turning on the holo-viewers so that we can see you."

"It is my pleasure," she said. And in an instant every viewscreen aboard *Rimfire* showed them. Their graceful bulk filled the screens. Their wings were partially unfurled.

"They're magnificent," Ursy whispered in awe.

"Thank you," Julie Roberts said, not unaffected by their radiance but hiding her surprise well.

"We regret that our contact with your race was based on misunderstandings," she said. "Our first impressions were based on the belligerence of the men on board the vessel called *Murdoch's Plough*. They were armed, and their first reaction to us was to try to use their weapons."

"What did you do with them?" Julie asked.

"Unfortunately, they are dead," the alien said.

"And why did you seize control of Erin Kenner and Denton Gale?" Julie asked.

"As you know, we are not completely invulnerable," she said. "After our experience with the crew of *Murdoch's Plough* we acted with caution. We did not, as you know, kill the Kenner and Gale things. We merely looked into their minds and saw that not all men are evil, as were the men we first encountered."

"I'm not buying this," Ursy whispered to Mop, who had come to attention, one ear raised, as he listened to Julie's conversation with the alien. "Captain, ask her why they killed the doctor?"

"As for the incident aboard your ship," she said, "it is regrettable, but you must remember that we were attacked by the first men we encountered. When your technicians began to bombard the Kenner and Gale things with what you call ultrashock, my companion assumed that we were being attacked once more."

"She heard you, Lieutenant," a rating said.

The alien was still speaking. "Now, Captain Roberts, while we wait for the Kenner and Gale things to become themselves once more, we ask your indulgence. Our intentions are to take this vessel to a landing on the large land mass in the planet's northern hemisphere. There we will be more comfortable, for the atmosphere aboard your ships seems quite close and stale to us."

Erin Kenner, able to hear through hairy, floppy ears, looking out onto the scene on the bridge of the *Rimfire* through Mop's eyes screamed out, "She's lying. I'm here. Don't let them go. Blast them now. Blast them into empty space."

Erin knew that in one of *Mother*'s cabins was the huge and complicated electronic construction that she had thought of as the Amplifier. She'd seen its incredible power. She was certain that they were going to turn the power of the Amplifier on *Rimfire,* but even though she made Mop aware of her by pretending anger, she could not do more than influence Mop's actions. And he was just a hairy little dog.

CHAPTER TWENTY-TWO

"We have no immediate need for the man things," The She told The He, as they left the gig and made their way from the hold of the converted destroyer to the *Mother Lode*.

They left the bodies of Erin and Denton lying on a bed aboard *Murdoch's Plough*. The only movement was the rise and fall of their chests in deep, even breathing. To the aliens the bodies represented raw material. For a moment she regretted wasting the life force of the female by leaving it aboard the big ship. He put the Denton Gale thing into deep sleep for possible use in the future, after they had solved the annoying little problem represented by the warship that was observing them from a distance that was well within the range of the force of the Amplifier.

They had agreed that they would take no chances. Once they would merely have paralyzed everyone aboard *Rimfire* from a safe distance, doing it instantly to prevent the use of the ship's weapons. Now they had to use guile, but soon, once they obtained the raw materials aboard *Rimfire* and began the reblossoming of their world, their full powers would be restored. Surely, she thought, that must be true. It was logical to think that some of the vast power they had once possessed came from the world that they had rebuilt. It was certain that the power of the Amplifier would be magnified when it was grounded on the planet, using the mass of the world as a resonator. The blast of stunning force that would then engulf the *Rimfire* would leave the arrogant Captain Julie Roberts and her crew impotent. At their leisure, the aliens would draw upon the raw material and begin the work of restoring their world to its former beauty.

She didn't wait for permission from the Rimfire. She fluxed the *Mother Lode* downward at reckless speed, screamed the ship into atmosphere, slowed as the outer plates began to glow with heat, and landed at the exact geographical center of the large, northern hemisphere continent. Her companion leapt into action, beginning to rig the grounding device that would allow the power of the Amplifier to resonate throughout an entire planet and be multiplied.

"I get life signals, two of them, from the destroyer," a technician announced. "They're the right size for Kenner and Gale."

"Very well," Julie said.

"Ma'am," Ursy said, "they're up to something."

"Ursy, we're the first to have seen a living alien species," Julie said. "Are you advocating destroying them without giving them a chance?"

"I don't mind becoming a part of history," Ursy said, "but I don't want to be history starting now."

The tone indicated an incoming radio signal. It was the female's voice, and it rang with arrogance. "My dear Captain Roberts," she said. "Now we can talk. I have many wonderful gifts for your rather backward race."

"That's very kind," Julie Roberts said, "in view of the fact that I see no technology on what you say is your world. In fact, I see only a raw and very primitive planet which supports no life."

"Ah, but your human eyes see only surface things," she said. On another level she was communicating with her companion. He was being very slow in readying the Amplifier for the stunning blast of power. It would be necessary for her to keep the attention of the humans diverted. "It is in the advancement of the mind and its hidden powers that we can help you most," she said.

Ursy Wade was turned half away from the weapons control console looking at the view screen, gazing raptly at the magnificent female alien. The eyes of the others on the bridge were also dazzled by her beauty.

Only one pair of round, brown eyes was otherwise occupied. Mop the dog was confused. He seemed to be hearing Erin's voice, but he could not see Erin. He was sitting on the edge of the weapons control console and Erin kept telling him to do something that he couldn't quite understand.

"Listen, you little son-of-a-bitch," Erin stormed, "listen to me. You're hungry. You're thirsty. Look."

Her anger made him aware of her. He wanted to please her. He was just having difficulty understanding.

"Buttons, Mop," Erin screamed. "Push buttons and get a goodie."

Mop licked his chops, thinking of nice, chewy tidbits. He turned, lifted his head to the weapons control panel.

Erin thought of them, on the planet's surface, imagined them readying the Amplifier, knowing the power of the instrument when it was combined with their wills. Erin had seen the Amplifier accelerate vast chunks of asteroid to speeds that, upon impact with other masses, made the darkness of space blaze with light. She remembered the alien's casual cruelty, and let her hate for the being become anger, through which she caused Mop to stand on his hind legs and press a certain button.

The alien's voice continued to boom forth from the speakers. She spoke of the wonders that mankind could accomplish once he had mastered the gifts that they would bestow.

"Food, Mop," Erin yelled. "That button. No. No."

Mop shook with frustration, showing his sharp little teeth and his red tongue, then tried again to please his Erin. His paw pulled a protective cover away from a switch and swept downward. The switch clicked. A blinking red light came on, but Ursy Wade was mesmerized by the alien's magnificence and by her rose promises.

Two of the preliminary steps to activate a weapons system that had not been used in a thousand years had been taken. There remained only two steps, two buttons to be pushed.

* * *

The female alien heard her companion say, "One last step and I will be ready."

She continued her soothing speech of good will and cooperation to the bemused humans aboard *Rimfire*.

"Tell me when you are prepared," she said to her partner. "It will be my pleasure to activate the force."

"Candy, Mop," Erin promised. "Push that button and there will be candy." She envisioned a tidbit of chocolate, one of Mop's favorite treats and one he didn't get often, for candy was not good for him.

Mop pawed at a yellow button. A click. A soft, warning gong.

"Ursy, what the hell?" Julie Roberts yelled, as she heard the gong telling her that a planet buster was armed and ready for launch, waiting only the last order to fire.

Ursy jerked around to face the weapon's control console in time to see a hairy little dog paw at a button that pulsated light the color of blood. She seized Mop by the scruff of his neck and jerked him off the console.

"Captain," came Jack Burnish's voice, "we have just fired a planet buster."

"Get that thing, Ursy," Julie Roberts ordered with fierce intensity.

It wasn't much of a world. It was raw and new, but it had good air and enough water to supply the needs of a couple of nearby desert planets, if such worlds existed. Most importantly, in a galaxy glutted with glowing bodies and blazing bodies and dark bodies and useless, sun-scorched planets of rock, and gas giants and frozen hulks it was a world that, some day, could support human life. A water world was the most precious thing in an uncaring galaxy and this one would be destroyed in a matter of minutes as a missile blazed toward it carrying a weapon that would first penetrate through the relatively shallow crust and then explode with a force that would spew the molten core of the world into space as the crust shattered.

Ursy's fingers flew. "Damn," she said. For switches that had been on ready were turned off. *Rimfire*'s missile

defense system had been downloaded from the ready status
that she had programmed in. "Oh, damn," she said.

"Ursy!" Julie Roberts yelled.

"Oh, my God," Ursy moaned, knowing that she was
too late.

She was telling him laughingly how easy it was to dis-
tract the inferior humans. He paused in his work to enjoy
her domination of them. She was distracting them with the
power of the words she had learned from the Kenner thing
while he prepared the instrument that would destroy them.

She felt an elation that made her seem, to the feeble-
minded humans who were watching her image on their
screens, even more beautiful as she became one with her
world once more, as her senses reached out to the barren
lands and the sterile seas and envisioned them as they
would be soon, when she and he had the raw material to
begin the implantation of life on their world. And after
that they would have the most advanced starship built by
the puny men and charts to tell them where there were
many planets teeming with raw material.

The world was beautiful, indeed. True, it was smaller
than it had been, but it had enough mass to give it orbital
and gravitational stability and to hold an atmosphere. She
let herself be one with it even as she continued to beguile
the humans aboard *Rimfire*.

Sensing her inner ecstasy, he merged with her, to better
share their triumph.

So it was that they felt the impact of the planet killing
missile together. They felt the missile penetrating, bur-
rowing through the crust of their world. It was only as the
eroded head of the planet buster entered molten lava and
continued for long seconds before the intense heat deto-
nated the warhead that she realized the true horror of what
was happening.

She screamed and, wings pumping, soared to bang
forcefully against the overhead on *Mother*'s bridge.

"No," he whispered, for it was happening again.

The planet shuddered. The molten core of a world burst
upward and outward through thousands of weakened areas.

The sky burned red. The destruction crept toward the *Mother Lode.*

She was the first to gain the open air. She lifted her wings and leapt to fly upward. He was soon with her, his more powerful wings beating hard as he passed her so that the erupting, fiery havoc overtook her first and encased her as it had done once before. Her screams of agony quickly ceased to have a physical source as she knew the torment of immobility, of imprisonment inside a mass of cooling core material.

"My God," Ursy Wade said, as she watched a world explode into fragments.

Julie Roberts gave quick orders. *Rimfire* blinked away from the exploding world, lest she be struck by the debris that was spreading into space.

Ursy Wade took one quick look at *Murdoch's Plough* before the blink and, after *Rimfire* was back in normal space she activated a detector. To her amazement, the converted destroyer was still there. The instruments showed masses of rock and debris scattered all around her, but she was still there, apparently whole.

Mop leapt into Ursy's lap, licked her hand.

"My God," Ursy said, "do you have any idea what you did?"

"You bet your sweet ass," Erin Kenner said, unheard.

EPILOGUE

Although the lights were low in the luxurious cabin aboard the sleek X&A destroyer converted into a private yacht and equipped with mining gear, Mop the dog's built-in alarm told him it was time to get up. He lay in his bed with his feet up in the air, his head hanging over the edge of the soft mattress, hairy ears brushing the thick carpet. He rolled to his feet, yawned and stretched, scratched behind his left ear with a quizzical expression on his face, and then walked to the big bed. He released a few experimental grunts and when there was no movement he crouched and leapt up onto the foot of the bed because when it was time for Mop the dog to get up it was time for everyone to get up.

He crept softly upward, peered into the sleeping faces, made soft, grunting sounds in his throat. Still nothing. He went back to the foot of the bed, lay down with his head resting on a covered leg and waited patiently for about two minutes. By that time he was convinced that it was more than time for *everybody* to be up and about and giving some love and attention to a little dog. He began to scratch at the covers, found an opening, burrowed underneath and chewed gently on a set of shapely, bare toes.

"Unnnnn," Erin Kenner Gale groaned, moving her foot.

Mop pursued, pushing his way under the covers, and began to get toes again.

"You hairy little varmint," Erin said, reaching down to pull Mop up beside her. "All right, all right. I'm awake, you animated alarm clock. Get Daddy."

Mop wriggled in excitement. His most pressing duty aboard ship was to see to it that everyone got out of bed in the morning to give a little dog a pat or two. He scampered across the bed and lapped a big, wet, doggie kiss right on Denton Gale's lips.

Denton sat up, sputtering, wiping his mouth. He reached for the dog, who playfully leapt away and then came back to growl fiercely and gnaw gently on Dent's hand.

"What would we do without you, Mr. Mop?" Dent asked.

"Get a little extra sleep, I imagine," Erin said.

Dent leaned over to give her a good morning kiss.

"Go brush the doggie slobber away," Erin said.

"He's your damned dog," Dent said, seizing her and pushing her down onto the bed. She struggled to avoid his kiss. Mop got in on the fun and managed to lap one across her mouth as she twisted her head to avoid Dent's lips.

"Well, what the hell," she said, relaxing, putting her arms around Dent, accepting his kiss.

The *Yorkshire Terror,* named in honor of a hairy little dog who had mastered the buttonology of the weapons' control system on an X&A explorer, was orbiting alongside a ring of debris that had been, not once but twice, a world.

After breakfast, Erin and Dent went to mining control and began a search. Two days later they were about to give up when the detectors sang of gold, gold in plenty. They latched onto an extra large asteroid and soon *Terror*'s mining equipment was digging out a vein so rich that in less than a week the number one cargo bay was laden with ore.

The search went on. Another good ore bed was mined.

Terror's instruments were far superior to those of the old *Mother Lode*. She could sit off from the asteroid belt and search hundreds of chunks of rock for gold and other things without moving. In less than three months she was laden to capacity with rich gold ore.

Erin started the generator charging, wanting to be able to blink well past the Dead Worlds before having to halt for charge again. Dent was sleeping. She sat in the command chair, feet up on the console. Mop dozed, curled into a ball in an open space behind the computer keyboard. Erin closed her eyes, let a pleasant drowsiness take her. Somewhere aboard the converted destroyer a relay was activated and an air filtering system came on with a whoosh. The sound caused Erin's eyes to jerk open and cast around for the source of the sound.

Moments like that came to her now and then—pure panic. It had been almost two years since she'd last been in the star-crowded area near the galactic core, but the memories were still vivid. Out there in a ring around the sun was *their* world. Somewhere among the masses of shattered rock and space-cooled masses of the planet's formerly molten core *they* were there.

Mop, sensing Erin's momentary distress, moved close to her and offered his right paw. She shook it tenderly.

"Yep," she said, "Mr. Mop. Mr. Mop the hero."

Mop grinned, not because he was a hero—he didn't understand hero—but because he liked Erin to hold his paw.

"They could not have survived that," Ursy Wade had said, after the planet buster burrowed its way into the mantle to burst the world open like a dropped melon.

But they had survived just that once before.

"I don't want to go out there again," Denton told Erin, after they had answered X&A questions repeatedly for over ninety days. The questions had been asked behind closed doors because a curtain of secrecy had been thrown over the *Rimfire* incident by the president of the United Planets Council.

"But how, Miss Kenner, did you, ah, reenter your, ah, body after the aliens, whom you claim could, ah, 'stash you away' as you say in the brain of a very small dog—"

She had said, "I don't know."

The inert bodies, the bodies of Erin Kenner and Denton Gale, were removed from *Murdoch's Plough* to the sick bay aboard *Rimfire*. Denton Gale regained consciousness within hours of his arrival aboard the X&A ship. Erin Kenner didn't move, other than to breathe evenly and deeply, until a small, hairy dog sneaked in when a medtech opened the door. He jumped up onto Erin's bed and licked her politely on the cheek and Erin sat up in bed and said, "Hi, Mr. Mop. What do you think?"

Ursy Wade said it was like a movie where the dying heroine is revived by her lover's kiss.

"Are you calling me a bitch, Ursy?" Erin asked jokingly.

"Hey, you could do worse than Mr. Mop," Ursy said.

"I think we both did, once," Erin said, winking at Ursy and nodding toward Jack Burnish.

"Now that's a real *dog,*" Ursy said, grinning.

All that joking was after Julie Roberts had thrown a fit on Erin for having used Mr. Mop to launch a planet buster. Julie was still a bit stiff toward Erin even when she heard it all from Erin and Dent. *They* had been, after all, the only living aliens ever to be encountered by man. Julie knew that there were people on Xanthos who would feel that she had lost a great opportunity to advance man's knowledge, people who would feel that she should have risked everything up to and including ship and crew to keep the aliens alive and to stay in contact with them.

But she'd seen the exposed facial bones of the ship's chief med-officer. She saw a holo-tape from the library of *Murdoch's Plough* documenting how the aliens had built a planet from scraps. She had heard both Erin and Dent describe, while under the influence of a hypnotic drug that made them incapable of either falsehood or exaggeration, the thinking process of the aliens, their attitude toward human life.

Julie had decided, by the time *Rimfire* blinked back to Xanthos with the converted destroyer locked in her generator field, that Erin had been right to put the aliens back into cold storage. She didn't know what they had been, although there were some fanciful speculations aboard *Rimfire* when the holo-tapes of the female's extended speech were shown. Some of the more scholarly and a few of the more religious ones had some interesting theories based on her statement that her name was "Legion."

"It must be pointed out specifically," said Ursy, during one heated argument, "that they never created anything. They just moved atoms and molecules and stuff around. So if you say they were divine angels, you're as full of

shit as a Christmas turkey and, furthermore, not just a
little bit blasphemous, because these were evil mothers.
Evil.''

"There were angels who were once divine, but then
were not," said a sub-commander called Preacher, because his main form of relaxation was studying the Bible.
"She said her name was Legion. That phrase was used
once before, when Jesus cast out devils and put them into
a herd of swine.''

"Whether or not she was a devil, she was a devil,"
Ursy said.

Julie didn't want to waste her life in idle speculation.
They were gone. She just wanted them to stay gone. In
fact, she recommended that an X&A cordon be placed
around the asteroid ring to keep anyone from stumbling
onto their bones the way Erin and Dent had until a small
fleet of X&A ships could reduce the asteroid belt to motes
in space. She was overruled. Perhaps, she thought, they
didn't believe what they heard back there on Xanthos far
from the eerie star fields of the Dead Worlds and the asteroid belt that lay beyond in the glare of the old, malev-
olent core stars.

"I want you two to go back out there," Julie told Erin
and Dent, after the courts had awarded the converted destroyer to Mr. and Mrs. Denton Gale in lieu of a salvage
settlement from the defunct Haven Refining Company.

"I don't want to go back out there," Erin said.

"I can't go," Julie said. "I have orders. You can. And
you must.''

Erin shuddered. "You want us to go bone hunting
again.''

"That's the idea.''

"And if we find anything?''

"That ship you own has a laser cannon as powerful as
those aboard most fleet ships of the line.''

"I think I understand," Denton said. "You're afraid
that sometime in the future some unlucky prospector might
find a few fossilized bones and take them aboard his vessel.''

"I know someone who did just that," Julie said.

"It's a job for X&A," Erin protested.

"Honey, X&A is made up of people. And Headquarters is made up of that peculiar type of people who think that longevity guarantees wisdom. We're in a period of time when the Service is commanded by ground pounders. What can you expect?"

"Oh, shit," Erin said.

The *Yorkshire Terror* was charged. Erin decided to make one last check. She put the ship on flux and used up several weeks in a spirited circumnavigation of the asteroid ring, the sensors set to the density of fossil bone.

"We're spinning our wheels," Dent said. "The bones we found were in the crust of the original planet. When they reassembled it, everything was mixed together. Maybe some bones survived the impacts, but I'd guess that they were either shattered into tiny pieces or went into the interior and became molten when the pressures heated the core. I fail to see how the bones we found were preserved in the first place. You saw the holo-tapes of the blowup. The crust shattered. The core burst out. If they got caught up in the molten material, they were simply vaporized. There would be no bones left."

"You're saying that they might just be floating around in space?"

He shuddered. "God, I hope not." He smiled at his own reaction. "I think they're gone, Erin. Gone for good. At best, enclosed in megatons of cooled core material."

"If I had the power," she said, "I'd vaporize every asteroid into space dust the way Julie suggested."

But she didn't have the power. The *Terror* blinked past the Dead Worlds to Haven where her cargo brought three-and-a-half million U.P. credits. Added to the money already in the banks, that made Mr. and Mrs. Gale not filthy rich, but rich enough so that they didn't have to go out looking for gold unless it pleased them to do so.

They were quite rich enough to buy a demure little Yorkshire damsel who, when she was introduced to Mr. Mop, licked him sensuously on the nose and began to lead him a merry chase that resulted, when she was ready, in a squirming litter of four little Mops and Mopettes.

"I think he's got the right idea," Dent said, lifting a

pup in both hands, much to Mrs. Mop's concern. "What do you think? Think we should follow his example?"

"You want me to have a litter of pups?" she asked.

"Whatever," he said, reaching for her.